Abuse of Privilege

John S Langley

Print ISBN: 978-1-7391381-0-3

To my Mum & Dad and all that came before.

To my wife Janet, my longsuffering soul mate

... she knows why.

To my sons Robert, Iain and Michael

... they should know why,

To my brothers Robin and Andrew

... they can't possibly know why.

"Grant me the strength to accept the things I cannot change, the courage to change the things I can, and the wisdom to know the difference."

Mark Wilson in pensive mood
miss-quoting Reinhold Niebuhr

"Don't you believe that some good can come out of bad?"

Hathos, Cusco, Peru

'But Mommy everybody's doing it!'

Teenage exasperation oozed from every pore and flowed in the direction of the older woman who held up her hand as if to hold back the tsunami of angst and signal that it was her turn to speak.

The pool boy was catching leaves from the surface of the pool. His bare muscled arms moved the large net languidly. It was a job he'd done thousands of times before and hoped to do thousands more. He was on autopilot, his mind on a surfboard catching the big waves off the coast of California. That didn't stop him from being attentive to his paymaster though and with a nod of the head the older woman signaled for him to leave. This was family business.

After a tough day the older woman had been looking forward to a few moments lounging by the pool while the cook prepared their evening meal. Toned, evenly tanned and in a red bikini she was not used to being shouted at but she knew, or thought she knew, her daughter and that kids had special privileges when it came to abusing their parents. She accepted this natural law of nature and calmly raised her sunglasses uncovering her hazel brown eyes,

'I don't care who's doing it,' she said, 'you're not, my dear.'

The use of the term "my dear" was, whether it was meant to be or not, like a red rag to a bull to the already indignant teenager. The teenager's name was Kerry-Anne, just plain Kerry to her friends, and her mother should at least have had enough respect for her to call her that rather than reverting to "my dear". It made her feel like a little dog that had just been patted on the head or worse, a little child. She was old enough to be going on to college wasn't she, she was a mature woman for goodness sake.

Kerry-Anne swallowed back the words that first came into her mouth, she knew that letting her mother get under her skin so easily was tantamount to admitting defeat and she wasn't prepared to go down without a fight. She still had cards up her sleeve.

'Daddy says I can go,' she said.

Her mother moved her expression just a fraction but enough for Kerry-Anne to read that her point had hit home - divide and rule was a tactic that had worked for her in the past although she was careful not to overuse it.

At that very moment the glass door that separated the pool area from the internal air conditioned lavish and large interior slid smoothly to one side and a man emerged.

He was above average height, straight backed, be-suited, with crew cut dark hair and was tanned like his wife. He paused to turn and slide the glass door back into place. No point allowing the expensive cool of the inside to be lost into the heat of the early evening. He wore a suave smile and was about to loosen his tie when he picked up the first wisps of the frosty atmosphere between mother and daughter. He didn't know what was going on but he knew that something was and he had a feeling he was going to find out more about it very soon. He wondered briefly whether he still had time to exit graciously and not get involved. Unfortunately, he realized, he was too late and such an option was out of the question.

'Daddy, so nice to see you,' said Kerry-Anne sidling over to give him an over-exuberant hug.

He extracted himself gently from her embrace and looked towards his wife for explanation.

'Your daughter,' he knew he was in trouble when his wife substituted "your" for "our", 'your daughter wishes to go backpacking around the world with no knowledge of where she's going, or staying, or how long she's going for or how she's going to pay for it all.'

Kerry-Anne had bitten her tongue just long enough to allow her mother to finish.

'Daddy,' she said, her eyes puppy-dog size as she looked up at him, 'everybody who's anybody at school is backpacking this summer. It's almost a part of the curriculum.'

Her father thought of the money he was spending on her education, the self-confidence the school had the reputation of producing in its students. He supposed it was possible that such a venture could be a step along the path to personal independence. He had high expectations of his daughter's future and was committed to giving her the best of foundations. However he didn't have to be the intellectual genius that he was to recognise that his wife wasn't happy with this idea. It wasn't the money, that wasn't a problem.

'I've got a route all worked out,' continued Kerry-Anne, 'I'd love to show it to you, and I've looked up hostels I can stay in, googled the reviews to pick out the best, and I'll only be away for 37 days.'

She felt the precision of this last number added to the solidity of her case. It was always these little points of detail that made the difference she found. It was exactly the same with her school assignments although she got a lot of informed, specialist help with them. Getting straight A's had become more a case of knowing who to use to help you research and write them rather than what you actually needed to learn. After all wasn't the mark of a great leader their ability to pick great helpers and then get the best out of them.

She could see her father was impressed with her riposte. She could also see that her mother wasn't… yet.

'It is just impossible,' said her mother, 'you don't realise how unsafe a world we live in. The risks are too high. It's for your own good. Travelling alone is too dangerous. We'll get you on a cruise somewhere, George can go along too, he'll keep out of your way, he's very unobtrusive.'

George was one of the family's bodyguards and had shadowed Kerry-Anne many times during her life.

'Cruises are sooo boring,' said Kerry-Anne despairingly, 'and George is not unobtrusive, he's huge and he's always in the corner of my eye. I just can't get away from him, he's just a grown up version of Nanny.'

Nannies had played a significant role in Kerry-Anne's upbringing. She had been looked after and feted all her life and taken it all for granted. But now she was beginning to feel like she was just a pawn in somebody else's game, that she'd been passed around from one pair of safe hands to another; from nanny to driver to teachers and back again. Well it was time for that to change. She was grown up now and could look after herself, she was sure of it, if only she were given the chance.

She still had a couple of more cards to play and realised now was the time.

'But I won't be going alone,' she said, 'Emily is going with me.'

'Really!' said her mother, 'and what do her parents think about that.'

Time for a slice of honesty.

'We haven't asked them yet, there's no point. If you don't let me go then she can't go. You know what an unbelievable opportunity it would be for her. Of course we would offer to pay her expenses, that would seal the deal I'm sure,' she paused, saw that her mother was thinking, 'so you see, if you say no, you don't just rob me of the opportunity and make me look foolish in front of all my friends at school who have more … er… different parents, but you also rob Emily of a once-in-a-lifetime character building experience,' she paused, it was time to go "All In", 'We're best friends but with me going to Harvard and Emily squeezing into Stanford we'll be, like, 3,000 miles apart! This is our last opportunity to, like, do something together that we'll remember for the rest of our lives.'

That was it, all the cards were on the table. She knew her mother was already supporting Emily's family through her philanthropic work, though she didn't know why. How would it feel then if it became known that she had snatched such an opportunity out of Emily's grasp. And it would become known, Kerry-Anne would make sure of that. She smiled at her mother, sure that she also fully understood the embarrassing consequences of a refusal.

'Hmm' said her mother, a little impressed by her daughter's manipulative tactics in order to try and get her own way, but still concerned for her safety. She had a lot more experience of the real world than her daughter. It was tough out there. Tough and dangerous. But maybe you only learnt through your own experience. She couldn't protect her daughter forever. If she was going to amount to something, as both she and her husband were determined to ensure, then Kerry-Anne had to start spreading her wings sometime. Perhaps now was the time after all. It would be a big change for Kerry-Anne to move away to the East Coast. Harvard was a tough place to get into but also a tough place to make your mark once you were there. She'd be chaperoned of course. They hadn't discussed the details yet but she and her husband would make sure Kerry-Anne was looked after and protected, whether she like it or not. Maybe a little leniency now would help with the battles ahead. Maybe gaining a little more experience of independent living before hitting the elevated hotbed environs of Harvard to study Economics was no bad thing. Maybe it would make her a bit more people savvy, increase her street cred in the eyes of her new peers.

'I'll think about it,' she said and then looked at her husband, 'we'll think about it,' he smiled reassuringly, 'now go and ask cook how long it is before dinner's ready.'

Kerry-Anne smiled inwardly, she knew she'd won. Now was the time to make a hasty retreat before either of her parents thought up any new objections.

As she closed the sliding glass door behind her and began to make her way towards the kitchen she began to compose her immediate "to do" list.

Firstly, she had better decide on a route that could be done in exactly 37 days.

Second, she would have to find some hostels worth staying in, and take enough money to ensure that she could default to a good hotel if needs be.

And thirdly, and quite importantly, she would ask Emily if she wanted to come along. She was bound to say yes, she was sure of it

Chapter One

Listen, this really needs to be clear from the start, I'm not a very nice man.

Some of the things that I do are not nice and no matter how hard you try you can't stop some of the bad moments seeping in through your pores, getting into your system and lodging there, waiting to creep into your dreams, waking you up at night, affecting your sleep.

Maybe I should start by telling you who I am. My name is Mark Wilson. I'm an employee of an organisation known as 'The Store'. 'The Store' is an organisation that operates outside and between borders, an organisation that does the difficult in-between work that all countries need but that no government organisation dare soil their hands with.

After a prolonged absence of career-threatening length I'd returned to work and was awaiting the call that would launch me into my next assignment.

I waited with mixed feelings; keen to get going again, but anxious of what kind of situation I was going to be catapulted into.

Sitting in my flat twiddling my thumbs and

waiting for the call had long outgrown its novelty value. I'm not very good at doing nothing and particularly not when doing nothing gives me too much thinking time. So as I distraction I'd donned trainers and running gear and gone out jogging.

London may be one of the biggest cities in Europe but it still has a healthy number of green spaces. I entered one of them through the open wrought iron gates.

It was a rainy Monday but I didn't mind. The rain splattered my head, ran down my neck and cooled me as I ran.

I was halfway across the park when I felt my phone vibrate. I took it out of the pocket of my running shorts and saw my call-sign "Agaricus" flashing on and off on the screen. I felt relieved. I had been re-activated and summoned to 'the Office'. I turned immediately and ran back to my flat, more quickly now, and got washed and changed. I was ready to go.

The prospect of a journey on the London Underground however filled me with dread. I wanted to stay fresh and am not one of those subterranean creatures that voluntarily and perhaps even enthusiastically leave the daylight and expansiveness of the surface behind them and descend into the dimly lit claustrophobic crypt-like bowels of the London Underground network. It never fails to amaze me that I, an apparently intelligent human being, together with millions of others of my fellow species rush and push for the pleasure of cramming ourselves through guillotine closing doors into an offensively close proximity. And, once underway, suffering the unpredictable wobble and lunge of the carriage that creates the perpetual danger of throwing us into the midriff, armpit or arse of absolute strangers or worse, them into ours.

Not only that but each of these predicaments is all too frequently interrupted by a bored, disembodied voice that crackles through the static to say,

'We apologise for the late running of this train. It is due to a point's failure … a signal failure … an electrical failure … a plumbing failure … or some other failure that we can't even be bothered to put a vague, meaningless name to.'

Such announcements are almost inevitably followed by the universal salve that, I suppose, was developed by committee and communicated to all Customer Service staff in expensive training sessions, in lavish training centres, that is designed to cool our collective fevered brow,

'… but we do hope that this has not caused you any inconvenience.'

Personally I'm not convinced they do care whether it's an inconvenience or not.

Even in the face of all this hard-won experience I admit that I still embark on a journey on the London Underground with the optimistic expectation that it will run on time, after all it often does!

However on this occasion I didn't want to take the risk.

I took a taxi.

Stepping out of the cab I tread carefully to avoid the fresh lumps of chewing gum ejecta that were splattered haphazardly about the pavement and walked down one of London's few quiet backstreets to a fairly nondescript door, the black paint peeling off it. I knew that although looking abandoned and uncared for the alleyway and door were being constantly monitored both by trained eye and technology.

I gained entry and proceeded through two bullet and blast proof internal security doors by using a combination of ID card, fingerprint recognition and the day's pass-code.

Once inside a deceptively sleepy ex-SAS man cast me a lazy eye.

'Welcome back Mr Wilson,' he said, 'please sign here and then just stand on that white line over there and look towards the camera for the usual retinal recognition.'

I smiled and did as he bid. I was back in familiar surroundings undergoing familiar protocols. It was somehow reassuring.

'Thanks,' I said, 'It's good to be back.

After the formalities were complete he said,

'They're expecting you, sir, although you're slightly later than anticipated,' he waved me towards the stairs, 'I'm sure you remember the way.'

I nodded, proceeded to the 3rd floor and made my way along the echoing corridor to Office number 31

Chapter Two

I knew the penalty for lateness was to be kept waiting – a kind of 'returning-the-favour' penance. I made myself as comfortable as possible and wondered whether 15 minutes would be deemed sufficient to ensure that I understood my place in the pecking order, or if it would take longer

I'd come see someone called AB and was seated in his ante-room. Although so much is high-tech these days, most of the real work being done virtually, the trappings of the office were reminiscent of an earlier time, the choice of décor down to individual taste.

The wait wasn't the mind numbingly boring interlude intended however as, rather than just sitting anxiously twiddling my thumbs, I passed the time of day with Samantha, the good-looking PA who'd been expecting me. We knew each other from earlier times.

Steering a course through inconsequential small talk she delicately avoided any reference to the length of my absence from active duty. It was therefore with a tinge of regret that I noticed one of the small lights that were embedded in the polished mahogany surface of Samantha's desk begin to blink green.

'AB will see you now,' she said.

'Thanks,' I said. 'Let's hope he's in a good mood today.'

She gave a small half smile and showed me through the sturdy oak door and into 'the presence'.

A clean-shaven face glanced up from a glowing computer screen, one of several scattered around the room. An arm appeared and casually waved me to a seat.

'Thank you Samantha; that will be all.'

Samantha turned to leave the room,

'Ah, and no interruptions for the next 25 minutes please.'

Samantha nodded, closing the door noiselessly behind her.

After a few more moments of keyboard tapping AB leant back stretching his shoulders by putting his hands behind his neck and sighed.

'Would you like a drink?' he asked getting up to pour himself a single malt from a cut glass decanter, two fingers.

'No thank you sir, it's a little early for me,' I said, determined to keep a clear head.

There are some men born to action, others who are not. There are people like me, destined to forever inhabit the grimy recesses of the engine room, blessed with a talent for the oily rag, and others who inhabit the first-class lounges, quaffing the very best wines, puffing on Havana cigars and putting the world to rights. There are those with that unshakably self-confident demeanour, accents and vocabulary that betray their private education at Eton or Harrow followed by Oxford, Cambridge, St Andrews or Sandhurst. Within this group there are those whose intellect is so recognized and admired that they have license to observe from the sidelines, commenting with assurance on the faults of others. These select few make life and death decisions from the comfort of Victorian green leather armchairs and think it hard lines if things don't come off quite as intended, such failings being put down to the shortcomings of the operatives, 'You just can't get the staff these days'. They may suffer a moment of melancholy when reflecting on the loss of life that their decisions have caused but soon manage to put the thought behind them, aided by a glass of properly aged brandy, and they move on to apply their intellect to the next case in point.

Such men AB, or Sir Anthony Baxter to give him his proper name, was used to dealing with this every day. He had become one of the go-to men when thought needed to be converted into action, especially for those tricky little things that needed to be done but could not be seen to be done by the establishment.

'I have a little job for you,' he said, without the courtesy of preamble, 'I believe that you might be a good man for this one,' he paused, 'it's an easy one.'

He didn't bother to smile, he'd made his point, he was reintroducing me gently.

'Thank you, sir.'

AB shrugged his shoulders and looked me in the eye. The silence hung.

'I was sorry to hear about your wife,' he said, 'cancer is such an indiscriminate disease.'

'Yes,' I said, thinking of my wife's brave but ultimately losing battle.

This was the reason for my absence. My wife's cancer. We'd tried everything. She was so wonderful. Her last words to me were, 'promise me you won't stop living.' Of course I promised her that but I did for a while. My daughter became my rock when I should have been hers. Now I was picking up the reins again one faltering step at a time. The kind of work I did didn't make it any easier but this was what I did and I couldn't face trying something else right now. Not unless AB decided I was damaged goods and let me go.

'Yes,' I repeated, 'it's not nice.'

He smiled back. He was not known for high

emotion and I reckoned he was trying to be reassuring. AB was my lifeline back. This was a straw I had to hang onto.

'Are you ready?' he asked.

'Yes sir,' I said, trying to mean it.

'I have looked through your assessment reports,' he paused, his soft grey eyes assessing, 'hmmm.'

AB leafed through a thin file of papers on his desk, stood up, walked to the window and looked out, his back towards me.

'It's a strange world out there,' he said to nobody in particular.

He stood for a few moments in inner contemplation. I found it unnerving, as if I was intruding. Then he slowly shook his head and returned to his desk.

'This job we have for you,' he said, having obviously made up his mind, 'although apparently straightforward it does need a light touch, careful handling.'

Chapter Three

I couldn't help respecting AB. He did a job I could never do, would never want to do. Hobnobbing with the rich and powerful whilst retaining your own personal integrity was no easy feat but he did it and he did it well.

He moved away from his desk and we sat on comfortable leather chairs either side of a low coffee table.

'There is a powerful client of ours who needs a hand,' he said, 'names and positions et cetera are not what's important. The most important thing to understand is the nature of the help and the limits and boundaries we are required to operate within.' He paused and raised an eyebrow. Although I'd got the message he clearly wanted some sort of reassurance from me.

'Yes sir, I understand, help… within boundaries.' Not the most effusive of confirmations but the best I could muster under the circumstances.

'Good,' he said, taking a sip of the single malt and letting it roll around his tongue, savouring the sharpness, the nuances of taste, before finally swallowing it down.

'Our clients have, let us say, very demanding roles,' he continued, 'and in common with many people who have very demanding roles their private lives take second place. In this particular case it seems to be the mother-daughter relationship that has suffered the most. It's difficult at the best of times but when its under stress it's even worse.'

I eased myself back in my chair, AB was warming to his briefing and I was happy to listen attentively.

'It's quite a familiar tale, a daughter raised by nannies and looked after by a team of others, then off to an expensive private boarding school with a name that would sit well on any resume.'

'The few proper talks that occur between parents and child are more like business meetings; diarised, stilted, and controlled. The best that money can buy is in no way a guarantee of affection although an apparently self-confident, independent young lady seems to be the outcome of all this expense. The girl is both intelligent and creative together with what one might be forgiven for calling a degree of arrogance, or even bravado, a feeling of personal superiority and invulnerability. Even so the daughter,' he paused, 'who by the way is called Kerry-Anne, you do need to know that.'

'Thank you, sir,' I said.

I was trying to build up a picture, absorbing each informational crumb that AB was releasing. He may at times sound facetious to the uninitiated but I knew each detail counted if I were to understand the true nature of this assignment. I was in his hands. Information is power and it was up to him how he chose release it. My job was to listen and to assimilate.

'More precisely, now that she believes that she's all grown up, she's tried to drop the double-barreled forename and is known to her friends as simply Kerry. Her parents still call her Kerry-Anne.'

'So now to continue,' he said, 'at this point in her life Kerry is determined to be and to become herself, to part herself from the shackles of her protected childhood and to demonstrate her independence, to prove to her parents, and perhaps even to herself, that she can make her own choices and decisions. She wants to demonstrate to everyone that she is no longer a child. The wide world is beckoning and Kerry is eager to answer the call,' he paused, 'but all is not going to turn out well for poor Kerry,' he took another sip of his whisky, 'what she wants to do is to travel, to go backpacking I believe it's called?'

I nodded in reassurance that he had indeed used the right word for this youthful concept of adventure. He continued,

'She would never have been allowed to set out alone, of course, and she enticed a fellow classmate to tag along. This was a girl called Emily, a young lady who needed little encouragement to join the fun.'

'One by one Kerry removed or resolved her parent's objections and left them to anxiously walk the knife-edged tightrope between seeming to allow their daughter some freedom whilst at the same time ensuring that she was guarded and protected at all times. In a rather ill advised move, although with the best of intentions, a new bodyguard was engaged to shadow Kerry, someone she did not know and would not recognise. This was obviously done without the knowledge of the daughter and the individual concerned was given explicit instructions to ensure she remained unobserved and in the background, reporting back on Kerry's progress on a daily basis and only moving out of the shadows if it became necessary to intervene to ensure Kerry's safety, or if so instructed by Kerry's parents or their representatives.'

AB sighed, it was the sigh of a parent.

'Kerry was also gifted a new smartphone. She would probably not have been quite so delighted by this unexpected present if she had known that it had been purposefully set up to track her location, in real time, anywhere in the world. The mother knew that her daughter would keep the phone with her at all times, holding it close, guarding it as though her life depended on it. Ironic really.'

Fresh ice cubes clinked in his cut-glass tumbler as AB took a refill.

'The parents were extremely keen that Kerry believed that she had been entrusted with the freedom she so ardently craved. With the precautions in place they probably thought "What could possibly go wrong?". She wasn't going alone, her every movement was being GPS tracked, and she was being secretly chaperoned by a professional bodyguard,' he smiled, but there was no humour in it, 'Now that's what I call giving your precious and precocious teenage daughter a true taste of independence.'

I could tell he didn't mean it.

AB shook his head slowly from side to side,

'Ah, kids,' he said, 'Youth is so inadvisably entrusted to the young.'

I was sure I'd heard that somewhere before but I couldn't remember where. I moved in my seat. There was a small creaking sound.

'Am I boring you?'

Oh shit, AB did have a way of keeping you on your toes, of ensuring he had your undivided attention.

'No sir,' I said truthfully, I was glad to be back, 'Not at all sir.'

He nodded.

'In any event let me hurry this little tale along. Two young girls with backpacks, dollars and credit cards. Each egging the other on to experience new delights and adventure, it's fun for all.'

'Their trip goes swimmingly until they arrive in Peru, Lima's Jorge Chavez International Airport Arrivals to be exact. Here two unfortunate things happen. Firstly, Kerry thinks she spots a familiar face in the Customs Hall and, immediately assuming she is being shadowed without her knowledge or permission, is determined to give this interloper the slip. The bodyguard is either too drowsy or too preoccupied to realize what is happening and consequently too slow to react.'

'Secondly, the girls speed through immigration and emerge into a crowded Arrivals Hall. They then proceed to grab the first taxi driver to offer his services. In their enthusiasm they almost drag him to his vehicle and speed off into the gathering gloom of the city.'

AB drew a Havana cigar from a wooden box. He rolled it between his fingers before snipping off the end and, holding a Ronson lighter aflame in one hand, languorously sucked it into life.

'Like all travelers to South America the girls had been warned to watch out for unlicensed taxi drivers and told of the unsavoury consequences. Unfortunately their impetuosity overcame any semblance of care or caution that they may otherwise have displayed.'

AB took a draw from the cigar, slowly exhaling to watch the smoke trail upwards towards the ceiling.

'They ask the taxi driver to take them to the Hilton Hotel in central Lima, a rather deluxe form of backpacking, and sit excitedly in the back of the cab chattering and laughing together, complementing each other on their cleverness and the speed of their escape. They have never been to Lima before, in fact they have never been to Peru, and so have no idea of the correct route to the hotel and simply put their faith in the driver. It is only when the taxi stops in an unlit street that their bubble of joy is burst.'

'Bundled unceremoniously from the taxi they are hauled down into a basement room with only a naked light bulb dangling from the ceiling, a single unkempt bed, a bucket in one corner and a sink by the door. They are now rightly terrified. Their kidnappers retrieve and scrutinise their passports and other belongings.'

AB took a long pull on the Havana, put his head back and blew comfortable ringlets of smoke upwards. I am not a smoker but if I were it would have to be cigars.

'Teenage girls,' he said meditatively, 'they are such trouble.'

Chapter Four

'The girl's captors,' AB continued, 'quickly succeeded in scaring our two young ladies. They are now under no illusion that their predicament is neither fun nor exciting but on the contrary is real and threatening. The kidnappers take their time to investigate the girls' belongings. Then they talk to each of them separately, using their best thickly accented English. They probably softened the teenagers up a little bit as part of the interrogation and then they left them alone together to contemplate their fate. Remember these girls had never experienced anything approaching this in their entire young lives, they must have been completely disorientated as well as being well out of their depth.'

'By this time they have seen three different captors; the original taxi driver and the two that took over and now have the girls under their control. Although none of them would qualify as members of Mensa the two that held them in the basement quickly realise that Kerry-Anne is the prime catch. You can imagine how overjoyed they must have been at this unexpected twist of fate. This is definitely the golden egg that they could only have dreamed of. On this basis they put their greasy heads together and come up with a plan.' he paused, 'But you must be wondering what the girl's bodyguard was doing whilst all this was going on?'

'The very question that was on the tip of my tongue,' I said too quickly. I regretted it immediately, knowing that it sounded a lot more facetious than I had intended. But it was too late to take it back.

'That attitude of yours,' said AB, shaking his head, 'it's going to get you into trouble if you're not careful.'

I knew he was right.

'Yes sir, sorry sir.'

'Anyway, the truth is that the bodyguard, the paid replacement, had panicked. Her first reaction was to consider her own position. She knew that this did not look good and that she would be held directly responsible for losing sight of them. Her employers were unlikely to be sympathetic to this turn of events. However, she had as yet no idea of the full course of events. As far as she knew the girls had simply moved quickly and were safe and sound and on their way to an hotel. She felt she could easily find out which one by using the tracking. It therefore didn't seem too serious a problem and so, to buy herself some time, she texted a report that simply said "Safely arrived at Lima airport" which may have been factually correct but hardly gave the complete picture. She then spent the next 24-hours trying to pick up the trail. 24 hours in which the kidnappers wreaked havoc upon the girls.'

'The following day Kerry's companion, Emily, was dumped outside the American Embassy and our becoming-worried bodyguard belatedly texted "Contact temporarily lost. Nothing to worry about. Am on the trail and will confirm when found".'

'She was wrong and, as far as I understand it, is currently unemployed and contemplating a change of career.'

His gold cufflinks blinked in the reflected sunlight as he reached out his hand for the whisky tumbler, still half full.

'I assume Emily had a message for Kerry's parents and that it involved a demand for money,' I said.

'Very perceptive of you,' said AB.

I winced but felt I deserved the put down.

AB put down his glass, ice cubes melting.

'The fact is that a lot of the information I am giving you is pieced together from interview with Emily post her release and yes their demands, made directly to the parents, were very much the usual;

don't involve the police, will make further contact in the next 24 to 48 hours, don't attempt to trace us in the meantime etcetera, etcetera … very boring in its predictability.'

'But?'

'But indeed,' he stroked his chin, 'to start with everything followed the obvious track; a telephone call in broken English to the parents, listened into by the FBI and the parent's legal team of course, the mother's demand to speak to Kerry in order to reassure the frightened girl, Kerry's teary voice querulous in her isolation, all her arrogance stripped away, the cry loud and clear "Mommy please help me".'

More cigar smoke spiraled its languid way upwards.

'The demand was high at $10 million and the parents received advice that, although protracted negotiation may reduce the sum, a swift armed intervention was the best route to a safe return of their child,' he paused, 'It's not good practice to give into these things, it just encourages more of the same.'

'During that first call the parents were prompted through their ear pieces to ask for 24-hours to find out whether they could raise the money and the kidnappers agree, adding that the next time they call they will specify the transfer arrangements. I'm told that the sour taste of slavering greed was almost tangible from the kidnapper's side.'

'24 hours was plenty of time for an armed group of four men to track down the signal emanating from Kerry's smartphone.' AB looked to the heavens, 'Unfortunately the hit squad only succeeded in locating the phone in a backstreet skip in one of Lima's more rundown areas. The phone was in an envelope with a message attached to it written in Kerry's own handwriting and presumably dictated to her "We told you not to try this. The price has just gone up or your girl will be sent back to you piece by piece." The writing, understandably, became less steady towards the end.'

'Even though kidnapping is a horrible business this calendar of events is not unusual,' I offered, 'although it's a dangerous business to send in the troops.'

When it's somebody else's child it's easier to be detached.

'I suppose the parents simply capitulated,' I said, 'they could argue that the raid wasn't their fault or their doing. The kidnappers must have been cock-a-hoop, they'd out-smarted the hit squad and were now going to demand even more money than they'd hoped for. They'd look after the girl, there's no point hurting a chicken that's about to lay you some golden eggs.'

'Yes, yes quite so,' said AB. 'the whole thing played completely into their hands. It must have felt like winning the lottery,' he paused, 'the strange thing is,' he said, 'they did not call back.'

He took up the whisky glass, gulped down the remainder.

'When powerful parents become distraught the situation can easily become incendiary. Alarm bells rang loudly, resources were allocated, searches were prepared and guns were loaded. In the absolute worst case, that is if the daughter could not be returned intact to the loving bosom of her family then, at the very least, there would be some bullet ridden corpses to show how hard they'd tried.'

'Fortunately, just before any more testosterone-fueled damage could be done, the next call came through. The voice was very different, the English more fluent and polished. The ransom demand was unexpectedly reduced to $500,000 without explanation. This was extraordinary in the circumstances. The only stipulation was that the intermediary sent to complete the deal and pick up the girl must not be North American. We don't know why. It wasn't questioned as it seemed a very small price to pay for a safe return.'

'I was contacted personally yesterday. And now here you are. You have only to hand over the ransom, collect the girl in whatever state you find her and deliver her back to her parents. After that you get a five-day break, all-expenses-paid, as a thank you for carrying out this arduous task. Any questions?'

It hit me all of a sudden, an American girl! My wife…

He read my mind, 'I know the American connection isn't ideal considering your recent experiences but I'd like you to handle it. To be honest, at such short notice, you're the best that I've got to offer.'

Thanks for the vote of confidence, I thought. I wasn't sure whether he was being complimentary or not. Probably not.

'There's the normal more detailed briefing scheduled for you,' he said, 'good luck and do keep in touch. You know how we like to know how you're getting on.'

Our 25 minutes were up. Samantha tapped politely at the office door. I got up and left.

Chapter Five

It was now on to the more difficult and detailed part of the briefing.

I was directed to a designated room down in the basement area. The room was flooded with white light and I was peppered with files, videos and talks.

The briefing staff were hyper-professional and proficient as usual. They worked on a 3 phased approach; they told me what they were going to tell me, they told me, and then they told me what they'd told me. This was then followed by sessions of questions and answers and tests.

I don't want to blow my own trumpet but I think it is fair for me to admit that one of the few positive attributes I possess is the ability to assimilate and absorb information quickly. I guess that's one of the reasons I'm doing this job.

It is normal in my game to adopt an assumed identity. This has the advantage of acting as a barrier between ourselves and any vindictive repercussions from individuals or organizations that may be dissatisfied with our services and also, and most importantly, a way of protecting our immediate and extended families.

My assumed identity for this assignment was Mr Paul Carpenter. Only minor changes were needed to my craggily handsome features in order to adopt this new persona. My hair was cut hedgehog short and dyed blonde and I was given a pair of tortoiseshell glasses with wide frames to wear and the wardrobe of a London stockbroker.

Occupation-wise I was a "Sales Executive", whatever one of those is, and to support this I was given a briefcase of samples, evidence that the purpose of my visit to Peru was the pursuit of new business in order to make my pretended bosses back home happy and justify myself a big non-existent year-end bonus.

In addition I was allocated a loving wife, Fiona, and two young children, Tom and Sam (a girl), the wee scamps, and the promise that if my home phone number was called at any time a suitably anxious "Fiona" would be there to answer it.

As importantly I was kitted out with a new phone with tracking, a watch and a few other bits and pieces. The obvious benefits of being issued with a gun were outweighed by the impossibility of smuggling this unnoticed through airport security even if I were happy to pay any excess baggage charges that might apply.

Finally I was ready to go, plane tickets in hand, post-haste to Heathrow airport, Terminal 5.

Once in the US I had people to meet including Kerry-Anne's parents and entourage and Emily, newly released from captivity and probably traumatized.

On my way to the airport I did manage a quick un-scheduled stop at a "friend's" for some additional things that I thought might come in handy. As my dear old mother used to say, you never quite know what's going to happen and it's always good to be prepared for the unexpected.

Chapter Six

I really don't like waiting, it's one of the most boring and wasteful of activities and, of all the possible forms of waiting in the universe, waiting for an aeroplane has got to be one of the worst.

When I arrived at the airport at the time demanded by the airline, and under threat of being thrown off the flight if I dared to disobey, I had to wait.

I had to queue to check in my baggage, crawl my way through the various levels of passport and boarding controls, drag myself laboriously through Security, X-ray and hand baggage surveillance procedures only to then have the pleasure of a personal frisking because I had forgotten to take my bloody watch off.

There was no sense of achievement in navigating my way through this frustrating maze of overpopulated checkpoints as it just moved me into a different phase of the waiting ritual, like moving up a level on a computer game.

Following the crowd sheep-like I walked mindlessly around the airport shops, browsing at things that I didn't want to buy; trying to work out, just for fun, whether any of the prices were actually cheaper than on the High Street and if so by how much. My answers still didn't tempt me to purchase.

Once tired of this form of amusement I found a café and decided to see how slowly I could drink a single regular-sized cup of cappuccino compared to my previous record of 2½ hours. Impatience got the better of me after only 60 snail-sliding minutes so I succumbed to an all-day brunch, piling on the calories by eating a meal I didn't need at the wrong time of the day.

Following increasingly surly looks from the servers I reluctantly vacated the café and proceeded to buy currency, exchanging hard earned Pounds Sterling for US Dollars at an exorbitant loss.

Even after these distractions had eaten their seconds from the slowly ticking clock I still had plenty of time to waste so I found, and tried to make myself comfortable on, a hard plastic seat with a view of one of the electronic Departure Boards. I sat staring at it. Waiting.

London Heathrow airport Terminal 5 was busy as usual and after a while I switched my attention to people watching. There was nothing else to do.

A teeming, ever-changing mass of people milled around me, each individual I picked out appeared to be much less bored than I was. There were holiday smiles on young faces, enthusiasm exuding from the collars of business suits, anxious mothers repeatedly counting their children, men stubbornly carrying bags that were clearly too heavy. It made me feel worse.

God, I'm a sad person I thought, perk yourself up for goodness sake!

The first leg of my journey was a British Airways Boeing 777 flight to JFK, due to leave London at 6pm and arrive in New York, taking into account the zonal time difference of -5hrs, at 9pm local time. It was an eight-hour flight.

There are two distinctly different ways to fly to New York from London Heathrow. One involves champagne, good food, at your seat service, several kinds of entertainment at your fingertips and a seat that converts into a comfortable horizontal bed in which you can ease yourself into peaceful slumber. The other has cramped seats, screaming kids, plastic knives and forks, crappy wine better suited for sprinkling on your fish and chips and a nil probability of a good flight's sleep. Both of these different worlds occupy the same plane; one is Business Class, the other Economy.

I was on the latter.

The logic went something like this: 'It wouldn't be right for you to stand out from the crowd, especially at the start' or more hurtfully, 'You're simply a courier, a paid agent of the ransom provider, an outrageously rich ransom provider perhaps, but one that is also keen on fiscal prudence.'

Thanks.

Although the statement about my lowly position in the pecking order may well be true, having it so clearly enunciated did nothing to lift my spirits. I comforted myself with the thought that some Economy Flights aren't that bad at all and at least I wasn't paying for this one.

Unfortunately my reluctant joie de vivre was nipped in the bud when I finally boarded the plane and found that, sitting next to me, was an overanxious young mother with her toddler son.

The child seemed determined to live up to his membership of the "terrible twos" club. The situation was made even slightly worse by the fact that his Spanish-speaking mamma spoke little or no English and my Spanish linguistic skills were close to zero.

I tried to placate myself with the knowledge that at least I had an aisle seat and could therefore make an escape more easily if I needed to.

At first I tried, I promise I tried, to play the part of the English gent, to be understanding of the mother's difficulties and to smile encouragement as she attempted in vain to control her errant son in such a confined space. I'm sorry to say that my patience ran out quite quickly and that the last straw was when my rather dapper travelling ensemble was splattered with assorted pieces of half-chewed ejecta from the child's meal.

I was struggling to look on the bright side any more when it occurred to me that here was an opportunity to test one of the things that I'd picked up from my friend's.

I want to say at this point that I would not have done what I was about to do if I was not desperately in need of some relaxation before my arrival in the US. I had to be compos mentis the minute I stepped off the plane even though I intended not to sleep and my body would think it was 2am. Also I'd approached the cabin crew and asked if I could change seats or make a late payment for an upgrade, the answer to both enquiries had been a firm 'No'. In addition I want it to be understood that I have a child of my own, I remember the toddler years and I love kids and I wouldn't do anything to any of them that would result in any lasting harm. Honest, I mean it.

Anyway, I bided my time until the stewardess had cleared away the leftovers from our meals. This reduced the amount of ammunition available to the terrible two-year-old although he had already moved on to a different game; arching his back, yowling and digging his rubber-soled shoes (why hadn't she taken them off?) into my thigh.

I got up and reached out my toilet bag from the hand baggage I'd placed in the overhead locker and made a quick visit to the bathroom, the wait for an available cubicle acted as a relief.

Once inside I removed the particles of projected food from my hair and took out a small bottle from the toilet bag. I had to correctly judge the reduced dose necessary for such a small child. There would be no permanent damage. I made my preparations, the sedative would be administered from a finger ring via a small and, I hoped, unobtrusive scratch to the skin.

I returned to my seat smiling and the next time a small chubby leg kicked out in my direction I took hold of the calf and administered a small prick to the leg. The toddler stopped yowling and turned to give me a look of large-eyed surprise and then he looked down at his leg and I released it.

'Lo siento,' said the mother and shook her head, pulling the child back.

'That's okay,' I said reassuringly.

Within five minutes the toddler had fallen silent, collapsed in his mother's arms, sleeping like a baby.

For about 30 minutes all was peace, quiet and calm but then the mother grew anxious. This was clearly not normal behaviour for her offspring.

At first she gently shook her son and when he did not wake up she looked at me and shrugged as if to say 'He does not do this'. I could see the worried look in her eye and realised there was only one thing to do.

A further trip to the bathroom, a consoling pat on her hand and a rearrangement of pillows as she drifted off into a well-earned sleep.

The next time the stewardess passed us she stopped to look at the sleeping madonna and child, smiled and said,

'They must be exhausted poor things. Children can be so demanding at that age, don't you think?'

'I guess they can,' I said.

'Oh yes,' she said, 'we see a lot of it in our job. Some children this age don't sleep at all, not for the whole flight.'

'Both of them look to be happily settled now,' I said.

'You're lucky,' she said and moved on.

I smiled. Some people make their own luck.

The rest of the flight was uneventful except that every now and again I had to remove the sleeping woman's head from my shoulder and make sure she wasn't drooling on my shirt. Eventually I tired of this and sought out extra pillows from the stewardess and constructed a kind of cushioned barrier between us.

As I've already said we were due to land in New York at around 9pm local time although my body would think it was 2am. I'd already switched my watch to New York time and as it had a second time zone function I'd adjusted that to keep track of the time in the UK, 5hrs ahead.

I've found the best way to cope with time differences is to take the pain immediately, force yourself to follow the local clock and try to ignore what your body is telling you. On this occasion this meant forcing myself to stay awake. This had the added advantage that I could keep an eye on my travelling companions, make sure their breathing remained regular, that kind of thing.

Although I think I did doze at one point I more or less managed to keep my eyes open by watching movies, drinking sips of water and stretching my legs every 20 minutes.

Travelling is not a passive sport. You need to be disciplined in order to try and ensure your internal body clock doesn't slow you down. I didn't have time for that.

From its inception in the late 1940s and up until 1963 New York's JFK airport was popularly known as "Idlewind" after the golf course that it had displaced.

In 1963 it was renamed to commemorate the United State's assassinated 35th president John F. Kennedy. Over 50 million passengers pass through the airport every year.

Our British Airways flight docked at Terminal 7. My maternal travelling companion had awoken as anticipated about one hour before we were due to land and had come round slowly and comfortably.

I was happy with that.

Her son however did not awaken so easily. But I knew what I was doing and a few gentle nudges from me did the trick and he awoke gently and without undue noise. His fully-open dark brown eyes and exuberant stretching and yawning re-assured his young mother. As I said there was never any intent on my part to harm this adorable toddler – I'm not a monster.

'He sleep good,' she said.

'Yes,' I said.

'He must like flight.'

'Yes,' I said, 'It must be that.'

'Maybe fly more often,' she laughed 'need sleep.'

See, I'd done them both a favour!

'Maybe,' I said, although without my assistance I hoped that for the sake of other adjacent travelers she didn't really mean it.

When I stood in the predictably long and

exceptionally slow-moving queue at Immigration and Passport Control I reflected that I had resisted the temptation to tick the "yes" box on the green immigration form in answer to the question "Are you a terrorist?" and reminded myself of the case of the British teenager who, filled with youthful over exuberance at his first landing in the good 'ol US of A, had thought it a bit of a lark to do this. As US border officials are not chosen for their sense of humour he was stripped naked and thoroughly examined both externally and, excruciatingly and humiliatingly, internally. This was followed by 48 hours of none-too-friendly custodial care at the end of which he gratefully accepted the suggestion to get on the next flight back to the UK rather than stay in a country where he did not feel welcome.

It doesn't pay to mess with, or try to share a joke with, a member of America's Immigration Force. You wait and wait in the non-American queue patiently and respectfully and answer only the questions you are asked, clearly and promptly. It was tough for me to do this but needs must and I eventually found my way to Baggage Reclaim and out into the Arrivals Hall. I was back in the USA.

Chapter Seven

For my first night back in the US I was staying at the Hilton New York JFK airport hotel which was only 1.6 miles from the airport so I sought out the free shuttle bus, remembering to tip the driver as he helped unload my bags at the hotel entrance.

The lobby of the Hilton was minimalist and clean. The guy on reception found my reservation, which was a relief, and I took the elevator to my sixth floor neutrally decorated "King Room" with its double bed and en suite bathroom.

It was 10pm local time and I decided I needed at least one further hour of wakefulness before collapsing into bed. The choice was between visiting the fully kitted out fitness centre and pool or finding the bar.

The bar was almost empty and I took a stool by the counter with the idea of keeping myself awake and amused through idle conversation with the bartender. Leaning an elbow on the cold stone surface of the counter for support I waited to be served.

A young woman of medium height, brown eyes and shoulder length hair approached me wearing the standard Hilton hotel livery. Smiling in that tutored customer friendly way that only involves the mouth and is not reflected in the eyes, she asked,

'What can I get you?'

To save time I gave her my room number straightaway and asked for two Budweiser. Over the next 45 minutes and two more Buds (you have to pace yourself on these trips) I learnt that her name was Teresa, that she was originally from Costa Rica, that she was holding down two jobs, was full of energy and was pretty bright.

I also noticed that her body was curvy and sensual. In a way she reminded me of my wife and that was nice. Even though it was wrong I did also note the rise and fall of her ample chest. I think it was the tiredness causing my defenses to lower. My wife had actually told me to stay alive after she had gone. I wasn't sure if she meant it. I wasn't sure that I could. And when I caught myself ogling a bartender all I felt was dirty.

Back in my room sleep, when it came, was like falling into a deep dark hole. Indistinct images swirled around in my dreams giving me nothing to hold onto, nothing to do but disappear into the blackness.

Chapter Eight

I awoke early, suddenly and hungry but before I went to find a good breakfast I called 'home' using my password "Agaricus". Choosing this time rather than the night before meant that the local time in London was sociable. That's the thing with 'the Store', they like to know what you're up to.

My go-to was Samantha, AB's PR,

'Hello,' I said, 'just checking in. Safely ensconced in the hotel in New York and meetings scheduled with no re-arrangements or delays as yet.'

'Fine,' said Samantha, 'how are you holding up?'

'You mean with the jet lag, the huge amount of data I'm having to assimilate, the stress associated with having a young girl's life in my hands, the lack of leg room in Economy…?'

'You know what I mean,' she said.

There was no avoiding the question. It was my first assignment back, if I wasn't coping I would have to be replaced and that would only get more difficult as the assignment progressed. I don't think she was enquiring through any sense of empathy, it was a purely professional question.

'I'm coping just fine,' I said, 'no need to worry about me, Sam.'

'Oh, but I do worry,' she said.

Somehow this attention felt more of a hindrance than a help. It wasn't comfortable having someone looking over my shoulder wondering if I was 'OK'. I'd rather be left alone to get on with the assignment but I knew that wasn't the way things worked. My location would be tracked and I'd have to check-in regularly or be chased, increasingly fiercely.

At breakfast I chose the Eggs Benedict, that luxurious concoction of poached eggs on so-called English muffins, sandwiched with bacon and smothered in a Hollandaise sauce that is truly an inspired American invention. Washed down with strong black coffee it made for a great recuperative. Let the day begin, I was ready.

There was a message waiting for me at reception. Somebody wanted to meet me inside Grand Central Station in around 20 minutes so I organised a late check out from the hotel and jumped into a taxi.

The taxi driver was a laconic New Yorker and regaled me with the inadequacies of his children who, he said, refused to listen to his sage advice and as a consequence their lives, in his opinion, were in freefall into the sewer. It made for an easy trip as the story took the form of a monologue. I hardly needed to respond although for politeness' sake I tried to give a passable pretence at interest and nodded and tutted occasionally to indicate my sympathy with his plight. He deserved his tip.

Grand Central Station, more correctly called Grand Central Terminal, is located at the intersection of 42nd Street and Park Avenue in midtown Manhattan.

The terminal covers 48 acres, has a total of 67 tracks and a world-record number of platforms at 44.

It is a fabulous place and I have to say a great location for a meeting. The main concourse is familiar to any avid filmgoer and is truly cavernous at 38m high, 84m long and 37m wide with giant versions of the Stars & Stripes on prominent display.

My meeting however was down on the Dining Concourse and I walked down one of the many connecting ramps looking for the Starbucks coffee shop, a landmark that even a jet lagged limey should be able to recognise.

Regretfully passing signs for the Harlem line, Hudson line and New Haven line and repressing the urge to simply wander and explore I sought out the familiar green and white branded frontage.

I was wearing a black overcoat, blue shirt, no tie, black trousers and shoes, a uniform that labelled me as either a businessman-on-the-way-to-work or as an uncool-man-trying-to-blend-in-and-failing.

I must have been closer to the latter as I had hardly passed over the threshold of the coffee shop when my arm was taken and I was led to a corner table. Passively I accepted this form of greeting although simply saying "Hi" would, in my humble opinion, have been a more friendly approach.

The table was at the very back of the coffee shop and even though surrounded by an ever-changing flow of commuters it was somehow both quiet and isolated. The risk of being overheard was consequently small. Busy places have advantages when privacy is required.

'Ya'll like a coffee?' asked one of my be-suited hosts.

There were two of them. The first was of large build, clearly worked out and was about 6 feet tall. His hair was cut extremely short and he was probably in his late 20's. The second, who had taken my arm, led me to the table and was now offering me a coffee, was clearly the more senior man. His face showed both age and experience underlined by a welter of scar tissue that lay above his right eye in a horizontal line about 2 inches long. They both wore sharp grey suits, highly polished black shoes, white shirts and red neck-ties. I felt distinctly underdressed.

'Sure I'd like a cappuccino please, no sugar.'

The elder man nodded to the younger who

obediently made his way to the counter.

'Y'all 're easy to spot Mr Carpenter. We got pretty damn accurate photographs and oh, bye an' bye, we were also granted permission to hack into youse'all GPS so as we could see ya'll coming right along.' He held out his smartphone, 'Clever damn things, don't know what we ever did without 'em.'

He glanced over at his companion, making sure that the coffee was on its way, then he continued, 'So Paul, guess'n it's okay to call you Paul? You'all limeys can be such pricks with your'n manners'n all.'

I nodded, he could call me Paul and we Brits are pricks when it comes to manners.

'Well Paul mah name's George, George Landers and that there young boy over yonder getting you your coffee, that's Richard. I like calling him Dick but he don't get the joke.'

So this was George Landers, Kerry-Anne's long time shadow cum bodyguard. His appearance lived up to his billing.

'Nice to meet you,' I said and stretched out my hand. He looked down at it but didn't take it. I withdrew it, a little offended, which I guess was the point.

'Purely business Paul, purely business. We'all'r not going to be digging too deep into your business and we'all'r going to be jest completing ours. This is a bad situation Paul, real bad,' after shaking his head he said, 'Don't know why our employers don't trust us to do what you'all'r goin' to do but that's their call. Maybe they want to keep it nice'n separate from their own team. What you think Paul?'

I knew that Kerry-Anne's captors had made specific demands as to the type of go-between they wanted and that George definitely did not meet those requirements. It appeared however that George did not know about that and I saw no reason to enlighten him.

'I don't think anything,' I said, 'it's not my job to think. I just do what I'm told to do and I do it as well and as quickly as I can.'

'Don' we all,' replied George looking at me quizzically. Maybe he did know more and had been testing me, 'don' we all.'

Call me perceptive but I'd already realised that George wanted me to know that he was not the kind of guy to be taken for granted. I knew from my briefing that he had acted as Kerry-Anne's shadow for a lot of her life and he must have been personally put out when he wasn't allowed to shadow her on her backpacking trip. He didn't seem like an I-told-you-so kind of guy but the way things had worked out he could be forgiven for thinking that.

Richard curtailed any additional pleasantries by

returning with the coffees; two espressos and one cappuccino, regular size. They clearly didn't want to spoil me.

'Everything okay?' asked Richard, 'need anything else?'

'That's just fine for me,' I said.

George didn't even bother to reply, just took the cup that was offered to him.

'We like our jobs, don't we Richard?' he said instead. Richard nodded, 'and we appreciate the people we work for an'all an' we don't like them being upset. We want our girl back quickly and intact, you get my meaning, Paul?'

I got his meaning and I said so although I thought that his clarity of expression could do with a little work. But I kept that to myself. No point ruining a blossoming friendship.

As we sipped our coffees George explained the errand that they had been sent to discharge. He reached down and retrieved a small leather man-bag that nestled underneath the table. He handed it to me.

'Inside there are two packages, both sealed,' he said speaking very deliberately. This was business and he didn't want any misunderstandings, 'right now our job is to jest hand them over to you.'

I was expecting only one package but I hid my surprise. I would find out the reason for the second when I opened them later, back in the hotel.

'Thanks,' I said.

'Now, to make sure you'n me'r startin' off right, I want you to check them packages'r still sealed. Wouldn't be nice of you to accuse us of any tampering.'

I didn't foresee any reason I would do that so I started to say, 'That won't be…'

It was Richard who put his hand on my arm this time, 'Like George said, we would surely appreciate it.'

I was beginning to see that this young man had potential. As I had no reason to antagonise either of them I unzipped the bag and inspected the contents without removing anything. It all looked okay to me and I said so.

Richard held up his smartphone and spoke into it describing the place, the date and the time with laudable clarity and brevity.

'Now, Mr Carpenter if you could just repeat the date, time and place, state what we have given you and the condition.'

Wow, I thought, these guys are serious about wanting reassurance. The stakes must be pretty high for them.

I politely complied, confirming my current identity and all the other information they requested. George and Richard rose to go, their coffees unfinished.

'You just stay here a while an' enjoy yer cappuccino,' said George, 'I'll be acontacting you agin, but this time ah'll come along to your hotel. Ah'll be in the lobby at 15:00 hrs, be ready.'

'Hmm,' I replied.

'Have a nice day now ya'hear,' said Richard as he got up and turned to leave.

In a few seconds the two of them were lost in the milling sea of humanity that perpetually flows through Grand Central.

I finished my coffee slowly, enjoying the busy ambiance of the place. Looking around casually I checked the faces and the movements of the people. There was nothing suspicious that I could see. No one seemed to care about me, or my friends, or our conversation, and that was just the way it should be.

After leaving the coffee shop I wandered aimlessly through the throng enjoying the thrill of being in this iconic space.

People flowed around me, each purposefully pursuing some individual design, talking on phones as they walked, bumping, dodging. With my head still a little woozy from the jet lag it felt almost like water rafting and in a pleasantly disorienting kind of way it felt good.

Chapter Nine

Once back in the hotel room I examined the packages George and Richard had given me in more detail.

The first was the additional pair of samples that I had been expecting and I added them to the ones that were already in my hand baggage.

The second was an envelope containing $50,000 in mixed notes and 4,000PEN or Sol, Peru's national currency.

The money was something of a pleasant surprise and a windfall that, when the time came, I might choose to omit from my end of assignment expenses report.

When I thought about it I realized what a helpful addition it was as it ensured that I was well placed to pay my way out of any unforeseen unpleasant situation that I might find myself in.

Feeling like I needed some exercise I visited the hotel gym and pool, the physical exertion and the refreshing coolness of the chlorinated water invigorated me and helped my body ignore the time difference. I had already forgotten what the time was back in the UK and didn't want to look for fear of negating my personal progress towards acclimatization.

The swim had also given me an appetite although I didn't want a heavy meal as I was due to fly out from New York later that evening. A bar lunch would fit the bill and I was pleased to see that it was again Teresa who was serving.

There weren't many people there at that time of day, the early afternoon lull, and I had the chance to resume our small talk and asked how often she went back to visit her home in Costa Rica.

This was simply meant as a passing remark, out of a little bit of curiosity but mainly just to keep a conversation going. The fierceness of her response however made it clear that I had accidentally hit on a raw nerve. She worked long hours she said, and still money was tight, did I think she had the freedom to go home anytime she wanted?

I had brought the man-bag, the one that George had given me, down with me from my room. Now empty, my idea had been to find a way of quickly disposing of it. In present circumstances an alternative thought occurred to me; that I should offer it to Teresa – as a peace offering.

A burger, two beers but no fries later I slipped $40 inside and offered her the bag. Her face lit up in surprise.

'Are you sure?' she said, 'it looks like real leather.'

I hadn't given it a thought, it probably was. I nodded.

'I don't think anyone has ever given me anything like this before,' she said.

She seemed to mean this literally and I smiled, it's amazing how little it can take to make someone else feel good.

Glancing at my watch I saw it was approaching the time I was due to meet George again so I took my leave, whilst the going was good, and went back to my room to clean up and be ready.

I had just emerged from the bathroom when the bedside telephone rang. I answered it.

'Mr Carpenter?'

'Yes.'

'There is a man here in the lobby waiting for you, sir.'

He was 10 minutes early.

'OK, could you put him on please.'

I explained I would be with him 'in five'.

'Bring youse'all's passport,' he said without explanation.

'OK,' I said, not wanting to ruffle his feathers, 'no problem.'

Down in the lobby George's short cut grey hair and sharp cut suit weren't difficult to pick out. I approached him my hand outstretched.

'Hello again,' I said.

'Mr Carpenter? Could ah trouble ya'll for the time,' he said, ignoring both my hand and my comment.

He was reverting to a previously arranged security question, acting as if this was the first time we'd met. I wondered whether he was working for two masters and trying to satisfy both of them. It was better just to play along, perhaps he was wired.

'It's almost time to start your Christmas shopping,' I said.

'It's never too early to start,' said George, 'please follow me.'

It may sound ridiculous but trading a pre-set question and answer is still an easy way to get over the hurdle of initial identification.

George led me down into the bowels of the hotel's underground car park full of sharp-edged shadows and yellow artificial light. Parked in a far corner was a black Mercedes C-Class. He opened the back door.

'Get in,' he said.

He remained outside with the door held open.

'Passport,' he said.

I handed it over. He took out his phone.

'Look this way,' he said.

It was like going through airport security except more intense. I thought it was all a bit unnecessary and contrasted sharply with the casual nature of our first meeting. However there is always that moment of doubt and I didn't like to think about what complexities would ensue if somehow I failed to pass these tests. I had faith in the technical abilities of 'The Store' to get all this right. But still.

He took a photo of my passport as well, pressed a few buttons, called a number.

'Yes… okay … sure … will do.'

He handed me back my passport.

'We'rn not happy y'all are here,' he said seriously, echoing my previous thoughts that he must be put out by my presence, 'but these here choices are not fer me to make so ah guess ah'll jest hev to welcome you to the good'ol US of A.'

This time he put out his hand and I took it gratefully.

This was hardly a great start, or re-start, but I could understand it. This was an American family so surely it must be an American problem to be solved by a wholly American solution. It must have cut deep into his and other people's pride that a non-negotiable requirement for a non-American go-between had been made and accepted. I'd try hard not to upset him any more than I had to.

'So now?' I asked, as politely as I could.

'Now's time to talk to some people,' he said.

'OK, let's get going,' I said, starting to close the car door. George stopped me. I was surprised.

'What's wrong?' I said, 'Where are we going?'

'Nothing wrong,' said George, 'we're right here.'

With my mind fogged by jet lag this took a moment to sink in.

'They're here at this hotel?'

'We're where we need to be,' he said, 'let's go.'

He led me towards an elevator shaft and as we stopped before the closed silver-metal doors he said,

'We got us a conference room. Got all them fancy facilities we gonna need. You ready?'

'Yes,' I said.

I'd prepared myself as well as I could ahead of these conversations. There were important things from all sides that needed to be said.

Chapter Ten

It had not been made clear to me who precisely Kerry-Anne's parents were and to be honest I thought it probably better not to know, but with all these security protocols they must be important. That just made my task more difficult.

I followed George obediently into the elevator, then up, out and along a richly carpeted corridor. When he got to where he wanted to be he stopped, knocked and we entered a large suite.

I was guided to the centre of the main room. It felt clammy and my jet lag slightly disorientated me and made me feel dizzy. George escorted me to a chair and once seated I took a few deep breaths and slowly but surely my head stopped spinning. George was looking at me. He probably thought I was nervous.

'You wan' a glass a water?' he said.

I was sitting at a fairly large light-coloured wooden table that could comfortably sit eight and he was sitting next to me.

'No,' I said, 'but I would like a coffee, black, no sugar, strong.'

'Too much coffee ain't good fer a person,' said George. Nevertheless he signalled to the only other person in the room. I glanced across. It was Richard. I wasn't sure he was loving this role of providing me with hot drinks, but whatever his feelings he didn't let them show and turned obediently towards what I guessed must be a kitchen area.

He returned promptly and placed a steaming cup of coffee in front of me. George tutted, found a coaster, and slid it underneath.

'Young'uns,' he said.

We sat for a few moments in silence while I nursed the coffee and George waited.

There was a knock at the door. After looking through the peephole Richard opened the door and two people entered, one guiding, one following.

The second figure was lead to the seat opposite me.

'This here is the bodyguard that was hired to shadow Kerry-Anne and Emily,' said George, with evident disdain, 'we reckon'd you'd meet her first.'

The order was up to them.

'Yes,' I said, 'thank you.'

'Then ask away Mr Carpenter, she'n all yours.'

Across the table sat an athletically built woman in a navy blue trouser suit and white blouse, open at the neck. Her hair was long and dark, her eyes blue and she looked distinctly uncomfortable.

I decided small talk wasn't necessary and jumped straight in.

'What is your name?' I asked.

'Joyce.'

Sparse, but it would do. I wasn't checking her resume.

'Organisation?'

She looked across at George. I picked up the signal.

'OK,' I said, 'it doesn't matter, just tell me in your own words what happened.'

She looked at me earnestly and started to speak, my guess was that she'd spent a long time rehearsing what she was about to say.

'Well now I'm highly qualified and experienced in surveillance,' she began, 'that's why I was chosen for this task.'

I wasn't interested.

'I spent many years…'

I interrupted.

'Could we just get to the arrival in Peru,' I said, maybe my previous disorientation, which the black coffee was doing a great job of dispelling, had left a residue of grouchiness. Now I was here I just wanted to get on with this assignment as quickly as possible.

'OK,' she said, a little put out, 'So we'd passed along nicely through a few countries already and I was getting used to the girl's behaviour. They was predictable like all youngsters is and I was keeping a good distance, changing my appearance reg'lar and carrying out my surveillance, reporting back right on time on every day an' sometimes more often, doing the job I was taught to do, thorough like, cos like I said I've got a lot of…'

I waved my hand. She stopped and started again.

'The flight to Peru had been just fine, I could keep an easy eye on where they was sitting an' most of the flight they was either chatting or watching movies. When we landed we made our way through passport control and on towards baggage collection. I didn't have no bags cos I didn't wanna be caught out waiting jus' in case their bags come off first.'

She paused looking, I think, for acknowledgment of her smartness. I just looked back blankly.

'Them girls always put their backpacks in the luggage. I don't know what they got in there but they sure was large.'

'Tents, sleeping bags,' I suggested.

Joyce laughed.

'You got these girls all wrong. These girls was not backpacking on a budget they was backpacking on a credit card an' a credit card with lots of credit on it. These girls was not sleeping in no hostels, these girls was sleeping in hotels… and nice hotels at that.'

'OK,' I said, 'please carry on.'

'Well when the bags was comin' up the chute I notice Kerry-Anne like glance across at me. I didn't think nothing of it cos when youse waiting youse glance around just to like pass the time. I did make myself a mental note howsever to get some glasses or something like that just to alter my looks a little for the next day.'

'Had you noticed Kerry-Anne or Emily glancing at you any other time?' I asked.

'I can't say that I did,' she thought for a moment 'no I can't say that I did.'

'You know that Kerry-Anne has had a shadow most of her life,' I said and I heard George grunt, presumably in agreement, 'so if anyone could pick up that they were being shadowed it would be her. I'm guessing she's a smart kid, she'd know the signs, she'd know the tricks.' George nodded.

'Yea, but she'd never seen me before,' said Joyce, 'and I'm experienced…'

'I know. You said. What happened next?'

'It was a busy flight we'd just come off, a Boeing 747 that was pretty much full, so there was quite a crowd around the baggage reclaim belts an' people were all pushin' and shovin' soon as they see what they thought was their bags… an' well…'

Joyce trailed off.

'An' well what?' I said.

Joyce looked away.

'It wasn't my fault,' she said, 'they was there one minute an' gone the next.'

She spread out her arms. If she was looking for sympathy, empathy or understanding then she'd come to the wrong place.

'So what did you do?'

'I moved into and through the crowd thinking they was still in there jus' being hidden like, by the other people. But I didn't find them.'

'What did you do then?'

'I got through security quick like and carried out a thorough search of the Arrivals Hall an' the external concourse, the taxi queue an' all that an' then I went up to Departures an' searched there to.'

'And?'

'Well, I didn't find 'em.'

'And then?'

'Well, like I said they was predictable so I knew they'd have hightailed it out of the airport to some nice hotel. I had access to the tracking on Kerry-Anne's phone so I knew I could find out where they'd gone and catch up with them real easy.'

'Why didn't you immediately track her whereabouts instead of running around the airport?'

Joyce put her hands palm downwards on the table in front of her. She looked crestfallen.

'The reception in the airport wasn't good,' she said, 'you have to switch providers when you arrive in another country and the reconnection hadn't happened yet.'

I wondered whether she'd panicked.

'I guess you knew you'd be blamed if it was found out that you'd lost contact,' I said.

Her head drooped.

'I knew I'd be blamed,' she said, 'but it wasn't necessary. I thought I'd catch up with them soon enough.'

'And when you did get your phone working?'

Her head drooped further and she muttered something.

'Sorry,' I said, 'I didn't quite catch that.'

'I had to check in,' she said, 'when my phone was working I checked in.'

'You mean you sent a text?'

'Yes,' she whispered, 'I sent a text.'

'And what did the text say?'

'It said something like "Landed safely in Peru".'

I waited.

'It was true,' she said.

'But not the whole story.'

'I knew I'd get blamed. I was sure it wasn't a problem. I just needed a little more time. After I sent the text I went to the tracking.'

'And you located them?'

'I located them. They were moving. They must have been in a taxi. Just like I thought. They must have jumped the queue somehow. Probably slipped someone a few dollars.'

'And then?'

'I put my phone in my pocket and went to get a few toiletries and then joined the queue for the taxis. I reckoned by the time I got a taxi they'd have stopped at a hotel and I could catch up with them.'

'And then?'

'When I got into the back of the taxi I looked at my phone and their signal had gone. I didn't think that was too much of a problem 'cos in places like that things like that happen. I knew the hotel chains they favoured so I picked one. I figured if I'd picked wrong I could make a base and track them down no problem.'

'But..'

'I did my best, I did the sensible thing, I trailed from hotel to hotel. Then I thought I'd just sleep on it and sort it out when I was fresh.'

'But that didn't work out.'

'No,' she said, 'so I sent a text.'

'But it was too late.'

'It wasn't my fault. I was just unlucky.'

'What happened then?'

'I was recalled and fired.'

'Thanks for coming in and talking to me,' I said.

'I hope I've helped. I've tried to help as much as I can. I'm experienced…'

'OK, thanks,' I said.

'…and I'm looking for another job.'

I looked at George. He shook his head.

'I'm not from round here,' I said, 'sorry but I can't help.'

Joyce shrugged.

George nodded to the guy who had accompanied Joyce into the room. Before taking her out again George handed Joyce an envelope.

'For your help,' he said.

After she'd left George asked,

'What do you think?'

'I think it had nothing to do with luck,' I said, 'it might be forgivable to lose sight of your mark but it is unforgivable to then choose not to move into emergency mode. Kerry-Anne's phone was active and could have been tracked, help could have been summoned. In the time that Joyce thought about her own neck the situation was running out of control. By the time she decided to act it was far too late.'

George looked at me and smiled. A genuine smile for the first time since we'd met.

'You been in the Forces?' he said.

'Yes,' I said.

'Thought so,' he said, holding up his hand to let me see his veteran's ring.

'It's like a big family,' I said.

'Ah like to think that family is wider'n home,' he said, 'maybe stretches 'cross countries, boundaries an' oceans.'

'Maybe it does,' I said.

Chapter Eleven

'Can y'all take another coffee?' asked George.

'Yes, please,' I said.

I got up from the table. Stretched my back, my arms, and my legs and started to move around the table.

'Keep away from the windows,' said George.

Richard was down on his knees messing with wires and cables.

'What now?' I said.

Richard got up from his knees and placed a conference speaker phone in the middle of the table. He started pressing buttons, listening to the static noise and looking at the coloured lights.

'Kerry-Anne's parents,' said George. He pointed to the speaker phone. 'It ain't that it'll be face to face or video call,' he said, 'ah'm sure y'all understan'.'

Security was being overdone in my opinion, but I was only a paid hand so who was I to comment. After all the last time they chose to use an outsider, against George's best advice, it turned out badly for all concerned. I'm sure they would not have chosen to do it again, especially if it involved hiring somebody from outside the USA. But this time their hand had been forced. I hadn't been expecting the red carpet treatment, and I wasn't getting it.

Richard completed the preliminary set up and pressed "Call". It was answered after just two rings.

'Yes.'

'We're ready at this end,' he said, 'Are you hearing me clearly?'

'Yes, and you?'

'Yes. Just leave the line open'

'OK.'

Not exactly chatty but efficient.

With my fresh coffee alongside me we sat and waited.

After 3 or 4 minutes we could hear rustling and throat clearing at the other end of the line and then,

'Mr Carpenter?'

'Yes.'

'You have George alongside you?'

'Ah'm here,' said George.

'Good, so we'll begin. My name is Andrews and I will be speaking on behalf of Kerry-Anne's parents. We understand you may have some questions Mr Carpenter and of course we are keen to help you in any way we can. We all want Kerry-Anne returned as speedily as possible,' he paused, there was some background noise which I took to be voices, 'Just one question before we start, Mr Carpenter, how much do you know about Kerry-Anne's parents?'

'Almost nothing,' I said.

'Good,' said Andrews, 'we're keen to keep it that way. We understand that you are the best at what you do so you can now go ahead and ask anything you like but please remember to be respectful.'

I wasn't sure I deserved the accolade. AB had told me I was just about the only one available at such short notice. I was also fresh back in harness and AB had told me that this was "an easy one". It didn't feel like it right now. What it felt like was walking over a field of eggshells while having your hands tied behind your back and wearing clogs. I'd do my best to tread carefully.

'I'm interested in Kerry-Anne's personality,' I said, 'how she might act in unfamiliar circumstances and why it was that a new bodyguard was chosen to shadow her.'

There was more muttering. My guess was that the parents were there but preferred to have this conversation mediated. Did they always have to be so careful? Theirs must be a pretty claustrophobic existence if they did.

'Kerry-Anne has a strong personality and is becoming more and more independent in her views and actions,' said Andrews, he paused, 'sometimes she can act precipitously and her actions do not always lead to the desired outcomes.'

Sounded like most young women of her age. It certainly reminded me of my own daughter and the scrapes she used to get herself into.

'Under pressure she normally keeps her composure,' Good, 'and tries to find a way out.' Not always so good in situations like this. Sometimes it's better to just sit tight and bide your time until somebody comes to collect you, someone like me for example.

'And the bodyguard?'

George was squirming beside me desperate to say something. Something like 'I told you so' probably. But he held his tongue.

'Herum, that was because Kerry-Anne had explicitly asked not to be shadowed. It was thought that to appear to be acceding to her request whilst providing a sensible level of safety and security was apposite. Kerry-Anne was of course familiar with all the normal staff so to go outside to a reputable agency was the logical next best course of action.'

'But it didn't work out.'

I couldn't stop myself. George bit his lip.

'Have you other questions?' said Andrews.

'I understand,' I said, 'that the ransom demand has changed significantly. Can you talk me through that.'

'Hrrum, yes, it has changed,' said Andrews, who had a habit of clearing his throat, 'the first demand was for \$10m. To be honest with you,' that would be nice, I thought, 'that was achievable but all the professional advice was to play for time, we thought we knew where Kerry-Anne was being held.'

I noticed he was distancing himself from the 'professional advice' and as it had led to the badly failed attempt made by an armed retrieval squad I didn't blame him. The attempt had bordered on humiliating and could have led to a very, very poor outcome.

'After our Plan A failed to deliver the desired outcome,' a nice way of putting it, it had been a complete disaster and upped the ante at least tenfold, 'we decided to await the next contact and take it from there. In the meantime sources of funds were explored and significant monies moved into accounts that could be immediately accessed.'

'So you were anticipating a significant increase in the size of the ransom demand.'

'Yes,' said Andrews hesitatingly.

'And you were going to pay?' I asked, 'no more alternative approaches?'

I was being as gentle as possible, but I needed to know.

'That was the idea,' said Andrews unconvincingly.

'But the demand, when it came, was a surprise.'

'Yes again,' said Andrews, 'they made us wait, you can imagine the way the anxiety levels were increasing around here and the impulse to do something,' I could hear muttered voices behind him, it sounded like 'Just get on with it', 'we kept our nerve,' he said, making it sound like a personal achievement, 'and when we did get renewed contact we were ready.'

I interrupted.

'But the voice sounded different?'

'Yes.'

'And you were sure it was genuine, not some secondary scammers who had somehow moved in?'

'We were and are sure, the information exchanged could only be known by her captors.'

I was going to choose to believe this. If I didn't then everything came off the rails right here, right now.

'OK, tell me what happened.'

'The voice was deep and guttural,' said Andrews, 'and talked slowly. A new demand for money was made of $500,000. We kept our surprise to ourselves and hid the increased anxiety we had been feeling. We're professionals, Mr Carpenter, we know how these situations need to be handled.'

Really, I thought. Maybe he had FBI and CIA operatives looking over his shoulder and wanted to keep them sweet. Maybe he was just a proud American. Maybe he had absolute faith in American superiority. Maybe he was just deluded.

'Before we accepted the demand the voice laid out the other stipulations. First, the girl had to be physically collected, no drop off point, no directions to a specific hiding place. Second, the money transfer had to be electronic and at the time of collection,' he paused, 'these were easy terms to accept,' he said.

I bet they were, I thought, they were a doddle compared to some of the scenarios they'd have considered whilst waiting for the renewed contact.

'Third,' he continued, 'hrrum, the intermediary must not be American and must not be associated directly or indirectly with any government agency. He was very clear on this last point. Fourth and last, if there were any other sign, any sign at all of these terms not being met to the letter then Kerry-Anne would not be coming home.'

I heard a gasp behind him. I presumed it was Kerry-Anne's mother. Although she knew all of this, hearing it repeated must just have reopened the wound. If it were my daughter I would have gasped too.

'Finding someone with the skills and experience to be parachuted in as an intermediary was no easy matter, but urgent. He was effectively asking for a civilian of non-American decent but we could not risk sending in an amateur,' he paused, 'and that's where you come in Mr Carpenter, that's why you're here. To be honest we don't like it but we've all agreed, after all that has passed, that we must simply follow the demands as stipulated.'

I still wasn't convinced that there wasn't some Plan C cooking in the background. This was America and Americans were proud, gun-toting people.

'Thanks,' I said.

'All the arrangements have been made, George will pass on to you your agenda and tickets, good luck, Mr Carpenter.'

I wasn't quite ready for the conversation to end so I soldiered on.

'I have of course seen photographs and videos of Kerry-Anne,' I said, 'but it may become necessary for me to validate her identity. Is there a question I could ask that only she would know the answer to?'

There was a long pause.

'What do you mean "it may become necessary" ?' said Andrews.

'I'm just trying to be as prepared as possible,' I said, 'it's better to be ready for any eventuality, however remote.'

There were sounds of movement and then a woman's voice.

'She's a straight 'A' student,' said the voice, 'the only subject she has ever failed at is State History. Will that do?'

Not really, I thought. Asking someone to remember a failure was not the most appropriate thing in this situation. But I decided not to push it.

'That's fine,' I said, 'is there anything more you want to ask or tell me?'

There was more movement and then a strong male voice.

'You been in the Army, Mr Carpenter?'

'Yes,' I said. In this position I'd have said 'Yes' whether it was true or not.

'You done this kind of work before?'

'Yes, many times.' The 'many' may have been a stretch but this kind of situation was far from new to me. It generally worked out OK as long as everyone kept their heads and no-one did anything stupid.

'Have we already made mistakes?'

This took me by surprise. It was a strange question to be thrown at me out of the blue, but I decided to be honest.

'Yes,' I said, 'you sent in an armed retrieval team that failed. It was predictable and you were outsmarted. You were lucky to get away with that.'

There was silence. Then Andrews was back.

'It was the best advice from our best experts,' he said, 'how dare you…'

I interrupted.

'I was asked a question and I answered it,' I said.

The strong male voice came back.

'Are we making any mistakes now?'

'No, you were asked to send in a non-American, I'm definitely that, and someone not a part of any government authority, again I fit the bill. Right now you're co-operating and making getting your daughter back as easy as possible. In this situation that's the best you can do. I would, though, give you one piece of advice.'

'What's that?'

'Don't double up on me. No armed forces in the shadows. No surveillance. No interference whatsoever. I just go and do what's been asked. No more no less. I assume your taping this call so I know that you'll have what I just said on record. That's my advice.'

Silence. A female voice

'You're asking us to trust you with our daughter's life. We don't know you, we've never met you, we know next to nothing about you.'

'I'm asking you to trust that the deal you've made is real and that by letting me complete your part of it you're giving yourselves the best chance of getting your daughter back quickly and safely, that you're giving yourselves the best chance of this all working itself out positively.'

Muttered conversation, some voices raised. Andrews came back on the line.

'Alright Mr Carpenter we'll do it your way but in the name of god I hope you're right.'

I hoped so too.

When the call had ended and all the equipment was tidied away, George said,

'Ah'll tell you this Mr Carpenter, you got some balls!'

I didn't see it that way. I saw it as self-preservation. The last thing I needed was some gun-toting know-it-all hiding in the shadows with his finger on the trigger. Nope, sink or swim, going it alone was definitely the best strategy.

We had one more person to meet and that was Emily.

George told me that this last interview would be face to face but her flight had not yet landed. She had asked to speak to me one-to-one and reluctantly that had been agreed to, although George and Richard would remain within hailing distance. I asked if the room was bugged. He shrugged. I asked that if it were would it be deactivated during my talk with Emily. He shrugged again.

To make use of the time I told George that I wanted to talk to him privately. He said that was OK but it was probably best if we did that back in my own room. I guess he meant because that one wasn't bugged.

Chapter Twelve

George Landers sat opposite me. Now in his fifties he was obviously a man who'd lived quite a life and, like me, probably seen a lot of things he wished he hadn't. His grey hair was cut short. His unusually bright green eyes shone out at me from tanned, wrinkled skin. He sat comfortably, legs crossed, with the sleeves of his white shirt rolled up to the elbows, his red tie loose. I tried to look relaxed, an emotion I wasn't feeling right at this moment, and wondered how best to start. He did it for me.

'Ask me whatever y'all want,' he said, 'I ain't fixin' to hold nothing back. This gal Kerry-Anne is as good as my own little girl. Them bastards that got her have a whole heap of shit coming their way, you can be sure of that.'

I didn't want a fight. My job was just to hand over the money, collect the girl, bring her back. That was all. No repercussions. No revenge. No vendetta.

My immediate reaction to this 'howd'ya do' from George was to make sure to keep him well away from the front line. I didn't know him so I didn't know how itchy his trigger finger might be. The best thing for me to do was to try and convince him I could be trusted to do this job competently … and on my own.

'When I get out there,' I said, 'I'll need to meet Kerry-Anne before I hand anything over. Like I said to her parents I've seen lots of photographs and family videos so identification should be straight forward but it would be good if I had a simple question I could ask that only Kerry-Anne would immediately know the answer to. I got that one from her mother, but asking her what she failed … come on, that's not the best idea is it ? You got anything better?'

He gave me a thin smile. I took it as reassurance that my thoroughness was appreciated and that he agreed that what I had been offered so far wasn't the best.

'You really ever done this before?' he said.

Maybe I was wrong.

'Plenty of times,' I lied.

'An' how many times did the thing go the way y'all expected 'em to go?'

This was a tricky question. If it sounded like I said too many then I was clearly incompetent, if I said too few then I was clearly lying. I went for noncommittal.

'You know the way of it, George. You're ex-FBI aren't you? You must have been well-schooled in the art of exchange.' I thought a bit of flattery might help things along.

'Oh yea,' he said, 'near'n a twenty year man. Loved the job, though it took its toll. It does that to a person over the years,' I knew about things that took their toll. As an ex-soldier I'd got a memory cabinet full of things that were still taking their toll, chiming in my restless dreams at night, 'Ah did all the training an' then when I came out I was happy to find work with Kerry-Anne's parents. Did a lot of looking after people, including a lot of looking after Kerry-Anne. I cain't say she appreciated the attention but ah reckon it wuz a smart thing, look what happens when you leave it to an amateur. Yea, an' to answer your question ah know a hell'uv a lot about exchanges, ah sure do. I just hope as hell that you do too… but ah ain't convinced.'

His green eyes burrowed into my skull. I was on trial as far as he was concerned and although I'd got in the room I hadn't yet passed the interview.

'Them parents of her'n make decisions aplenty an' most of 'em'r good, but not all'n 'em,' he said, softening his glare, 'They should've let me go like I told 'em. Ah been looking efter Kerry-Anne since she were knee high. She know me, Ah knows her. Ah could've been sure to keep a distance but still be looking. Yep, that wuz a poor decision alright and ah ain't wanting there to be no more, that's why you 'n me have to understand each other. You git me?'

I got that this was personal as well as professional for George and that he was not going to just sit back and leave me to it.

'So ah'll give yer all the help ah can, but you gotta do somethin' fer me.'

'And what's that?' I said, 'After Kerry-Anne herself it's her parents I'm beholden to. You know that.'

You can have too many clients I didn't need another one.

He laughed.

'Did yer notice,' he said, 'how they'all talk about her?'

I had, but I wasn't going to admit that to him.

'What do you mean?' I said.

'Like she was some kinda project, like they was moulding her to be what they want her to be, like she ain't allowed to be imperfect like you 'n me?'

I took the point. I was very definitely imperfect. I didn't know about him.

'Maybe they just want the best for her,' I said, 'they've probably got her best interests at heart.'

George grunted.

'Shame they've never been a ask'n of her what she wanted,' he said, 'now you gotta keep me informed too ya'hear. Ah'm not bein' shaken off looking efter

Kerry-Anne agin an' I'll tell yer this Paul, she had better be in good shape when you bring her home.'

It seemed to me that George was too close to this, it would be too easy for his professional judgement to be impaired were Kerry-Anne was concerned. Anyway I'd got his message and I'd think about when, how or if I'd respond to it.

'Poppy,' he said.

'Poppy?'

'Her first pet, it was a rabbit, got taken by a dog, neighbour's rottweiler, she cried fer two days, there'll not be many but Kerry-Anne remembers that.'

A bit gruesome but nevertheless better than what I had.

'Thanks,' I said, 'I'll use that. Anything else?'

'As long as you 'n me understand each other then that's all,' he said.

He waved his hand. The conversation was over.

It was becoming very clear to me that I was not seen as top dog on this assignment. The respect I was being shown was about the same as would be granted the most menial of lackeys. That wasn't to say I wasn't being held accountable for a successful outcome... oh no, everyone was happy to lay that on my shoulders... if anything went wrong the scapegoat had already been identified!

His telephone rang. Emily was here. It was time for me to go and talk to her.

Chapter Thirteen

Before going in to see Emily I was met in the corridor by a thin balding man in a casual suit. He had travelled from California with Emily. He didn't need to tell me he was a lawyer nor that he was there to protect Emily's interests. It was plain just by looking at him..

'You must understand, Mr Carpenter, that Emily has had a traumatic experience. I think we can both appreciate that in the interests of her health this interview may turn out to be brief.' He looked towards the door and nodded, 'I think you should know that I am strongly against her decision to talk to you alone,' I could see his point, in his position I would have been against it too, 'but she has convinced her parents that she must talk to you and that she must, for her own peace of mind, do it on her own. I suppose it allows her the opportunity to speak more freely but I do wish to point out that there may be areas that are just too painful for her to revisit and I ask that you respect that and not push too hard, instead stop, or if you must then move on and do not press the point.'

As I've mentioned before, I'm not a monster,

there would be no reason and nothing to gain by me traumatizing an already traumatized teenager. Anyway, I was pretty sure the room was wired and if things got too emotional we were bound to get speedily interrupted.

'I understand,' I said.

It was Emily who had demanded to see me one-to-one. I would have been happy for her to be chaperoned and supported. Now she sat in front of me demurely dressed, looking distraught and gazing down into her lap. To me she looked very young and vulnerable. If I had any doubts about why she wanted this conversation private she dispelled them immediately.

'It's all my fault,' she said.

She was as taught as a bow string. I decided to ask her some questions that I hoped would make it easier for her. I started by going back to the beginning.

'Emily could you tell me, in your own words, how you came to embark on this backpacking journey with Kerry-Anne,' I paused, 'and take your time, I'm in no rush.'

This wasn't completely true but if the interview were to be anything other than very short I had to help her stay calm.

Without looking up she began to speak,

'We weren't real friends you know. We knew each other of course, we were in the same year and we shared a lot of classes but we weren't really close. I guess you could say we got on, liked to talk about the same things.'

She wrung her hands unconsciously.

'And then she tells me about this trip and how she's determined to go on it to teach her parents, especially her mom, that they don't have to treat her like a kid anymore. I knew exactly what she meant and after a few weeks of her making such a big deal out of it and hearing her tell me of all the tears and tantrums she had had to turn on to get her own way she made me understand how important it was to her.'

She paused.

'And then, you know, I was really surprised when, one day in school, she told me that she knew for sure that she wouldn't be allowed to go alone and said she really wanted me to go along with her, that if I said no then all her hopes and planning would be dashed and she'd never get this opportunity again, that her parents were shipping her off to Harvard and that once there they'd make sure her life was all study. She wanted to see something of the world and this was her only chance.'

Emily glanced up at me through long, false, lashes,

'The deal was that she would see to it that at least most if not all of my expenses would be paid for by her parents if I agreed. Eventually what I did agree to was to talk to my parents about it. I knew my mum and Kerry's mother knew each other quite well and I was sure they would talk to each other as well.'

'As things worked out it didn't take my parents long to decide that this would be a good opportunity for me,' she said, 'I don't think they would ever have paid for anything like this themselves and they actually encouraged me to go along.'

Clearly her parents had had no reservations in agreeing to a free trip of a lifetime for their daughter. I guess they reckoned that by keeping Kerry-Anne safe and secure, which her parents were bound to do, then Emily would be protected as well.

The story that she proceeded to hesitatingly unfold simply confirmed most of what I already knew and although she added tones of light, shade and colour these were of no real additional value as far as I was concerned. Nevertheless I adjusted my glasses and tried to smile reassuringly, whilst inwardly wishing we could get on with her story a wee bit faster.

As she talked Emily played incessantly with her

shoulder length hair, she was a brunette, and eventually she reached the part of her story that I had been waiting for.

'When we arrived in Peru, in Lima's airport, Kerry spotted somebody in the crowd that she thought she'd seen before. I told her that I didn't think so but she convinced me that, even if it wasn't, it would be fun to pretend we were being followed and move fast to give her the slip, kinda scat fast you know. It was just a game. We were probably imagining things anyway.'

Maybe Kerry recognised Joyce and maybe she didn't, I thought, but one thing was for sure, it wasn't a game. I kept my face neutral and nodded encouragement.

'Travelling First Class we were able to get our backpacks from the carousel pretty quickly. It was a real problem squeezing everything we wanted into the one bag and still being able to lift it. We knew already that we'd taken too much stuff and were dumping things every time we stopped somewhere. Anyway we pretty much flew through baggage and customs, you know, and the next thing was to make sure we got a quick exit from the airport so when a guy came up to us and asked if we needed a taxi we just said yes and followed him outside.'

She let her face fall into her hands. It was pointless asking if they had had any warnings about rogue taxi drivers, or if they had checked for any license card. She spoke again without raising her head, the sound muted.

'He took us to a car in the parking lot and we threw our bags gratefully into the trunk and got into the back seats. We were mega excited and told the driver which hotel we wanted to go to.'

I interrupted.

'Can you describe the taxi driver?'

Emily lifted her head.

'Oh yes,' she said, 'He was a small man, brown and lean, looked like he could do with a good feed. His face was pinched like, lots of creases and wrinkles. He wore a dark red shirt open at the neck. We didn't pay much attention to him at first. He was just a taxi driver.'

"Just a taxi driver" like I was "just a guy asking questions". People who do things are easily overlooked, I thought, although I was impressed with the description.

'He was on his phone a lot of the time and got quite animated. We didn't understand what was going on and although the ride took us through increasingly grimy looking streets, broken buildings and past seedy looking people in dirty clothes we thought he must just be taking us a shortcut.' Emily looked at me, making eye contact for the first time, 'There are some parts of New York City that are not that much better,' she said.

'It was when we pulled up outside a downtrodden looking building that we really started to worry. I remember holding on to Kerry's sleeve and shouting at the driver "Why have we stopped here, this isn't the hotel!?"'

At this point we took a little break. I brought her a glass of water. The tears were beginning to well up in the her eyes when she chose to continue.

'The car doors were locked and when the driver turned he had a knife in his hand. We freaked out, I mean really freaked out, you know.'

I didn't know, but I could imagine.

'Then it got kinda crazy and ugly and blurry. Somehow someone else was there with us in the car. It felt like we had bags over our heads. I couldn't see or hear any more. It was like falling into a black hole. I guess I must have fainted.'

Drugged more like, I thought, maybe a fast acting injection. It wasn't unusual for memory to fail when trying to remember such incidents. It was clear to me however that wherever they had been taken was pre-planned and a reception committee had been waiting.

Emily clenched her hands together and I could see the whiteness of her knuckles as she continued.

'When I came to I was in a small room. I think it had plain sort of creamy-coloured walls, although the paint was peeling off in places, and a bare concrete floor. There were no windows. There was a brown wooden door and alongside that was a white sink with chrome taps. Apart from a single bed the only other furniture I remember in the room was a round wooden table and two hard chairs.'

'In the corner nearest to the sink was a galvanised bucket. That was our toilet,' she crinkled up her nose in disgust at the memory, 'When I got my focus back I realized I was lying on the bed and I reached out my hand and felt Kerry lying alongside me.'

'There was what looked like quite a small, fat man sitting in one of the chairs at the table watching us. When I looked at him I thought I must still be dreaming, he looked like the devil, he even had horns!'

She stopped.

'Please go on,' I said.

'After I got over the initial shock I could see that he was wearing a woollen head mask. It was grotesque, like something out of a horror movie. I can still see it,' she shuddered, 'it had a yellow face and was red at the neck and covering the top of his head. It even had what looked like a green-tipped goatee beard at the chin and two small green horns protruding from the forehead,' she paused, reliving the memory, 'and there were black slits in the yellow face, trimmed with red, that formed holes for the eyes and mouth. I remember the eyes glistening, the wetness of the slightly open mouth as the man sat staring at me.'

This sounded bizarre, the guy must have a pretty warped sense of humour. At least by hiding his face he was indicating that he did not have any immediate intention to do any permanent harm to anybody.

Emily's story seemed to confirm that the kidnap was intentional and its purpose was to deliver dollars to its perpetrators. In the same situation, after the initial surprise, I think I would have found the set up re-assuring. It was clear however that Emily had not.

'I felt Kerry stir as she came round,' Emily stared out into the middle-distance as she tried to remember, 'I'm pretty sure that the man at the table actually smiled behind his mask as he offered us coffee. His English was very good, quite clear and precise. He called over his shoulder and a second man came in. He was much taller and thinner than the man at the table. He was wearing the same kind of mask but with a black face, and he brought in more chairs and then the cups of coffee. The chubbier man introduced himself as Matias and Kerry and I sat up and took the drinks that he offered us. He spoke to us in a very gentle way and almost apologised for kidnapping us. I know I was very confused and I think Kerry was as well.'

'He had obviously had time to go through our belongings as our passports and phones, backs removed and SIM cards out, were laid out on the table in front of him. The second man was introduced as Hugo and was somehow much more physically threatening. Matias told us not to worry and that everything would be okay, we should just stay calm and answer his questions.'

'Even though he spoke softly and smiled reassuringly Kerry just lost it. She started screaming and shouting, yelling things like "Have you any idea who I am?", "How dare you do this, do you know what's going to happen to you if you don't let us go right now?" Rather than causing our captors any concern this seemed to increase Matias' interest in Kerry and he took her by the arm and led her out of the room, still protesting.'

'This left me alone with Hugo and although he said nothing I felt increasingly intimidated as he took his time to look me over from head to foot. Then he moved towards me and stretched out a bony arm and stroked my hair with his hand. As you can see I'm a brunette and I remember him saying something like "I like blondes best". I could smell him he was so close. I could feel his breath on my face and I just started to shake uncontrollably. I felt like I was frozen, unable to move, unable to scream. His hand moved and when I felt his course skin stroking my cheek I just panicked, I mean I just flipped. I jumped up, pushed past him, ran to the bucket and threw up. I could feel him approaching behind me "You a silly girl," he said "you want live you be nice." He reached over my shoulder and took hold of my chin forcing my neck round to look at him. I closed my eyes then I slapped his hand away.

He laughed.

Her voice broke as she continued.

'I panicked. I just started blabbering. I wasn't even conscious of what I was saying. I was just trying to protect myself.'

'Most people would have done the same,' I said reassuringly.

Emily started to cry. It wasn't unexpected. I left her to get control of herself again.

When she'd regained some composure she continued,

'I told him about Kerry,' she said, 'I must have said something without thinking that got his interest. He moved away from me and then left the room, locking the door behind him. When he returned sometime later the other man was with him. They had our passports in their hands, Matias asked me if Kerry's passport was in her real name. I said, of course, but I must have said something else earlier because he kept asking me, getting more and more aggressive and calling me a liar and telling me what they did to liars.'

'I broke down eventually. It wasn't a big surprise to me that Kerry travelled under an assumed name but I should have kept quiet. Once I'd admitted it they stood over me each shouting the same question "What her real name!?", "What her real name!?" at me, telling me I'd better tell them… and I did tell them, I did tell them, and they left me alone and they brought me food and they told me I had been a good girl.'

Emily shook her head.

'Oh, god,' she said, 'oh god.'

'Take it slow, Emily,' I said, 'we can stop any time you want.'

Emily sighed and then slowly but surely she continued.

'They must have googled Kerry or something because they became all smiles and said they needed to get a message to Kerry's parents and that the best thing they could think of was to get me to deliver it.'

'As I said they had our phones and so they put them back together. In the rooms we were in, concrete walls, no windows, there was no signal anyway but they told me to put in my pass-code and tell them which numbers in my contacts list were for Kerry's parents. I said I didn't have that on my phone. And I don't, I wasn't lying. Then they left me alone again.'

'I must have looked in a dreadful state and I remember crawling to the sink, pulling myself up and splashing my face clean as best I could. Then I curled up on the bed and the light went out.'

'Sorry?' I said.

'I thought they'd done it on purpose to scare me some more but Hugo told me later there had been a power cut and if it happened again they had kerosene lamps they could use. He even apologised to me, saying it wasn't unusual and I wasn't to worry and they didn't normally last long. I'd laid in the complete darkness for what seemed like hours before the single electric bulb fluttered back into life.'

Emily was shaking now, tears rolling down her cheeks. She was clearly reliving the memories in her head.

I wanted to know what she knew about what had happened to Kerry. Emily, after all, had been released and although fragile and traumatised was seemingly lucid and was right here, sitting in front of me, in one piece. I didn't know where Kerry was.

'When did you next see Kerry?' I asked.

Emily flinched. She took a sip of water, patted her cheeks with a tissue that I gave her to dry away her tears. I felt no better than one of her captors. I knew this must be hard for her. I just stayed silent to give her some time. Time I hoped we had.

'I must have fallen asleep because when I next woke up I realised that Kerry was lying next to me crying quietly. I wrapped my arms around her and we just clung to each other.'

She sighed. I think she was relieved that she'd now told me the worst of her story. She'd got that over with.

'It must have been the following morning when we were given a kind of breakfast. We hadn't eaten for a long time so we were very hungry and accepted what was offered without question. We had slept in our clothes and I was feeling uncomfortably dirty and sweaty but there was no way I was going to wash with Hugo and Matias around.'

'While we were eating Matias singled me out and asked me a few questions about where I lived, what my father did, who was paying for our trip. The questions seemed innocuous enough to me and I just answered them automatically. Kerry sat beside me in silence, just eating. There were some bruises appearing on her upper arm and her left eye was partially closed.'

That did not sound good. That did not sound good at all. They must have realized by now that Kerry was potentially their golden goose. They were idiots if they went about damaging such a prize.

'After breakfast I was taken into a different room and told to sit down.'

I interrupted, 'Emily, can you describe anything about this second room?'

She thought for a moment, 'I wasn't really paying attention. There were a lot of guns, I remember that, but I don't really remember anything else.'

'Guns?'

'Yes, the room was full of guns, there were racks and racks of them.'

This was new, I hadn't heard about this before. Maybe this safe house they'd taken the girls to was also somebody's armory. It was an interesting thought although I didn't think that it was worth probing too far as it would be unlikely that Emily knew anything specific about the weapons.

'Please go on Emily,' I said.

'Well it was in this other room that Matias dismantled my phone again and gave me back the parts. He also gave me my passport back. Then he examined me to ensure I had no bad cuts or bruises. After that I was blindfolded and told to keep calm, which I found very difficult. Somebody then grabbed hold of my arm and I was told to get up and walk. I was led up steps and along passages and eventually felt some fresh air on my face. It was glorious but short-lived because after a few more steps my head was pushed down and I was bundled into a car. I could hear the engine running.'

'The drive seemed to last forever and I thought they might be taking me somewhere quiet to kill me. I was really, really scared. Eventually the car stopped, the door was flung open and I was pushed out. I was just pleased to be still alive.'

A smile fluttered across her face as she relived the moment of release.

'When I realised I had been abandoned I ripped off the blindfold and found that my backpack had been thrown out alongside me. I picked it up and looked around. I saw an American flag and simply ran towards it.'

She stopped and took a drink of water.

It was enough. We knew the rest.

Once in the American Embassy she had at first been disbelieved and then believed, questioned and examined. Calls had been placed and arrangements had been made to get her home as soon as possible.

Of the two families contacted one had been shocked but relieved and able to talk to their daughter for reassurance. The other had been simply shocked, the shock turning quickly to anger and an urgent need for more information and immediate action.

'Thank you Emily,' I said, 'I can see that wasn't easy for you. Is there anything else you remember about any of the men? Or anything more about the last time you saw Kerry?'

'When I got home,' said Emily, 'I just went through like a deep cleansing. I washed and scrubbed until I was red raw.'

She looked at me, 'I often wonder what would have happened if I had been a blonde and not a brunette,' her eyes darkened, 'I mean, like Kerry.'

In my head I was saying 'You were lucky'.

Emily had only been in captivity for one night, had suffered no significant deprivation or maltreatment and had been released. The most difficult thing she would now have to contend with was survivor's guilt. I wanted to ask her if she had flashbacks like I do, if she had sleepless nights and nightmares. But there wasn't time and as far as my assignment was concerned it didn't matter.

Just before we parted Emily said,

'I'm supposed to go to Stanford in the Fall to study the Environment and climate change,' she gave a dry laugh, 'I had this idea that I could help to save the world but when it came to it I couldn't even save Kerry. I don't think I can go now.'

'Give it time,' I said.

I knew from recent personal experience that after suffering a traumatic event you needed time. Time to accept what had actually happened. Time to try and come to terms with it. Time to realise you've got to cope. Time to decide that somehow or other you're going to.

'It's worse than you know,' she said.

Really? I thought.

'Kerry's parents run a philanthropic scheme. I am a beneficiary. They were going to be paying the majority of my Stanford fees.'

Oh shit, I thought.

'And what have I done? I've ratted on their daughter and saved myself. That's why I needed to talk to you alone. What happens if they find out. Ooooh…'

I was pretty sure the room was wired. I prayed that there might have been an electrical fault or that Emily's voice hadn't been picked up clearly or that the recording didn't need to get to the ears of Kerry-Anne's parents. She'd problems enough.

'And if anything happens to Kerry…' she trailed off and then looked me directly in the eye and said, 'you've got to bring her home, Mr Carpenter, you've just got to get her home.'

I'd been thinking Emily's parents were the lucky ones. And they were. Their daughter was home and physically intact. But there were wider consequences. Their source of philanthropic support was in jeopardy, maybe even a real friendship was at risk of permanent damage. Their daughter was mentally under stress. The future must have seemed like a clear highway stretching out in front of them.

But fog had descended across Emily's road and she couldn't see more than a yard in front of her face. She was keeping secrets that would fester, assuming they hadn't already leaked out of this room.

'I'll do my best,' I said.

Chapter Fourteen

I had time to eat before my night flight to Lima so I went down to the bar. I wasn't really going to see if Teresa was there, why would I? No, it was simply that the convenience and casual atmosphere of a bar won out over the formality of a restaurant. I just wanted to relax.

I did look around when I entered the bar and before finding a table I did notice that Teresa was on duty, this time not on her own but with another male bartender. I wondered idly if she ever went home, she seemed to work extremely long shifts.

As luck would have it, it was Teresa who came over to take my order, it was a 50/50 chance after all.

'Hello,' she said.

'Hi,' I said.

She reached into a pocket of her hotel uniform and took out two $20 bills.

'I'm glad I've seen you again,' she said, 'I found these in that beautiful bag you gave me, you must have forgotten they were in there.'

I hadn't forgotten, I'd put the money in there for

her. I admired her honesty though and took the money. I didn't have much choice.

'What time do you get off,' I said on a whim, 'you seem to live here.'

She laughed, it was a nice laugh.

'I'm just on changeover now,' she said, 'Joe's just come in but I thought I'd return your money and take your order before I go.'

'Do you know any good restaurants in the area?' I asked, 'I'd like to stretch my legs and get out of the hotel for a while.'

She thought for a moment and then said,

'I don't know about fancy food,' she said, 'but there's a good Pizzeria just a block away, run by an Italian friend of mine.'

'Sounds just the ticket,' I said, 'will you show me?'

I'm not normally this forward. Especially not with attractive women. But there was something about Teresa and I was in need of a pleasant distraction right now. She could always say no.

She said yes.

The manager of the Pizzeria "Piazza Romana" was called Alessandro and as soon as he saw Teresa he came over to greet her.

'Ciao bella,' he said, throwing his arms wide, 'it has been too long.'

Teresa had a locker at the back of the hotel bar and had changed out of her work clothes. Beneath a deep green knee length coat, buckled at the waist she was now wearing a sleeveless white blouse with an open shirt collar, brown slacks and sensible shoes. Over her shoulder hung the leather bag I had given her.

Largely ignoring me, Alessandro took Teresa's coat and showed us to a table close to the open kitchen and pizza oven.

'What you want to drink?' he asked.

Teresa turned to me.

'The house Chianti is good,' she said.

'You order, I'll pay,' I said, 'I owe you at least 40 dollars worth of gratitude.'

She kept the shoulder bag with her and hung it over the back of her seat. She turned and touched it.

'You don't owe me anything,' she said, 'I think it's the other way around.'

'Nevertheless, you order,' I said, 'I'll eat anything.'

Alessandro scowled, 'You no get just anything here!' he said, 'you get the best,' he looked adoringly towards Teresa, 'only the best for you mio caro.'

Without looking at the menu Teresa ordered a carafe of Chianti, two Minestrone soup and two pizzas; one Margherita, one Pepperoni. Even when given a clear run Teresa was turning out to be a cheap date. Not that this was a date. I'm just saying she didn't take advantage that's all.

'Perfetto,' said Alessandro and glided away.

'He's all right really,' said Teresa, 'thinks he looks after me, was one of the first people I got to know when I came to New York, gave me my first job.'

'Why did you move?' I said, 'you seem great friends.'

'Hmm,' she said, 'we are and I'd like to keep it that way. That's why I moved.'

I was probably getting too much information too quickly. We were practically strangers.

The Chianti was surprisingly good, smooth with a nice rich berry flavour, the Minestrone soup was obviously a house special and had a nice thick consistency with pasta, beans, onions, celery, carrots, and tomato swimming around the interior while Parmesan cheese was grated on top. With fresh crusty bread it tasted great although I managed to spill a little on myself as a tried to safely navigate spoonfuls into my mouth. I was embarrassed to be so clumsy but it only seemed to amuse Teresa who had made much better use of spreading her napkin.

'So you've had a few jobs,' I said, trying to make conversation.

Teresa didn't seem to mind.

'Yes,' she said, 'I work and I save it is my master plan.'

She smiled, slurped the soup and made no mess.

'Your master plan?'

'Yes, of course, everyone has a dream don't they? So the way I will make my dream come true is through my master plan.'

'And what is your…'

I was stopped in my tracks by Teresa pointing towards the kitchen. One of the Italian chefs had taken a piece of dough and was spinning it into a disc, sprinkling flour from his fingertips throwing it like a plate into the air, catching it, spinning it some more until it was just the size and just the thickness he wanted and then he let it fall and rest on the floured steel counter. From a huge range of ingredients that lay within arm's length he then chose and applied thick tomato sauce, sliced mozzarella, more sliced tomatoes, basil, and extra virgin olive oil.

'Oh,' said Teresa, 'it's an art, so simple, so good.'

When he was satisfied the chef slipped the spread aluminium end of the pizza paddle effortlessly beneath his creation and, taking hold of the wooden shank of the paddle, turned to the wood burning arched opening of the yawning red hot mouth of the pizza oven and slid the embryonic pizza deep inside. He then turned back and repeated the process only this time with the mix of toppings required to create a Pepperoni pizza.

When the paddle was re-inserted into the oven and the first pizza was removed Teresa took a deep breath,

'Smell,' she said, 'isn't it wonderful.'

I sniffed. The powerful scent of baked bread mixed with the acidity of the tomatoes and mozzarella, the smell of basil, and the herbal touch of the oil hit me like a good memory. It was like the air was suffused with home comforts. I couldn't wait to taste it.

'That's the other reason I left,' she said, 'too much pizza, I was getting fat.'

I looked at her figure. She was curvy and sensual. I think she saw me looking because she laughed. I didn't know what to say, so I said nothing.

We shared the pizzas like old friends. Towards the end I asked,

'So this dream of yours, what is it?'

She leaned across and took the last slice of Pepperoni. I nodded that I didn't want to fight over it. Between mouthfuls she said,

'I am a proud Costa Rican,' I'd picked that up from our earlier conversations, 'but there was no life for me there so I came to America,' I didn't want to ask how, you don't do that, 'I want to build a future here but I do not want to forget my roots.'

Her brown eyes sparkled. She spoke seriously,

'There are many good things in Costa Rica and if I bring them to America I am sure people will want them. So my dream is to start a business, import and sales,' she said.

I smiled.

'Are you laughing at me,' she said, passion rising in her cheeks.

'Oh no,' I blurted out immediately, 'far from it Teresa, I'm smiling because your dream is so positive. I like it, I think you'll do it.'

'You do?' the passion subsided as quickly as it had risen. I breathed an inward sigh of relief, 'so that's what I work and save for. I need the money as a start up fund.'

'You're so clear on your business idea,' I said, 'can't you approach a bank for a loan to get you started?'

'Are you making fun of me?' she said.

I felt like I was walking a tightrope and couldn't understand why I didn't just keep my mouth shut. Somehow or other Teresa's positivity for the future had got me interested.

'No,' I said, 'no, really no. Tell me some more about your ideas.'

When Teresa talked of her plans she did it with sincerity and passion, she became animated, throwing in the odd Spanish word here and there when the speed of her thought outstripped the breadth of her vocabulary. It was fun to listen to and I let her infectious enthusiasm engulf me hoping that I might catch a bit of it.

Compared to her my plans were more about survival rather than growth, restarting things I'd put on hold. It made me wonder whether I'd got my priorities right and I made a mental note to take up my daughter's long standing offer and actually pay her a visit. Face to face beats phone calls and video calls hands down. To be honest I'd been avoiding visiting her because she reminded me so much of my wife. Maybe though it was now time…

'I will make it happen,' concluded Teresa, 'Even though I am from Costa Rica and right now I don't have the backing or the funds. I am working hard, slowly my savings grow, you believe me, Mr Carpenter, I am one determined lady.'

I didn't know how fast but Teresa was certainly moving in a clear direction. I envied her.

We finished off the meal with a coffee and the conversation turned to much lighter things; favourite movies, favourite songs, that kind of stuff.

When Alessandro brought the check I paid it despite Teresa's protestations. She really was an independent woman and I believed her when she insisted she wanted to pay her half. I won the argument by telling her that I'd been brought up to pay and that if she didn't let me then I would feel humiliated. She gave way grudgingly.

Outside I thanked her for the recommendation and for her company. We shook hands and went our separate ways. I felt refreshed as I made my way back to the hotel.

Chapter Fifteen

I've travelled so frequently that my case almost packs itself. George was going to drive me to the airport. I had a little time still before he was expected so I decided to call my daughter. I wouldn't mention Teresa because there was no reason to.

I've mentioned my daughter already. She lives in the United States with her partner and our relationship has been subject to, what is for me, an awkward kind of role reversal. Since my wife died we have shared tears and reminiscences of happier times, there were some thank god, but she has slipped into the role of mother hen and has been a support to me much more than I, as the parent, have been a support to her. I was uncomfortable with this and as a little time had passed I'd tried to distance myself a bit more, to give her more space to concentrate on her own life and, to be honest, to give me a bit more adult independence. I didn't talk to her about what I did, except in the vaguest terms, and I wasn't going to change that. I was far from sure that what I did would make her proud, my fear was quite the reverse. The only person I properly confided in was my wife. She sort of understood that after leaving the army, becoming adrift and washing ashore into 'The Store' that this work was something that I could and should do. Somebody has to do it or society will crumble into anarchy but like the untouchables in India, if you knew what I did, I wasn't the kind of person you were likely to invite round for dinner.

My wife used to worry about me but learnt that in order for her to cope she had to sometimes just leave me alone and wait for me to come back, because I would always try my best to do that. Love is like a magnet. She had a great job, made friends easily and once we had a family her life was filled with other things. I don't know why she stuck with me, it can't have been easy, but she did. That's why what happened was so unfair. She deserved rewarding not infecting. I deserved that not her.

Anyway, I didn't want to put my daughter in the same position as my wife had been in. Too much knowledge can be a dangerous thing and what you don't know can't hurt you, well at least not immediately. If you find out later it can break your heart. I was determined to not let that happen to my daughter.

She knew I was going back to work and I'd agreed to keep in regular contact. I dialled her number,

'Hello.'

'Hello.'

'Dad?'

'Checking in as instructed.'

'Hmm, I don't think you've ever done anything as instructed.'

She knew me so well.

'I'm back at work,' I said.

'Good, are you going to be doing any travelling?'

Her young life was full of my comings and goings. It was part of our small family's DNA. My wife was American but we lived in Scotland. I wasn't surprised when our daughter met an American boy at university in St Andrew's and followed him over to California. During her mother's illness she'd put her own life on hold for a lot of the time, done a lot of Atlantic hopping, staying in her old room, surrounded by her own childhood memorabilia. My wife had told her not to. She'd ignored her. Her stubbornness was genetic.

'Yes,' I said, 'I'm back on the road, or rather, I'm back in the sky.'

'Where you headed?' She was beginning to pick up an american accent.

'Can't say for sure,' I said, which was mainly true. I had to tread a line here, my movements were not to be broadcast but this was my daughter. She deserved to know something.

'Will it include the US?' she asked. I could hear a tinge of exasperation in her voice although she was used to squeezing blood out of a stone were I was concerned.

I couldn't lie.

'Yes,' I said, 'in all probability.'

'So will you have time to pay us a visit?'

Sheesh, what happened to aimless small talk? I was getting a grilling here. I could feel myself squirm.

'Could be,' I said, 'but my plans aren't clear yet. I'd love to meet up with you if I could.'

'You mean you'd love to meet up with both of us,' she corrected.

I backtracked. I had a normal level of parental 'he's not good enough for you' feeling when it came to her partner. Perhaps a smidgen more than normal. We'd been through a lot together and it did feel a little like this guy, don't get me wrong he wasn't a bad guy, was taking her away from me. Life happens, I thought. I had to learn to share. Maybe later.

'Yes,' I said, grudgingly, 'yes, of course I mean both of you.'

She ignored the grudging undercurrent and grabbed onto my answer at face value.

Clever girl.

'Good, Brett is keen to spend some more time with you, get to know you better. I've told him a lot about you.'

I had flashing mental images of Brett and me fishing together, bonding over a rainbow trout. I shook my head. I wasn't ready for anything like that, not yet anyway.

'Great,' I said, thinking that meeting up might be best put off to a later date.

'Dad.'

'Yes?'

'I love you Dad, I really would like to give you a hug.'

It was a second or two before I replied. That's kids for you, they just know how to get through. The probability of me finding the opportunity to visit, maybe even making the opportunity, had just shot up.

'OK, thanks, love you too.'

The call ended with me promising to keep in touch, to call regularly and to 'look after myself and not to try to take on too much too soon' whatever that meant. You can see what I mean about the role reversal. It was nice to have someone who seemed to care but it was also a burden. I'd always kept my family and my work completely separate and I certainly wasn't going to change that now.

Chapter Sixteen

George was waiting for me in the pickup/drop off area in front of the hotel. I put my bag in the trunk and climbed into the passenger seat. As we raced towards JFK Airport he had things he wanted to say,

'Listen, Paul, ah feel real guilty about Kerry-Anne. Ah shoulda down right insisted on goin' along on this joyride of her'n. An' if'n they still said a no then ah shoulda gone along anyhow's. Ah feel like ah let her down.'

I could tell he really meant it.

'I don't think there was much you could do,' I said, 'you're obviously loyal to her parents and they have to call the shots, don't they?'

He kept his eyes steadfastly on the road.

'Ah'm more loyal to Kerry-Anne,' he said, 'If'n ah had to choose then that'd be the truth'n it.'

We drove in silence for a while and then he said,

'Ah think ah should be a comin' along'a you.'

'You know that impossible,' I said

'Ah knows it, but t'ain't right.'

I realised that trading one external intervention, Joyce, that clearly hadn't worked out, for another, me, as the apparent solution, must seem crazy to George. It didn't seem all that great to me.

'It wasn't your or Kerry-Anne's parents or the FBI or the CIA's or anybody else's call this time it was the kidnappers, god knows why, and I think it's the right thing to go along with it. By doing what they say it makes Kerry-Anne's release as easy as possible.'

'Ah'd still like t'string along.'

'No,' I said, 'if you attempt to do that you'll put the whole thing in jeopardy.'

We'd arrived at the airport. He parked up and turned to me.

'If'n that be the case you'n remember what ah said. You keep me informed you here?'

I nodded.

'An don't you fuck up.'

The flight for Lima's Jorge Chavez airport left JFK at 22:45hrs, a Lanperu overnight flight on a Boeing 767 landing at 05:30 hrs local time; a further -1hr time difference and a 7 hr 45 minute flight time.

I was in Economy but had again secured an aisle seat. My body and mind were both tired, partly from the reaction to the time difference and partly from the scattered thoughts that would not settle and whirled around inside my head.

I knew I was going to be continually hopping between time zones and I had to try to protect my body from the potential dizzying biological confusion. Jet lag is, after all, a modern phenomenon, we are not built to travel around as quickly or as far as we do. Our technological development has outstripped our genetic one. The USA, for example, is so large a country that it has six main and different time zones; one in Hawaii, one in Alaska and four mainland continental covering the East to the West coast.

The time difference between Harvard and Stanford is 3hrs, Harvard being ahead. This may sound complicated and obviously makes internal travel, calling home and arranging Zoom calls for a certain time a bit of a challenge but it is nothing compared to the situation before 1883, less than 160 years ago, when many towns and cities set their clocks to their local solar noon.

Although noon occurred at different times the time differences between distant locations was barely noticeable because of the long travel times and the lack of long-distance instant communications. When the railroad and later the telegraph came along the problem was exposed when each station set its own clock. So to help the situation the idea of time zones was born.

To start with there were around 100 time zones, which improved but didn't really solve the problem. Later an idea originally introduced for coast to coast weather stations of 4 standard time zones was adopted and synchronised by telegraph at Chicago noon on November 18, 1883.

As a species we are constantly trying to cope with the consequences of our own cleverness, as often unsuccessfully as successfully. As far as modern travel is concerned some people cope better than others.

I was looking forward to what I hoped would be a reasonable meal, passable wine and sleep. Although contrary to the best medical advice I find alcohol the best relaxant in these circumstances and thought that if I included a few medicinal G&T's then I would be able to get to sleep no matter how uncomfortable the seat or my sleeping position.

But the best laid plans and all that…

It all started off so well. Sitting beside me in the centre of our three seats; aisle, middle, window, was a middle-aged lady who seemed pleasant and made the normal sort of idle small-talk as the plane prepared for takeoff.

I must have been more tired than I'd thought because once we were in the air I immediately fell asleep. I was woken abruptly however by a sharp dig in the ribs.

'Move it sonny!' hissed an American accent, far too close to my ear for comfort.

My sleepy mind struggled to comprehend. This person must occupy the window seat. Someone I had completely ignored up until now.

'I got to get to the men's room,' he yelped, and shoved me again for effect.

Groggily I made way, not best pleased with his mode of address. As the man's backside swayed away up the aisle the lady beside me spoke softly,

'I'm so sorry, that's my husband, Rich. He was hoping we'd have these three seats to ourselves, said he'd use his influence when we checked in,' she shrugged, his influence clearly didn't amount to very much, 'I'm sorry he was so rude, he's just like that,' she looked me straight in the eye, 'all the time.' She sighed before adding, as an afterthought, 'My name's Rita by the way.'

'I'm Paul,' I said and reached out to shake hands. Before this polite gesture of simple greeting could be completed however my arm was forcibly knocked away.

'Don't you go getting too friendly there boy.'

It was smiley face Rich returned from the loo. 'People should get the damned respect they deserve, that's what I say. Booked these tickets so far in advance they've been growing hairs on 'em. Kept asking for a bit of space so we could just get comfy like and not have anyone disturbing our peace or getting in our way. Least they could do for a ex-military man was my thinking.'

As far as I could see it was my peace that was being disturbed but I kept silent and stood up to let him pass. He eased his way through to the window seat, pressing past his wife in a non-to-genteel fashion and once in his seat he leaned back across to glower at me and to continue the one-sided conversation.

'I been in the American Army boy,' he said, just in case I hadn't got it the first time, putting emphasis on the "American", 'been defending the freedom and liberty of the likes of you. Seen things that'd curl your hair and that's for sure. Afore you were even born most like, and you think you got the right to squeeze in next'a me.'

It wasn't clear to me whether this was a question or a statement. I was already none too enamoured at being woken from my luxuriant slumber and being called "sonny" and "boy" had not improved things. Call me perceptive but I felt that these terms of endearment were not intended to compliment me on my fine youthful appearance despite my maturing years, but rather that they were meant to be disparaging, verging on insulting.

'Thanks for all you've done for me.' I said, as deadpan as I could.

'You darn right you're thankful. Without the likes of me doing what we did you wouldn't be on no commercial airplane enjoying this freedom to travel.' He paused to poke Rita painfully in the side, she winced but said nothing. I was guessing this was normal fare between the two of them. I didn't like to see it.

'I been telling Rita here we should'a been given priority in the allocation of these here seats instead of being forced to have a person like you sitting alongside'a us.'

A person like me? This guy was not good at making friends. Presumably a "person like me" applied to anybody who's body occupied space in the vicinity of the space he thought should be kept free for his own use alone, space that was somehow his by right. I was encroaching on his territory, a territory that he thought he had conquered and stuck his flag into. I was too tired to bother to reply, the options of apologising profusely or trying to find an alternative seat did not appeal to me and I didn't want to fight, not right now anyway. This seemed to rile him.

'What you do anyway?' he growled.

I sighed inwardly, but a cover story is a cover story.

'I'm a Sales Executive,' I said.

Rich laughed. Rita said softly, 'Don't Rich, please.'

'Don't you tell me what to do and what not to do,' he snarled, Rita winced. 'We both know what happens when...' Tears were forming in the corners of Rita's eyes and she bowed her head and gazed fixedly downwards.

Rich was clearly a bully.

I don't like bullies.

In my experience it seems that at least some of us humans have an unfortunate trait, a need to identify someone worse off or weaker than ourselves and make their life hell. To me bullies are people that use a combination of physical and mental intimidation towards someone who is least likely or least able to fight back. It is not unusual to find that the bully bullies because they themselves are being, or have been, bullied and are passing on the unsavoury legacy. But this is no excuse. Whatever the causes or the ins and outs the fact remains - I don't like bullies.

His wife dealt with, Rich turned his focus back onto me.

'Executive eh, just means you leave the work to everybody else and sales, pah, that ain't no real work neither.'

Having so easily demolished my title he paused to let the ridicule sink in.

'So what you sell, boy?'

Unfortunately for me my cover story was unlikely to give me respite from his chiding.

I haven't up until now mentioned the items of sale that were in my hand baggage. There is a good reason for this. I was hoping to avoid the subject. However Rich had asked the question and I suppose it deserved an answer.

'Toilet rolls,' I said.

His first reaction was one of astonishment. His second reaction, which followed micro-seconds after the first, was more predictable, he let out a loud, long, audible, guffaw.

'Well no shitting,' he said, clearly tickled by his own ability at spontaneous repartee, 'You sit there in your nice shirt, dressed like some slick businessman and you sell toilet rolls!'

I was pleased he liked the shirt.

'That is correct,' I said

As you can imagine the next 20 to 30 minutes were occupied by him giving full vent to his feelings on executives, salesman and in particular the unimportance of my particular calling. In a masochistic kind of way I was increasingly enjoying this distraction and decided to fuel the flames with such comments as,

… but where would we be without them?… or, we believe that health and happiness come from having a clean and sweet smelling rear… or, to add detail, our range includes quilted, layered, hardy and standard varieties in a range of attractive pastel shades…

He lapped it up and I tried to ensure that my demeanour showed the pain that I was suffering as a result of his piercingly brutal attacks.

It was only when I observed Rita's reaction to all this that my enjoyment subsided. She was not having a good time at all. It was easy to see that she would rather be somewhere else, anywhere else, than in the middle of this conversation.

We were approaching the time when our in-flight meal was due to be served.

In anticipation of this Rich expressed the need to proceed to the toilets and empty his obviously weak bladder.

Once left alone Rita could not have been more apologetic.

'It's okay,' I said, 'it's not the first time I've had to cope with this kind of reaction. It comes with the territory, so to speak.'

'But it wouldn't have really mattered what you did,' said Rita, 'he would still have found a way to humiliate and belittle it. He does it all the time, thinks he's being funny. It's awful. Makes me feel awful. He didn't used to be like this you know. He could be quite kind. But the army changed him.

Made him and then ruined him. His pals used to call him "Bull" because he was strong and dependable but that's all changed now. I don't know why and I don't know what to do,' she gazed at me through glassy eyes, 'I loved him once,' she said.

Rich returned with his cheery demeanour intact. I thought Rita's outpouring of feeling was too much information imparted too quickly, and to a complete stranger. It smacked of desperation.

Maybe there was something I could do. It was worth a try and would anyway give me a degree of satisfaction.

The meal when it arrived was a passably tasty prawn curry and rice and I managed to sweet talk my way to two bread rolls instead of the regular single allocation to bulk it up.

Although curry is probably best accompanied by white wine I had red. I just like red wine better than white, and this one was drinkable, especially the third small bottle.

Rich had more or less worn himself out by this time and had lapsed into quietness which was a great relief.

Some 30 minutes or so after the meal had been completed and the debris cleared away the cabin lights were switched off, making it more comfortable for those of us who wanted to sleep.

It wasn't long before I felt the by-now-familiar poke in the ribs and I got up to let Rich through. Rita was asleep and even Rich's clumsy exit did not wake her. I sat back down to let a few seconds pass and then I got up and followed Rich towards the toilets.

We had hit lucky, there was no queue and some toilets were vacant. As Rich pushed open the door of his chosen cubicle I moved quickly in behind him.

The rabbit punch to the neck stunned him and I caught him under the arms as he slumped forward. I then carefully lowered him into a kneeling position, his head down the toilet bowl.

Although it was a tight fit I managed to squeeze in behind him and close and lock the toilet door.

He was dazed but not unconscious and began to remonstrate volubly whilst attempting to push himself back up onto his feet. I held his arms tightly by his sides, put my mouth very close to his ear and using my best attempt at a mid-American accent I began to whisper in his ear, the constant background drone of the engines taking the edge off my amateurism.

'We been seeking you out Bull,' I felt his body tense at the mention of his army nickname, 'been hearing bad things.'

'Who the hell…' hissed Rich.

I increased the pressure on my hold and spoke through clenched teeth.

'We both know what you did, so you just listen up.' I had no idea what he had done, but he must have done something. If you've been in the Army for any length of time there are always some memories you would rather forget. I know all about that.

Rich was sweating.

'That was a long time ago, I was only a kid, didn't know what I was doing, I was just following orders.' I could almost taste his guilt, his voice almost a whine.

'Now Bull we don't want no bullshit do we? We been watching an' we gonna keep watching. Whatever you feel about what you done we don't wanna see you actin' the clown. You got that?'

'But I feel angry, I feel angry all the time.'

I had seen the American military veteran's ring that he wore on his finger.

'You wear that army ring, Bull. You don't wanna make people think we army guys're just some bullshit bullies do ya?'

I didn't wait for a reply and pressed a nerve in his thigh with one of my knees. He clenched his teeth against the pain.

'Do I make ma'self clear. You wear that ring with pride, you gotta show people that we're the good guys. D'ya hear me Bull?' Rich nodded, 'Just you remember this Bull "Life is not about waiting for the storm to pass, it's about learning to dance in the rain", you remember that.'

I had no idea what this psychobabble mumbo-jumbo actually meant. I'm not a very deep thinker but I'd heard this recently on a radio program and it had stuck in my head for some reason. I thought it sounded good.

It had become very obvious to me that Rich had not been able to contain the contents of his weak bladder for the duration of our conversation. As I didn't want to humiliate him any further I decided to end it there. I'd done my bit. I'd given him a shock and hoped that that might make a difference. If it didn't it didn't really matter as this meeting of minds had at least made me feel a bit better.

'Now you just keep looking down that toilet Bull, that's where your life is going right now. You just remember our little chat. I'm going to leave you to get yourself cleaned up. We'll be watching.'

I gave him a final whack on the head to discourage him from looking around and quickly made my escape, closing the toilet door behind me.

Rita was snoring gently as I eased myself back into my seat and closed my eyes.

I must have actually dozed off because I didn't feel Rich as he somehow manoeuvred himself past me and back into his window seat.

We were woken up for breakfast.

The cabin lights were switched back on and I blinked in the unaccustomed glare. Rich was very quiet and from Rita's reaction it seemed that this was unusual.

He asked politely for coffee for himself and for Rita. Trays and cups were passed back and forth, full then empty, with a comparative pleasantness.

I saw Rita look at him strangely and he reached across and took and squeezed her hand. I could see from her expression that, if this were to continue, it would take some time for her to get used to it.

The landing was smooth and I let them disembark in front of me, I was in no real hurry.

Along with my fellow passengers I joined the congregation that clustered around the baggage carousel.

As I gazed around I spotted Rita and Rich and had to smile. There seemed to be a small but non-zero possibility that, however unwittingly, I may have done something good.

It's well known that some people respond to bad experiences by sharing the hurt, normally amongst those closest to them. They get into a pattern of behaviour that they can't get out of, it becomes a part of them. A sharp shock can occasionally give a reason for change.

I had no idea whether I had provided such a shock or whether any positive effect would evaporate before the day was out.

The only thing I did know was that right then, right there, by the baggage carousel, Rich and Rita were holding hands.

Chapter Seventeen

I like to know something about countries I'm visiting for the first time. It helps me to have some wider context in the back of my head when I'm coping with whatever my assignment might throw at me. I had never been to Peru before so I'd done a bit of homework.

Peru is a west coast South America country with a Pacific coastline of 1500 miles and borders with Ecuador, Colombia, Brazil, Bolivia and Chile. It is the third largest country in Latin America with a land area of 500,000 square miles and a population of around 29 million people, with Lima, the capital, being home to around 8 million.

The national language is Spanish and Peru has a clear-cut class structure with the indigenous peoples occupying the bottom, and the descendants of the Spanish the top. The rich are very rich and the poor are very poor. Political and economic power has been in the hands of the small white and Mesitzo (people of mixed European and indigenous descent) elite for centuries. Not surprising then that it was the indigenous communities that were hardest hit by the armed conflict that erupted in Peru from 1980 to 1990 during which approximately 200,000 people were driven from their homes and an estimated 70,000 were killed.

Today it is corruption that tops the list of things that Peruvians are most ashamed of with poverty coming only fourth or fifth.

Family is sacred. Grandparents, married daughters, sons and their children often share the same house and pool their incomes in order to survive.

Crime has become a threat to all visitors to Peru. Pickpockets are common and visitors are advised to always keep cash in a money belt hidden under their clothes and not to wear expensive jewelry when out on the streets. They are further advised to use ATMs during the day when there are more people around and they are less likely to be mugged. Similarly they are advised to avoid walking out alone at night and to be aware and vigilant of their surroundings at all times.

On a lighter note Peru is also the home of the potato. The Incas cultivated more than 1,000 varieties. Peruvians have found many non-dietary uses for the potato ranging from a cure for ulcers, the dissolving of kidney stones, the soothing of burns and the use of mashed potato as a beauty product (applied to the face as a mask at night).

Guinea pigs are domesticated and are often to be seen running around the floor of rural dwellings. They feed on scraps and are commonly harvested, skinned, roasted and eaten by their erstwhile benefactors.

In general Peruvians like to dance and sing as evidenced by the many annual carnivals and are passionate followers of both bullfighting and football.

It is a land of history, of art and of culture, of pride and sometimes of despair. It is a country and a people that should not be taken lightly, but should be respected. It is a country that has known trauma, has survived difficult times but not forgotten them. As one of Peru's finest poets Cesar Vallejo rather fatalistically put it "the undertow of all our sufferings is embedded in our souls."

When I got through Lima's Jorge Chavez Airport Passport Control, Baggage Reclaim and Customs (the Green lane) it was a little after 6am local time. Nothing was going to be happening until at least 9am according to the schedule I had.

I therefore approached Tourist Information and asked if there were facilities within the airport where I could get a shower. I'd eventually slept OK on the plane, actually better than I normally do, but you still can't help getting off a nearly eight hour flight feeling like you need a wash and a brush up. I had the time and taking such an unexpected turn allowed me to look over each shoulder and see whether, despite my protestations, I had been given a tail. As far as I could see I hadn't. Good.

The showers were clean and the water hot, the towels were Egyptian cotton and the cost was reasonable. I emerged feeling better and in a fresh set of clothes.

Still wanting to make sure no-one was shadowing me I visited a number of the airport shops picking up some bits and pieces and then found a place to have breakfast. I went for a Chicharrone sandwich, a favourite in Peru and consisting of a freshly baked bread roll filled with lightly seasoned crunchy pieces of fried pork, crispy sweet potato, and a zesty onion relish. Accompanied by a mug of black Peruvian coffee it was delicious, almost as good as the bacon butties my mother used to make me back home.

Now feeling refuelled I thought this would be as good a moment as any to check-in to 'The Store' so I found a private corner and dialled in using my "Agaricus" identifier.

'I've just arrived in Peru,' I told an attentive Samantha, 'I don't appear to have company but I'd like you to keep an eye on that, an unwanted companion is the last thing I need.'

I could hear her keyboard clicking and then,

'As far as we know you're on your own,' she said.

'I'm worried that someone will get trigger happy,' and remembering the failed armed retrieval attempt, I added, 'again.'

'OK, concern noted, have you got anything more concrete than that?'

'Not at this moment.'

'How are you f…'

I interrupted.

'Tired, grumpy and irritable,' I said.

'Ah,' she replied, I could hear the smile in her voice, 'back to normal then.'

Mutually reassured, the call ended.

After I'd had a last look around for hangers-on I pushed through the glass-paneled doors and exited the airport, luggage in hand.

The sky was overcast but there was no rain and only a light breeze, the temperature was a pleasant 22 degrees Celsius. For a Brit it felt like a Summer's day.

Although I was keen to get Kerry-Anne home as soon as possible I was very aware that the pace of events was not under my control. It was important that I did not let my impatience or impetuousness surface. I had to go with somebody else's flow.

The next step of my journey was to go to the pre-booked hotel and check-in to my pre-allocated room. Then I was to sit and wait to be contacted.

I joined the queue for the fully licensed, officially validated taxis and was soon travelling through Lima's city streets confident I was being taken to the right place without any unnecessary diversions. I kept vigilant nonetheless. Better safe than sorry.

My room on the 7th floor of the Radisson Hotel ensured I had a base to work from, even though I was unlikely to spend much of my time there.

Once I'd settled in I checked for emails on my tablet and phone and moved my "sales samples" from my main luggage into a smaller bag. Once completed I was ready for collection from the hotel by whoever the unknown representative of my Peruvian hosts was going to be. With nothing left to do but wait, I lay back on the bed and, still fully dressed, fell asleep. Maybe I wasn't as acclimatized as I thought I was.

Chapter Eighteen

A loud knocking at the door of my room woke me up. I emerged grudgingly from slumber's soft embrace and answered it.

It was a woman.

'My name is Isabella,' she said, 'I think you were expecting me, no.'

'Yes,' I said, 'and I'm Paul, Paul Carpenter.'

'Yes,' she said, 'apparently you are.'

I was expecting someone but Isabella was a surprise. Despite the academic look the glasses she wore gave her, what I saw at once was that Isabella was a very attractive woman. Dark skinned, golden streaked luxuriant brown hair flowing down past her shoulders, piercingly green eyes and an impression of elegance from tip to toe. Maybe it was because I'd just woken up but I felt off-balance, this wasn't what I had been expecting. Full of self-confidence she brushed past me into the room. She had my attention.

'I hope you had a pleasant flight,' she said, making herself comfortable in one of the lounge chairs that sat either side of a low table. She crossed her legs.

She was wearing black high heels. I sat opposite her. 'no problems en route?'

I caught my breath. Closed my mouth.

'No, no problems,' I said.

'You are alone?'

'Yes,' I said.

'And where do you come from?'

'I flew over from London to New York about 36 hours ago. I'm Scottish,' I said.

She raised her eyebrows.

'Scottish, the home of golf, football and whisky.'

'The place where if it's not raining its between showers,' I said, 'it is certainly the home of golf and whisky but even I could not claim it to be the home of football.'

She smiled. Had that just been a little test?

'And who do you work for?'

'I am working on behalf of Kerry-Anne's parents,' I said, realizing that this was an interview, a vetting process that I was expected to pass, 'my organization is independent of any country and not a part of any enforcement authority, either in the USA or elsewhere.'

'And your real name is not Paul Carpenter,' she said, more as a statement than a question.

'No,' I said, there was no point lying, 'it's not.'

'Good,' she said, 'I do hope you realize that if you are lying you will be killed?'

She said this in such a calm matter-of-fact way that it took a moment to sink in.

'I'm not lying,' I said.

She waved a hand dismissively, 'We shall see but in the meantime we shall proceed and we welcome you Mr Paul Carpenter, the name will do, to Peru.'

'Thanks,' I said.

She got up and went to the hotel phone, called room service and spoke in fast Spanish.

'There are a few things you now need to know. It will take a few moments so we may as well be comfortable. Are you packed?'

This last question came as a kind of afterthought. It surprised me.

'I've hardly had time to unpack,' I said.

'Si, of course. Bring your bags in here where I can see them', she said, 'then I know you are ready.'

'"Trust nothing but your own eyes" is a good practical maxim that she seemed to have learnt already.

I retreated to the bedroom, recovered various toiletries and bits and pieces, put them back into my bags, zipped them up and brought them through to where she was seated, waiting for me.

'Good,' she said.

At that moment there was a polite knock at the door. It was room service carrying a tray with two coffees and a plate of what looked like pastries.

After they'd been laid on the table and the waiter tipped and left, she pointed to the plate.

'A Peruvian speciality,' she said, 'these cookies are called alfajores, two vanilla cookies with a caramelized milk sauce in the middle. It is an art to produce such a thing. Please try. I must warn you it is sweet but still delicious alongside the bitterness of your coffee.'

I played along. It was sweet, very sweet. It was delicious alongside the sharpness of the coffee. But I wanted to get on.

'Why do you want to see my bags?' I asked.

'Oh, so direct, I like it, we will get on well, you and I,' she said, 'the reason that I want to see your bags is because you are leaving.'

Had I after all failed the test, was it all over already?

'The girl is not here, Mr Carpenter. I think I will call you Mr Carpenter, it does not feel right to call you Paul, it is too familiar… but you must call me Isabella,' she put down her coffee and brushed a couple of cookie crumbs from her lap, 'no, we decided that it was better to relocate the girl so we will be taking you to Cusco.'

'Cusco?'

'Si, Mr Carpenter,' she reached into a concealed pocket and held out her hand, 'here, take these,' she said.

In her palm were two tablets. I took them from her with reluctance. I wasn't a big fan of taking medication from strangers, especially strangers who were dangerous. And there was no doubt about it, she may be elegant, she may be attractive, but she was dangerous. I had to keep my wits about me.

'One is a Sorojchi pill and the other is Gravol,' said Isabella, 'they are for the altitude. I understand it may be difficult to trust me, Mr Carpenter, but I assure you that, for the moment, I have your best interests at heart.'

She unfolded a leaflet she'd taken from the same concealed pocket and handed it to me.

'Read this,' she said.

I took the leaflet and read it through:

"Cusco - How to Cope with Altitude Sickness

Cusco, the old capital of the Inca Empire, is located at an altitude of 11,152 feet (3,399 meters) above sea level. It is not unusual for visitors travelling from Lima (at sea level) to Cusco to immediately experience fatigue, difficulty in walking, shortness of breath, discomfort in the body, dizziness, headaches, stomach aches, or even vomiting.

This response is due to the comparative lack of oxygen, scientifically known as hypoxia, which can manifest itself at altitudes above 7,874 ft (2,399 m).

Right after landing in Cusco visitors who try to walk one block can feel like they're trying to walk ten carrying a backpack full of rocks.

To prevent this happening to you there are some simple precautions you can take:

1. Stay hydrated - The body dehydrates quickly at high altitudes. It is important to drink lots of water before and during your trip to Cusco.

2. Coca - is the best natural medicine to combat altitude sickness as it makes it easier for the bloodstream to absorb oxygen and also combats fatigue, headaches and eases the stomach. It can be taken either by chewing the leaves (although they are bitter and numb your mouth) or by drinking coca tea.

3. Medication - by taking one tablet of the Sorojchi Pill and one tablet of Gravol an hour before landing in Cusco you can minimise the effects of the altitude when you land.

But don't worry, the body eventually gets used to the altitude and any symptoms will subside.

By following these rules we hope you will enjoy your visit to Cusco.
Welcome."

I understood. I took the tablets.

Chapter Nineteen

To get to Cusco we had to return to Lima's Jorge Chavez Airport. I may as well have stayed there although by taking such a convoluted route the chances of being successfully followed were reduced.

Isabella informed me that we were booked on a LATAM Airbus A320 flight that was going to leave at 11:25hrs and arrive in Cusco Alejandro Velasco Astete Airport at 12:48hrs, a 1 hour 23 minutes journey through the air. From the scare she'd given me about the altitude I was expecting a vertical take-off.

Once aboard I asked her how come her English was so good, in a lot of ways it was better than mine.

'I was educated in Europe,' she said.

'Europe?'

'What, Mr Carpenter, you don't think a girl from South America can be educated in Europe?'

'No,' I said quickly, 'it's just a surprise. I thought that maybe you'd gone to the US.'

'I am no fan of the USA,' said Isabella.

From her face I could see it would not be a good idea to press her on that so instead I said,

'But you came home.'

'Yes,' she said, 'there have been some bad times here in Peru. My father did not want my life to be like his. He wanted me to build my life in Europe. He was my father, I did what he told me,' she paused, 'when my father died I came home. I am from Peru, it is in my blood and fills my soul, I could not exist anywhere else.'

I couldn't stop myself from saying,

'But you returned home in order to kidnap teenage girls, American girls.'

The problem was that I could just not bridge the gap between what Isabella looked like and said and the dirty business I was here to try and resolve. For all I knew irreparable damage had already been done.

Fire flashed behind her eyes.

'That is enough,' she said, 'I have said too much, I apologise, let us speak only about our business from now on.'

She was an attractive, intelligent woman. She was impressive and easy to like but I wasn't there to make friends and the facts were that she was a kidnapper demanding a ransom. For my part the simple truth was that I was representing Kerry-Anne's parents, I'd brought the money and all I wanted was to have Kerry-Anne released and returned home.

When I stepped off the plane the altitude hit me like a brick wall, tightening my chest and making me gasp. Isabella left me in Arrivals. I sat down and wondered how I'd managed to run a marathon without noticing. She returned a few moments later carrying two cans. She handed one of the cans to me.

'These are cans of 95% pure oxygen. They can be used to give you relief if you're feeling dizzy. They operate like this.' She took the other can and held it about 6 inches in front of her face and pressed the top. I heard the hiss.

'You try,' she said.

Using the can she'd given me I followed her instruction. The relief was immediate.

'Just short bursts,' she said, 'or you will use it up too quickly. Now we go to the car,' she called a porter over, 'let him take your cases and walk slowly.'

I felt like I'd aged about forty years.

As we left the airport we passed an open door. Inside were two hospital beds and large tanks of oxygen. Both beds were occupied, one with what looked like a young athlete, the other with a more mature lady.

'You see,' said Isabella, 'the altitude is no respecter of age, sex, colour or creed. It is one of nature's levellers.'

A car was waiting for us outside and we drove to a small Spanish colonial style hotel near the centre of Cusco. Isabella took control and saw me safely checked-in and my bags taken up to my room.

'Now I will leave you for a while,' she said, 'get settled in, have a rest and drink the coca tea. I'll pick you up in 2 hours.'

There was a supply of coca tea in the reception area so I drank some before attempting to climb the stairs, there was no elevator.

It felt like climbing a mountain.

With this unexpected turn of events I thought I'd better inform 'The Store'.

'You're where?' said Samantha.

'Kerry is not in Lima as we expected, for some reason she's been moved. I'm in Cusco suffering from the altitude. I got to tell you, Sam, it feels like I've gone 10 rounds in the ring and come off second best.'

'Hmm, well there's not much we can do about that from here,' thanks for the sympathy, I thought, 'just stick with it.'

'I'm not telling anybody else about my movements until I get a clearer picture of what's going on. The last thing I want to do is panic anybody into unhelpful and precipitous action.'

I could hear her thinking.

'Understood. I'll let AB know. Personally, I think you're right, there are people stretched to almost breaking point, there's nothing to be gained from increasing their anxiety although they'll know where you are, they're tracking your phone just like we are.'

'Can you buy me some time?'

'I'll do my best to keep things cool,' she said, 'but don't leave it too long.'

'I'm doing everything I can to make sure the altitude doesn't get to me, that would really screw things up. I've got an aerosol of oxygen and I'm drinking coca tea that they've got in a big urn down in the hotel reception area. It must be expensive stuff because the cups they give you to drink it out of are very small.'

Samantha laughed. It was good to hear her laugh. It made me feel better.

'Don't be taking any drug tests,' she said, 'Coca tea contains a significant amount of cocaine and cocaine-related alkaloids.'

'No wonder I'm feeling better,' I said.

Chapter Twenty

Isabella called from reception at about 2:45 pm to let me know it was time to go.

'Don't bring anything metal or electronic, leave your phone, watch, keys, etcetera behind. Bring nothing but yourself and the clothes you stand up in.'

So at last we were going somewhere that they didn't want me tracked to. Assuming it wasn't just to bump me off and dispose of my body then this was promising.

I walked slowly out of the hotel and showed that I had disobeyed her instructions in only one regard. I had the oxygen can in my hand. She took it from me and handed it to the guy on the reception desk for disposal.

'That's OK,' said Isabella, 'I have another one in the car.'

She then scanned me for metal objects and electronics using a security wand before she allowed me into the back of a black limousine.

Once inside the doors were locked. Although allowing through some natural light the side and back windows were blacked out as far as viewing was concerned and the driver's seat was likewise blacked out by a separating panel. Communication from front to back was via an intercom.

'Please strap yourself in, Mr Carpenter, there is some food and drink in the cabinet beside you, please help yourself you must be hungry. The journey will take about 40 minutes, there will be no need to talk along the way unless you have questions. OK?'

I really had peed her off. Not a smart move.

'OK,' I said.

The food was ham and tomato sandwiches and the drink was mango juice. Although I had snacked on the plane it was only when I saw them that I realized how hungry I was. Eating and drinking also usefully occupied my time.

All I knew of the journey was that, from the direction of the sunlight entering the car, we were travelling roughly eastward.

From the roughness of the road and length of time travelled we had obviously left the central city behind us and soon began to climb further into the Andean foothills.

After the promised 40 minutes the car slowed and the screen separating front from back was lowered. I could now see over Isabella's shoulder and out through the front windscreen.

As far as I could make out we were approaching

the gated entrance to a large house which was surrounded by high whitewashed walls inhospitably topped with barbed wire.

Just outside the black metal electronic entry gates was a gatehouse and Isabella wound down the driver's side window and shouted over. A security guard responded hurriedly, his large frame wobbling as he jogged over as quickly as he could.

'I have one visitor,' said Isabella, 'a Mr Paul Carpenter.'

The guard was holding a log book and pen and looked uncertainly at me.

'Give it to me,' said Isabella.

She took the book filled in my details and initialed alongside.

Relieved of any responsibility the guard smiled, saluted to Isabella and turned to wobble back to his gatehouse.

'Welcome to the home of your host,' said Isabella as the gates slid apart, 'his name is Hathos and I ask that you, even under these circumstances, treat him with respect. He is a proud man and it would not be to your advantage to upset him.'

I had no intention of purposely upsetting anybody but at least I could now put a name to the man I had to complete the deal with – Hathos.

The metal gates closed noiselessly behind us, like a ripple disappearing from the surface of a pond, and I wondered if I would get out as easily as I was getting in.

The perimeter appeared to be circular or oval and curved away from us on both sides of the drive. Security cameras were mounted at regular intervals looking both inside and out. This was clearly a place where access, egress and movement were closely monitored.

We passed well-tended lawns, flower beds, shrubbery and the occasional AK 47-toting individual as the car climbed steadily up to the entrance.

When at last we stopped Isabella held open the rear door for me and I got out. We had pulled up at the foot of a set of wide stone steps that led upwards towards a pair of solid-looking wooden doors.

The doors stood ajar and two men stood side-by-side on the threshold.

'Come, let me introduce you,' said Isabella.

Here we go, I thought, as I ascended the steps. It felt like I was climbing a mountain. It was noticeably cooler than in Lima and as we got closer I could feel a warm draft from a heated interior flowing out to meet me. Once I'd reached the top I paused, gasping, to catch my breath.

'Are you alright?' asked Isabella.

'Yes, fine,' I lied.

'Then may I introduce Carlos,' said Isabella gesturing to a short man. He nodded. 'and Diego,' who was taller and thinner, 'they have travelled from Lima and will look after you while I go and talk with Hathos.'

'Hello,' I said to the two men. They each nodded and said 'Hola.'

Isabella strode off and left me to their tender mercies.

The two men's greeting had been about as warm as an ice bucket. They moved apart and gestured me to follow them inside.

Obediently I stepped into the marble floored interior and walked behind them as they guided me into a kind of ante-room.

The room had a number of leather armchairs and a small low-level table and I was invited to sit down. I did so gratefully and tried to make myself comfortable.

My two companions sat opposite me and immediately began playing with their mobile phones, ignoring me completely. I couldn't help wondering who they were and why they were here. What was clear was that they were suspicious of me and kept glancing up at me.

I took this opportunity to look the two of them over.

Carlos was a rather squat man, somewhere around

5'4" tall, well dressed in a white linen suit, dark shirt and white tie. He had swarthy features and a rather wide nose. His hair was black and slicked back tight to his head. He was clean shaven and had no particular distinguishing features that I could see.

Diego, on the other hand, was taller, easily over 6 feet, and painfully thin. His suit was brown and ill-kempt. He had a straggly beard and moustache and his hair was an uncombed mess. His complexion was bronze and he had a 1-2 inch long scar running diagonally across his left cheek.

After taking this all in I cleared my throat loudly.

'So guys what's the next move?' I said.

It was Carlos who replied, his English was good.

'We wait, Mr Carpenter. Now we wait.'

He moved his hands up and down in a "calm down" motion, 'Just sit quietly and wait,' he said.

I sat uncomfortably, shifting my position.

'You came here from Lima?' I asked.

'Si,' said Diego, 'we drive.'

'That's a long way,' I said.

'Very far,' said Diego, like a man who had done most of the driving.

'Over 600 miles,' said Carlos, 'and of course the climb, always up. 30 hours journey, 24 hours driving. But not so much altitude sickness.'

That had to be right. Climbing the 11,000 feet in 30 hours with the ability to stop along the way had to be easier on the body than jumping up in an hour and a half. Anyway it would not have been anything new for Carlos and Diego, they would have known what to expect and coped accordingly.

'Can I have a glass of mineral water?' I asked.

From the look on their faces I was clearly being a bother but Carlos said,

'Would you like whisky with that?'

'No just mineral water thanks,' I said, 'still not sparkling and chilled would be good.'

Carlos snorted and signaled to Diego who obediently got up, returning with a bottle of water, presumably from a nearby kitchen tap, in less than a minute.

I poured some of the cool water into the glass Carlos brought across for me from a nearby drinks trolley. I sipped luxuriantly. With the altitude and the situation combined the water tasted like nectar and I savoured it, feeling the coolness as it slid smoothly down my throat with rejuvenating effect.

Sitting with Carlos and Diego was an uncomfortable experience. They weren't chatty and we had nothing meaningful to talk about. The interesting thing was that they, if anything, seemed even more uncomfortable.

Chapter Twenty One

When Hathos was finally ready to meet me I was led into a high ceilinged room with wall high windows on one side. The windows opened onto a paved patio area with a panoramic view of the surrounding area. In the centre of the room a man was sitting in a comfortable red leather recliner and as we approached he stood up, stepped forward and put out his hand.

His smile was wide in greeting, as if we were old friends. My chaperones appeared to be almost ready to bow.

'Mr Carpenter, I'm so pleased to meet you at last, you may call me Hathos.'

Although he might have a strange name his handshake was knuckle crunching. It felt like I'd inadvertently put my hand in a vice and someone was over-tightening it. I made a mental note to make sure to count my fingers at the earliest available opportunity.

My overwhelming first impression of Hathos was that he was a big man, big in all respects; his height, his breadth, his smile. His presence in the room seemed to make it smaller, to centre it on him. Whatever charisma is, I thought, this man seemed to have it.

Once he released me we sat down facing each other across a glass topped coffee table, each in our own deep red leather armchair, he comfortable, me much less so.

'I hope that Carlos,' Carlos nodded to acknowledge that it was indeed he, 'and Diego have given you a suitable welcome?'

I did not know what a "suitable welcome" was but as they had not hit me I was quite willing to be generous.

'Yes of course,' I said and could almost taste the relief that flowed from the two men who were now standing behind me like naughty schoolboys. They had not been asked to sit.

'That is good,' said Hathos, 'it is important to me that all of my people have respect. There are too many who use their power improperly, don't you think, Mr Carpenter? After all you are entirely under our control but I see no reason why we should take undue advantage of that.'

So much for pleasantries, I thought.

I wasn't sure if any of what he had just said was meant as a question but felt that it would be polite to give a response.

'Quite right,' I said, 'and please call me Paul.'

'Thank you,' he said and waved to Diego, 'two whiskies'.

Diego dutifully went over to a drinks tray and poured an amber liquid into two cut class tumblers. Without asking he added one ice cube into each but no water. My time for undiluted mineral water was clearly over and with alcohol at altitude I knew I would have to be careful. He handed me a glass.

Hathos waved a hand.

'Ahora ve,' he said to Carlos and Diego and they left immediately.

'Salud,' he said and lifted his tumbler so we could chink glasses before taking a drink.

It was a very pleasant lowland single malt, smooth on the palate, light and delicate but with an underlying strength and a rounded finish. I liked it and took a second pull at the glass and then put the glass down.

Hathos looked across at me.

'I think, Paul, that I owe you an explanation,' he said.

An explanation! He had kidnapped two teenage girls, demanded money in return for their release and I was here to complete the transaction. Why on earth would he owe me an explanation? Just give me the girl and let us go, I thought.

'I am sorry that your clients were troubled with this unfortunate incident,' said Hathos, 'but I would like to assure you that it was not of my instigation. Once I found out I took immediate steps to rectify the problem.'

For "problem" he presumably meant the unprovoked kidnapping of vulnerable young girls and for "clients" he presumably meant their parents. In its sanitized form it didn't sound so bad, in reality it was horrendous. However I hadn't been expecting an apology and it threw me off guard.

'As a mark of my feeling you will know that I reduced the ransom demand to a nominal sum,' he said.

I suppose half a million dollars is a nominal sum for some people, certainly not for me, I thought.

'But now mark this and mark it well, Paul,' he said, his face turned hard and icily serious, 'my people must learn to do what I ask, and only what I ask. They are the only family that I have left. I am their father and as such I set the standards and I maintain the discipline. No one acts independent of my wishes. No one steps out of line. No one exceeds the limits that I draw, the boundaries that I set. This is the price of being a member of my family, of reaping the benefits and comforts that it brings.'

His change of demeanour was stark. Gone was the bonhomie to be replaced by a fierce self belief in what he was saying.

'Once I have accepted someone into the fold we are joined by blood, theirs to mine and mine to theirs. And no one can part themselves from such strong family ties and still live. It's that simple.'

He smiled.

It was certainly a clear and simple principle.

'It is good for my family to be so clear. They know the rules and if they stay within them they are protected. I nurture and feed my family. I help them to grow in the special skills that are needed in our mission. I believe we are a successful family, but we are still growing, still learning.'

'It is very important for you to know, Paul, that I and no one else may discipline or chastise this family. If anyone misbehaves within the family then I will find out about it, make no mistake about that, and I will deal with it.'

'If someone from within or, much worse, from outside my family takes my law into their own hands, whether their cause is just or not, they will suffer the consequences. No matter where they run I will find them and my retribution will be upon them. It may take time or it may be done quickly but it will be done. It may be carried out quietly or it may be dealt with publicly as a form of example. Let the punishment fit the crime, Paul, let the punishment fit the crime.'

'Now to our current problem,' he said, 'I have

searched diligently inside my family and I have identified the man who decided to act on his own, without my knowledge. The man responsible. Come...'

He got up and I followed him to the far side of the house and out into a stone flagged courtyard. It was mainly in shadow and a wall light threw an eerie yellow glow across the immediate area.

He put an arm around my shoulders and ushered me forward.

As my eyes adjusted to the scene I could see that about 5 metres away from us were three people. I recognised two of them immediately as Carlos and Diego. The third person was kneeling behind them making strangulated weeping noises.

'Come,' said Hathos.

As we walked towards Carlos and Diego they moved aside so that I got a clearer view of a small, bronzed, lean man who was tied and gagged and on his knees.

'Of course he has admitted everything, this ugly dog,' said Carlos in English.

'Take the gag away,' ordered Hathos.

The man held up his bound hands, he looked as if he were praying. He probably was.

With the removal of the gag a tsunami of words was released. Hathos held up a Canute-like hand and the flow of words stopped.

Hathos leant forward and spoke to the man very precisely,

'Paulo, escúchame, listen to me. Slowly and in your best English por favor. I would like my guest to understand you.'

The man concentrated hard. To plead for your life was one thing, to do it in a foreign language was quite another.

'Pleaz, pleaz, I have wife, family, pleaz, pleaz. Mercy, Mercy.'

Hathos turned and asked something of Carlos in Spanish. Carlos shrugged.

I thought I could detect doubt in the tone of Hathos' question.

Hathos turned to face me.

'You see, Paul, how I teach all my people to be international, to have mastery of many things, many languages.'

I looked at the man, black hair, brown eyes, wrinkled deep brown skin, small, lean to the point of malnutrition. No matter what his skills were he was unlikely to fit seamlessly into any international gathering of the cognoscenti.

Once again Hathos spoke to the man in Spanish as if he, Hathos, were a disappointed parent.

'In order to have forgiveness, we must first have a sin,' he said to me, 'and it is the nature of the sin that is the problem here.'

'Pleaz, pleaz…' wailed Paulo.

Carlos put his head down and whispered in Paulo's ear. The man started to shake. He looked up imploringly,

'I sorry,' he said, 'should not have…please mercy me, mercy me.'

'Should not what?' asked Hathos gently.

Paulo hung his head.

'I take girls. Want money. Stupid. Very stupid. Not do again. Forgive.'

'So, Paul, you see, we have our man. We have a confession. You have heard it.'

I wasn't convinced. The man was begging for his life, he would probably have said anything to please. And Carlos was also involved. Whatever he had whispered in Paulo's ear had made a difference.

But I wasn't going to argue. What good would it have done to say anything?

'As it was against your clients that this sin was committed,' said Hathos, 'and as you are their representative here, I ask you what your choice would be if you were in my position.'

Choice?

'Would you show mercy to this man, this man who you do not know, this man who I would guarantee would show no mercy to you if the situation were reversed. Well, what do you think?'

I looked at Paulo. He was a human being for

Christ's sake, not a dog. I wasn't even sure he'd done anything.

'I would show mercy,' I said.

Hathos laughed.

'Have you not been listening to me,' he said, 'or is it that you westerners, you act tough, but in your heart you are soft?'

He nodded to Carlos who took out a handgun.

Paulo continued to weep and beg for his life.

Hathos stood firm.

'Paul, you must tell your clients that you saw this with your own eyes. You can say that there is no need for any further retribution, you have seen it done here on their behalf by me.'

My instinct was to try and stop this happening but I was powerless. On what basis could I intervene? This was a human life being sacrificed and for what? In the belief that such action would placate the mob I represented back in the States. And would it? I had no idea, maybe this show of penance was going to turn out to be a waste of time or maybe it would mark an end.

I've seen some bad things in my life and I didn't need to see any more.

'I'm not going to watch,' I said and turned towards the house.

Diego blocked my path.

'Let me pass,' I said through clenched teeth.

He didn't move.

I turned to Hathos.

'Either let me go inside or this exchange ends right here!'

Hathos sighed.

'You can go nowhere without my permission, Paul, just watch if you please. I need you to be a witness.'

I wasn't in the mood to be a pawn in Hathos' game.

'I mean it,' I said.

Hathos paused, balancing risks.

He shrugged.

'OK, Paul, we are videoing all this anyway so it doesn't really make a material difference. But I insist that you relay to your clients that this event is real, there is no subterfuge, it is not staged.'

I looked at Paulo, this was definitely real.

I nodded.

Hathos waved his hand and Diego stood aside. He followed me in.

Behind me I could still hear the cries and then there was a shot.

And then silence.

I felt complicit even though when I thought about it objectively there was nothing I could have done. If I had intervened the chances were that I'd have only made things worse.

My priority was to find Kerry-Anne and to get her home.

Chapter Twenty Two

After what had just happened I felt I was in need of some insurance. I did not know what was going to happen next. I did not know where Kerry was. I did not know how the people back in the States were going to react and at the moment I was useless. I didn't know the whereabouts of any of the critical locations, I had no means of tracking any of the people involved.

I therefore decided to take a risk.

For better or for worse I have a talent for pick-pocketing. It has come in handy many times and I am good at it, up to professional standards.

I had watched both Carlos and Diego use their phones and had seen which pocket they had put them back into. The rest was easy.

After we had heard the shot and Diego followed me far enough inside I stopped abruptly and we stumbled into each other. I apologised for my clumsiness and although he was clearly displeased he brushed it off.

To me his appearance looked like a mess on legs but who knows, maybe he put substantial effort into achieving this level of dishevelment. There was enough oil in his hair to lubricate a bike and the style of facial hair he'd adopted was unique to put it politely. Perhaps in his own mind he was quite a catch for the ladies, perhaps I was wrong and he had a unique animal magnetism that an idle onlooker like myself could not be expected to appreciate at first (maybe even second or third) glance.

Whilst waiting for Hathos to return I told Diego I needed to use the bathroom. Grudgingly he showed me the way.

Once inside I downloaded the required stalkerware apps onto his phone and made adjustments in the settings to make them invisible to a casual user. For safety's sake I also memorized his and, from his address book, Carlos' number.

Replacing the phone was as easy as taking it, the only downside was that I had to get close to him again. The sickly sweet smell of cheap cologne was almost overpowering.

I hoped that like most other people he took his phone with him everywhere.

At least I'd done something and, who knows, maybe this extra bit of insurance would turn out to be useful.

Hathos returned shortly after.
He took me by the arm.

'Now you have seen my sincere intent to show contrition, Paul, we have other things to talk about.'

He lead me onto the front terrace, the sun was shining and the view was spectacular. The land fell away steeply to the west and south and from an elevated position such as ours we had a panoramic view towards Cusco.

'I come here to watch the sun set each evening,' he said, 'Each time it is different.'

Hathos raised and spread his arms wide as if in orchestration or in worship of the sun.

The scene was indeed splendid. The bright sun making its way towards a clear horizon.

'Sit,' he said, indicating a patio chair.

I sat and he pulled around another chair so that he could sit alongside me.

'It is the sun that gives us warmth and light and life and at the end of every day he disappears. Many times I watch the pin-prick of coloured lights that awaken in the city, shimmering like grounded stars, as the sun fades. Each evening I am here I bid farewell to the sun, my soul healer and health bringer and ask that I rest well and rise again tomorrow.'

The fact of the matter was that the picture he painted was flawed. Without the protection of the Earth's atmosphere this so-called health bringer would fry us to an ultraviolet crisp.

Hathos had just had somebody executed, could he really just move on as if nothing had happened?

I looked at his upturned face, his eyes closed. When he opened them again he pointed to something. I didn't understand so he got up and took me over to an ancient-looking wooden statuette.

'This is the head of the god Inti,' he said, 'the Inca god of the Sun. I put it here so that it has a preeminent position.'

He rested the palm of his right hand on the wooden totem and stroked the carved surface. From the polished gleam of the wood I could see that this must be a regular custom.

I knew I had to be careful of him. Although his behaviour was in some respects theatrical there was something in his demeanour that suggested a kind of dangerous sincerity and negated much of my natural cynicism.

He shepherded me back to our seats.

'The girl,' I said, 'I need to see her.'

He smiled reassuringly, all white teeth and gleaming eyes.

'Yes,' he said, 'you do. But rest assured the girl is safe. Would you like another drink?'

I declined. I just wanted to get on with it. But he was the boss, I was in his hands so had no alternative but to play along.

'So whose side are you on?' he said.

This question came out of the blue and took me by surprise. I did my best to come up with an answer.

'It's not my job to take sides,' I said, 'I just need to know what I'm supposed to do and then I do it. My job is to go between one side and the other, deal with both and try to ensure that everyone is as happy as possible at the end.'

'But there must be times when you have to make a choice.'

'Other people make the choices,' I said, 'I just do what I'm told. You wouldn't survive long in my game if you made your own choices and I've been doing this job a long time, a very long time.'

I was so convincing that I almost believed it myself.

'I would like to tell you a little about myself, Paul. It is good I think to know something about the person you are doing business with.'

I was a captive audience, if he wanted to tell me more about himself then so be it. I was not in favour, on the other hand, of him learning anything more about me.

'Do you know what ambition is?' he asked. I shrugged half-heartedly. I was pretty sure that the question was rhetorical.

'Ambition is aiming high. That is what I am

doing, Paul.' he paused to allow me to soak this in, 'I come from a poor family, that is unfortunately not so rare here in Peru. My parents lived a simple life, they worked and lived off the land. They were not interested in politics or ownership, they wanted only to be left alone, to work, to feed themselves and to look after their family. This is not so much to ask but here in Peru it can be impossible.'

He gazed off into the far distance of memory.

'Men with guns came to our village. I was only a boy then and did not immediately understand what was happening. I was soon shown the ruthless truth, our crops were burnt and people were killed. My own mother was shot and fell over me as she died, hiding and protecting me from the men and from their bullets. I should have died then, Paul. It is by luck and my mother's self-sacrifice that I did not. When all was quiet I crawled out from under her body. I stood and I ran. I cried as I ran. I cry for my mother still.'

Hathos appeared to be an intelligent man, there must be a reason he was telling me all this. I was a stranger who he would know for only a matter of hours and, if I were completely honest, a stranger who had little interest in learning this much about him. There must be a reason, but I couldn't see it.

Hathos continued, he was calm, measured and in control.

'I have no political allegiances, Paul, but I believe I have a sense of justice. My journey to this point has required me to learn toughness, ruthlessness even, and perseverance. I have learnt all of these things through experience, through trial and error. I will always be learning.'

'My father and my close relatives tried their best to raise me. Along the way I found I grew big and strong and had a voice that others would listen to. In this way I learnt and grew into a knowledge of leadership, about what it takes for men and women, individuals in their own right, to accept the authority of someone else. I have learnt that we all seek such leadership but we are also harsh judges of those that we choose to follow.'

'Most of all I have experienced fear and learnt of its power. You see, Paul, I have overcome my fear. I no longer fear death. I understand fear. I understand that death is less to be feared than life. I should have died that day long ago and now each new day is an extra day, a day that I should not have had, and a day to take the most from. I have seen death but I survived, I grew strong again, stronger than I had been before, stronger mentally as well as physically. All that I now do is a gift and I try to use that gift well.'

He paused, rose and moved to stand by his totem, 'Slowly we try to rebuild our villages and our lives.

The past has not been good to my community but I believe I can help in the rebuilding. Do not be fooled by the trappings of leadership you see around you, Paul, a leader must live his position or else he is not respected. Already I have helped to build a new school, a hospital. However I am young in these efforts and along the way mistakes are made.'

He shrugged.

'But where does the money come from to do these things? It comes from activities that defy the law. It comes from cross border dealing including with the United States. Do you not believe that good things can come from bad? We do illegal things, there is no other way.'

He paused.

'We are limited in our funds and maybe even in our abilities but there is no limit to our ambition.'

His voice had risen during the delivery of this monologue, his dark eyes shone as he looked for my response.

I said nothing. I did not know whether he was mad, deluded or worse; honourable. Whichever way you looked at it he was dangerous.

'You think me mad, Paul? I hope I am not mad. As the sun rises in the morning I hope there will be a new dawn for people like me. This country is my home. I do not want to leave it, but I do not want it to remain as it has been.'

'I hope, Paul, that we are moving towards a resolution of our problem. You may choose to believe me or not but I can promise you that the whole of this ransom will be spent on bringing education and improved health to people in the far north of this country. Good can come out of bad, Paul. Sometimes it is only by doing bad things today that we can hope to do better tomorrow.'

He was beginning to talk in sound bites. Did I believe a word of it? I wasn't even sure if I cared whether it was true or not. Maybe he was just putting on a show to while away the time, was self-delusional, or maybe it just made him feel better to say these things.

In point of fact, if I was reading between the lines correctly, Hathos smuggled contraband across various borders and probably did a bit of racketeering on the side. Put like that it was a lot less noble and grandiose than Hathos portrayed it and I could see why any attention from governmental agencies would be unwelcome.

'My work must not be interrupted,' he continued, 'it is too important to too many people..'

I could not stop myself, I said,

'Those are fine words, Hathos. But I don't understand why you are telling me all this.'

He paused, his eyes bored into me, seeming to

seek out my own flaws and weaknesses. It wouldn't have taken him long. I glanced away.

'It is because I need your help, Paul, that is why I tell you these things.'

So he was trying to convince me that he was good at heart because he wanted my help? What kind of help could I give him? What kind of help did he think I would be willing to give him? He had just executed, in cold blood, one of his own people. He lived in luxury far beyond those he purported to be trying to help. His activities were illegal and it was a stretch for me to actually take at face value anything he told me. I was here on behalf of Kerry, her parents and several others but not for him. Unless helping him was hugely in my own interests he was going to be grossly disappointed.

'What kind of help?' I said.

It was at this point that we were interrupted by Isabella.

Chapter Twenty Three

'Carlos and Diego wish to return to Lima,' said Isabella to Hathos, 'do you wish to see them?'

Hathos paused. We had not finished our own conversation.

'Very well,' said Hathos, and then to me, 'the air is beginning to chill, Paul, we will go inside.'

He was right about the temperature, as the Sun was lowering so was the thermometer. I was quite relieved to re-enter the warmth of the interior and pleased to see that a log fire had already been lit to heat the cavernous lounge.

By the time Isabella brought in Carlos and Diego we had resettled ourselves in leather armchairs. Carlos and Diego were not invited to sit.

Isabella left us, she obviously had more important things to attend to.

Hathos did not speak to Carlos or Diego, instead he said to me,

'I have a question for you, Paul,' he said, 'as you have seen I have done my best to find the person who was the instigator of this unfortunate mistake. It is possible however that I have not discovered the whole truth. So my question to you is this: do you have any information that I do not yet possess that may require me to consider further action?'

I was not expecting the question. Carlos and Diego visibly flinched. I had seen one man die, surely that was enough.

'The other girl for instance,' said Hathos, 'has she told you anything that I should know about?'

The memory of my discussion with Emily flashed through my mind. Her description of her masked captors fitted the appearance of Carlos and Diego. It did not fit that of the executed man. But surely this was not the time to escalate matters. I wanted to keep everything as simple and straightforward as possible. After all I still did not know where Kerry was being kept nor what physical and mental state she was in.

'I'm afraid Emily, the other girl, the one that was taken at the same time as Kerry-Anne but released to carry a message back to Kerry-Anne's parents, has been so traumatised by her misadventures that she has, for now at least, blocked all memory of what happened to her from her mind. I did talk to her directly but she was not able to help me. Supported by her parents and friends she is one hundred percent focused on putting it all behind her and getting on with her life.'

Complete fabrication of course, but needs must.

I hoped, whether Hathos really believed me or not, that this was a sufficient contribution to the necessary formula for bringing all this to an early end.

Assuming Kerry was in good health then I further hoped that her parents would be so grateful for her release and safe return that pursuing any further form of retribution would not be high in their minds and that, without their instigation, no further action would be taken on their behalf by any branch of the American authorities.

I saw Carlos and Diego physically relax. I think Hathos saw it to. But if he did he let it go.

'Buen viaje,' he said to Carlos and Diego.

They looked uncertain.

Hathos waved his hand and Carlos and Diego hurriedly left the room.

Chapter Twenty Four

'Why did you demand a non-American as your go-between?' I asked when Carlos and Diego had left.

'Trust and need,' said Hathos.

'I don't understand,' I said.

'Why do you think I don't trust North Americans?' he said, 'The relations we have always had between our countries is fraught, full of ups and downs. But I'll tell you one thing I trust the North Americans to be and that is vindictive. I trust them to act, and with force, when they feel slighted.'

'There is no doubt that it was a mistake to waylay Kerry-Anne. I cannot believe that Paulo knew who she was when he took her. I suppose that even if he had known he would have not understood the consequences. But I do. I know that those around Kerry-Anne will feel they must act.'

I couldn't help feeling that he was expecting others to act in the same way that he had told me he would if he had been slighted. I'd heard the mantra "we will defend ourselves against those who seek to harm us, avenge ourselves against those that have dealt us harm" or something like it, several times over during my time in America so perhaps he had good grounds to be concerned.

'As soon as I found out what had happened,' he continued, 'I stepped in and I will now do what I can to end this unfortunate episode as equitably as possible. The work I am doing for my community must not be derailed by this,' he tutted, 'so I hope you can understand why I could not risk a go-between from the United States. You have had eyes on you since you arrived, Paul, if you had brought others with you, if armed force had been tried for the second time, then I could not have predicted the consequences.'

I had also worried about that. Thank goodness no-one had gone rogue. Because of his emotional investment I had been particularly worried about George. But so far, so good.

'I could not have talked to anyone from the United States the way I have been talking to you. The States treat us like provincials, their superiority rammed home by their firepower. I would have felt that I could not trust them. I would have been worried about being stabbed in the back.'

It was difficult to know whether such prejudice was justified or not, learning from my own life experiences I'm fully aware that almost anybody can stab you in the back given the right, or the wrong, circumstances. "Don't trust anybody" isn't just for wearing on a T-shirt.

'Why didn't you just release the girl?' I said, 'wouldn't that have been the easiest thing to do?'

'Ah,' said Hathos, 'now we come to it. If you were American I don't think you would understand what I'm about to say to you and I don't think you would help in the way I'm going to ask you to help. You do believe, Paul, don't you that out of bad there can come good?'

He'd used this before. What I wondered was who had the right to define what "good" was and what level of "bad" was acceptable. But I wanted to keep things simple so I just said,

'I have a job to do, Hathos. I've brought you the money and all I need is for you to hand the girl over to me so I can take her home.'

Hathos held out a hand.

'Here take this,' he said.

It was a memory stick. I took it.

'As I told you we recorded what happened outside. Please give this to whoever needs to see it. Help me stop this escalating, Paul, or share the responsibility for what happens.'

I could imagine that there would be those back in the United States who might be comforted by what Hathos had done. There would be others who would not believe it without evidence. They could pour over the recording if they wanted. I would validate the reality of it if that helped.

'You can rest assured, Mr Carpenter, that Kerry-Anne would not have heard a thing. The walls within this building are soundproofed.'

My ears pricked up. Now he had my attention.

'The girl is here?'

Hathos smiled.

'Yes, of course,' he said, 'you have reached your destination. There are no more steps to take.'

'Can I see her?'

'Yes of course, although before you do I want you to meet someone.'

Now what, I thought.

Chapter Twenty Five

The man introduced to me as Doctor Alvarez wore a white coat, glasses and a stern expression.

'So Kerry is injured?' I said, my concern escalating.

'Nothing serious,' said Hathos, failing to make eye contact, 'Doctor Alvarez will explain.'

'I have examined the patient,' the use of the word "patient" did nothing to steady my nerves, 'and physically there have been some minor scrapes. These may be uncomfortable but they are not serious and are almost healed.'

He looked at me over the top of his glasses waiting to see if I had any questions.

'How extensive are they and how bad?' I asked in trepidation.

'I have been conscious at all times that the patient is a young lady and therefore my examinations have been sensitive and not invasive. I have looked only as far as the patient was comfortable for me to look.'

'And?' I said.

'And I have found minor marks and also, monitoring them daily, I have seen them heal satisfactorily.'

'Well that doesn't sound too bad,' I said.

'There was also some bruising,' said Doctor Alvarez.

Oh shit, what had Kerry been through?

'As you may know bruises can look a lot worse than they feel,' continued Doctor Alvarez, 'As the body heals and breaks down the hemoglobin, that gives blood its red colour, the bruise itself changes in colour. This is just a regular part of the healing process. I am happy to report that none of the bruising I have seen is still red or blue, or purple, or black. It is now at the stage were if you look closely enough you can still see some light brown discolouration but this is fading away day by day.'

He stopped. I waited a second or two to make sure he was finished.

'Anything else?'

'I have not assessed her mental state other than to note that she seems to be of a resilient nature,' he said.

I wanted to hit him. The way he spoke he could have been talking about a thoroughbred horse and not a human being.

'Thank you,' said Hathos, 'you can leave us now.'

Doctor Alvarez did as he was bid.

Without asking permission I went over to the drinks tray and half-filled a tumbler with whisky, no ice, and took a swig. Sod the altitude, I needed it.

'Before you saw Kerry-Anne I wanted you to know about this,' said Hathos, 'I did not want to give you any surprises.'

He paused to allow me to resettle myself.

'Are you ready to meet the girl?' he said.

Chapter Twenty Six

Hathos walked me through the house until we came to the end of a corridor. A man was sitting alongside a solid looking wooden door. At a nod from Hathos he got up and unlocked the door. Hathos ushered me into the room and I heard the door being locked behind me.

It took me a few moments to get my bearings. Although there was a large window in the wall facing me the curtains were drawn and the room was lit by only a bedside light. As my eyes became accustomed I could see there was a seating and eating area ahead of me by the curtained window and a door to my left that presumably led into an en-suite bathroom. To my right was a large double bed.

To begin with I thought the room was unoccupied but then I noticed a huddled figure, hardly moving, curled into the foetal position and lying on the bed.

So here she was at last, I thought, the object of my journey, the reason for all this. If I'd ever thought of her as a spoiled rich girl then she certainly didn't look much like that right now. Right now she looked like someone who was frightened.

I had already witnessed a death meted out as retribution for this, I didn't want to see any more.

I reached out my hand and touched her. She flinched. A shudder ran through her. For some reason I thought of my own daughter but I bottled up my feelings and spoke as softly and as kindly as I could,

'Kerry-Anne?'

She shifted her position, the white of an eye appeared, blinked and looked at me.

'Who are you?' she said.

'My name is Paul, Paul Carpenter and I have been sent here by your parents to get you home.'

She unwound herself and sat up hugging a pillow to her stomach.

'I don't believe you,' she said.

'I think I can prove that I've been sent by your family,' I said.

'How?'

'They told me something that only a few people know and certainly not your captors.'

She flinched at my use of the word "captors". I would have to tread carefully.

'What thing?' she said.

'Your first pet, do you remember?'

'Yes,' she said.

'It was a rabbit wasn't it.'

'Yes,' she said.

'And its name was Poppy.'

She stared at me.

'And how did Poppy die?' she said.

I wished I had a happier story but nevertheless it seemed to be working.

'Poppy got taken by a dog, a neighbour's rottweiler,' I said.

'Just like me,' she said, 'taken by dogs.'

She sat rocking backwards and forwards.

'Can I open the curtains and put some more lights on?'

It was approaching that twilight time, the edge of the day when both natural and artificial light could make a difference.

She nodded.

I wanted as much light as possible as I needed to look for marks.

With this better view I could see that Kerry was wearing sneakers, jeans and a long-sleeved, high-necked blouse. The clothes looked clean and her hair was tidy. She didn't appear to be wearing any make-up.

'Take me home,' she said in a whisper.

She moved to sit on the edge of the bed and I got a better view of her. Thankfully she looked neither undernourished nor dehydrated. She turned her face fully towards mine. Even though I was determined to keep aloof it was disconcerting.

It is a horrible thing to be in this kind of situation and have to suspend belief. I was almost sure this was Kerry-Anne but that wasn't enough. I had to be absolutely sure. It's a terrible thing when you can't trust anybody but I would have been severely embarrassed if I went ahead and handed over half a million dollars and then found that I'd been given the wrong girl. It had happened to others, the substitute normally being tempted by the expectation of asylum in whichever benevolent country they were dispatched to and the prospect of a better life. As part of my briefing back in London I had been told the way to remove this doubt.

'Kerry-Anne, I'm sorry but there is a question I now need to ask you.'

'Go ahead,' she said.

'When you were a little girl you had a favourite toy that you would take everywhere with you. What was it? What was it called? Can you remember?'

For some moments I thought she was not going to reply. That would have given me a problem I really didn't need.

'My little bear, fluffy and with big ears, my little friend Caesar.'

She crossed her arms and cradled herself as if giving the memory a hug.

That was all I needed. Thank goodness.

She sat quietly with her hands clenched into fists. I suggested we move to the seating area and make ourselves more comfortable. With a growing level of trust between us she agreed.

'Take me home, Mr Carpenter,' she said again, 'I want to go home.'

I hadn't transferred the money to Hathos yet and I was still to discover what else he might have up his sleeve. At this stage I didn't want to make any promises I couldn't keep. So I decided to try and be both positive and vague.

'Everything is going well,' I said.

'So can we go?' she said, 'I want to go home.'

I felt for her.

'I know,' I said, 'and I don't want you to worry, you're going home, there are just some final arrangements we need to make.'

Her head dropped. She started to cry. Quietly. Her shoulders shaking.

I wanted to rush forward and comfort her, but I had to keep it professional.

'Kerry,' I said softly, 'you've got to stay strong. We're so close now. There are no real obstacles.'

With an effort she pulled herself together. Stopped crying. Lifted her head. Looked me in the eye.

'How long?'

'Not too long,' I said, noncommittally. I could see the frustration etched on her face but I couldn't promise what I didn't know.

'Can I talk to my parents?'

'No,' I said, 'not yet.'

'Will you talk to them?'

'Yes, I have to go back to Cusco, I'll phone them from the hotel. The people here are very keen I don't give this location away. Is there anything you want me to tell them.'

She thought for a moment.

'Tell them it's all my fault, I should have listened to them. If I had then none of this would have happened. Tell them I want to come home ... and ask how Emily is for me.'

'OK,' I said, 'I'll let them know.'

'And Mr Carpenter...'

'Yes?'

'Don't over-exert yourself. It took me a while to get used to the altitude. If you're not careful it can knock you flat.'

All of a sudden she had moved into mothering mode. I guess it was in her best interests to make sure that I didn't get ill. That wouldn't help matters at all.

'OK,' I said, 'I'll be careful.'

Soon after that I knocked on the door and when I was out I asked to see Hathos.

Chapter Twenty Seven

Hathos turned his broad and muscular frame towards me, his skin brown-black. I was sitting back in the lounge, looking across at his cool, bronzed, well-built figure.

'I need a little more time,' he said.

'What do you mean?' I said, 'Although she was well-covered so it made it quite difficult, I didn't see any marks.'

'I'm afraid you're wrong, Paul, there are still a few faint marks,' said Hathos.

I nodded. The light in the room wasn't great and she was wearing a long-sleeved blouse and jeans, maybe there was a good reason for that.

'Nothing serious,' said Hathos, 'but I've told you already I've had experience of Americans and,' he continued with emphasis, 'with revenge.'

He strode to the window and looked out, his back to me.

'I can't control what Kerry-Anne might say when she is home and I can't prevent her going home. Even if that might have been a potential solution earlier it's too late for that now. I believe that to agencies trained in search and destroy I'm too easy to trace, so the best I can do is to reduce the chances of retribution. I've already reduced the ransom to a token amount, just enough so that both sides retain their dignity and now, and as importantly, I need Kerry-Anne to pass scrutiny when she gets home.'

He paused and turned back towards me, poured himself a drink, strode to an armchair and sat down.

'There's no easy way to say this, Paul. When I first saw Kerry-Anne she was dishevelled, scraped and bruised,' he sighed, 'can you imagine what would have happened if I had released her in that state. If you had a daughter and were to find her on the side of the road would you not wish to find out how she got there? Do you think they would have let things lie?'. No. They would have come hunting for the perpetrators. I cannot afford to be constantly looking over my shoulder. Or can you imagine me having this conversation with an American not knowing whether they were FBI, CIA or an employee of her parents? These things would have been impossible.'

I saw his point.

'So I'm asking you,' he said, 'I need you to help me.'

Bit of a turn up for the books, I thought.

'I need you to buy a little more time without causing alarm,' he said, 'just until the marks have completely gone. I need you to keep everyone happy in the meantime. The doctor says 48 hours should be enough.'

48 hours!

He stopped and looked at me. What was I supposed to say? I wasn't expecting to be asked to help him. What I had been expecting was to get in, transfer the money, pick up Kerry-Anne and get out as quickly as possible. I didn't expect to be the one given the job of delaying my own escape.

I could understand what he was saying though. The abortive armed retrieval attempt had given a glimpse of what future action might come his way if retribution was sought.

'Have we a deal?' asked Hathos.

I didn't see that I had a choice. If I said no he probably wouldn't let us leave anyway.

'And what excuse am I supposed to make?' I said.

Hathos smiled.

'I'll leave that you,' he said, 'that's your job.'

Thanks, I thought.

Chapter Twenty Eight

As I left the sun was setting, shimmering as it transmuted into a liquid orange, deepening, reddening as it disappeared below the horizon. Scattered clouds picked up the colour and as if in answer spread widely a blood red glow. Behind me a large dark silhouette stood with its arms outstretched to the heavens.

Isabella drove me back to Cusco. The journey gave me time to digest and ruminate on what Hathos had said and to think about his request.

I had no way of knowing the validity of anything that he had said, but I was convinced that he believed every word of it himself. He was committed to protecting what he had built at all costs.

His recent actions had purged me of any grudging respect that I may have had for him but it had proved he was a dangerous man.

But then again, why should it not be possible for someone to come through experiences like his and, although clearly scarred, actually want to improve things rather than just take a personal grudge-fuelled revenge on society. He wasn't portraying himself as a saint, and maybe he would be completely unsuccessful, but could you fault him for trying. The money had to come from somewhere. Without a proper education, rooted in the class of society that he was and with a character and ambition moulded through heredity and experience, nature and nurture combined, what alternative did he have.

He'd done well to remain sane, assuming that he had.

Even if I were to help him, how would I do it?

As we sped along I thought about what Kerry-Anne had said: "If you're not careful the altitude can knock you out". But I had been careful, I'd taken the preparatory medication, I'd drunk coca tea, I'd got an aerosol of oxygen to give me a boost if I needed it and I'd avoided significant exercise. I'd managed it OK and was still managing it OK. But Kerry-Anne's parents or any of their entourage back in the States didn't know that... what if I hadn't been so careful?

That gave me the idea.

Isabella dropped me off outside the hotel and agreed to be back in an hour. My job now was to get back to my room and my phone, call the States, reassure everyone, delay any possible return 24 to 48 hours without panicking anyone and then get back to where Kerry was being held to transfer the money.

All this was circling around in my head as I sat in my hotel room and switched on my phone.

It immediately started ringing.

Someone must be telepathic, I thought.

It was my daughter.

I decided to answer it.

'Hello.'

'Hello dad, just catching up, how's it going?'

That was a good question. After seeing the state Kerry-Anne was in I was still a bit shaken up. My daughter was only 5 or 6 years older and it was easy to remember her when she was Kerry's age. It hardly bore thinking about. But I wasn't going to share any of that.

'It's going fine,' I said.

'How has it been getting back to work? You're not overdoing it are you?'

I thought about the comfortably familiar surroundings of AB's office, of Samantha's professional demeanour, of the briefings, the interviews, the preparations, all of that had felt like objectively distanced, intellectual pursuits as easy as putting on an old pair of slippers. But then here I was facing the reality. Not just photographs or words on paper. This was when it turned from clean to dirty. I'd taken an instant dislike to Carlos and Diego, I'd met Hathos and been suitably impressed, but in a dark way, and I'd glimpsed Kerry-Anne, or a shadow of what used to be Kerry-Anne.

'No I'm not overdoing it,' I said, 'and the work is pretty much as I remember it.'

'Sometime,' she said, 'you're going to have to explain to me what it is you actually do.'

'It's a kind of engineering,' I said.

Which has some truth in it as I'm involved in engineering solutions to other people's problems.

'You've told me that before,' she said, 'but it doesn't tell me much.'

That's the idea, I thought. Since her mother died my daughter had got a lot more interested in what I did. Before that all she wanted to know was when I was going, when was I coming back and would I be bearing gifts. Now she wanted to know where I was going and why. I didn't like keeping secrets from her but it was for her own good.

This call wasn't giving me much comfort so I sought to change the subject.

'OK,' I said, 'and how are you and Brett?'

'We've got big news,' she said, I could hear the joy in her voice. This was better. This was probably why she called.

'Go on then,' I said, 'unlike Van Gogh I'm all ears.'

She ignored my attempt at wit.

'We're moving,' she said, 'buying our first house!'

What I wanted to say was, 'Have you thought about getting married first', but I didn't want to dampen her spirits with my old-fashioned notions.

'That's great,' I said, 'where are you moving to.'

'Oh, we're not moving area. We saw this place a few weeks ago. Brett inquired, we had a look around, we started negotiating straight away.'

'And you didn't tell me,' I said.

She paused for a second, and then,

'Dad, with so much going on at your end we didn't want to bother you until we knew the deal was done. We signed today.'

So I wasn't the only one who could hold back critical information, I thought. It must be genetic.

'That's great,' I said, 'when do you move?'

'Four weeks or so,' she said.

'No point in me visiting then,' I said, 'you'll be in turmoil.'

'Don't you use that as an excuse,' she said, 'you're welcome any time,' she paused before adding pointedly, 'and we're expecting to see you very soon.'

Nice to be wanted.

'This job's unpredictable,' I said, 'but I'll let you know if I get a chance.'

'When not if,' she said. She was sounding like her mother. I loved it. It made me smile. And I needed to smile.

'When not if,' I said.

Although the call had come out of the blue I realised that it had acted like a pressure release valve. Hearing about someone else's life, someone I cared about who was on the up, had given me a bit of a lift. Seeing the state that Kerry-Anne was in had not been easy but I was determined to get her out of her predicament just as quickly as I could. After all that's what I was here for, and it was the only thing I could do.

Chapter Twenty Nine

After speaking to my daughter I thought I had better check in with 'The Store'. After all they were my paymasters and I had big news.

It was the wee small hours in London so I wasn't surprised it took a long time to get an answer. When it was answered however Samantha sounded as fresh as if it were the middle of her day.

'I've seen Kerry-Anne,' I said.

'And?' asked Samantha.

'She's alive but has marks on her body.'

She got the impact of this immediately.

'Shit,' she said.

'The marks are fading but they want to delay her release until they're gone.'

'Who wants to delay?'

'Her captors.'

'Shit,' and then, 'Where is her head at?'

Good question.

'Fragile,' I said, 'she's clearly had a shock. I purposely have not probed too deeply into exactly what has happened to her since she was taken.'

'OK,' said Samantha, 'what's your next move.'

'I have to talk to her parents.'

'I would suggest you major on the good news; you've seen Kerry-Anne, she's OK, she's coming home. When will you hand over the money?'

'Within the next 2 hours.'

'OK, we'll track that, that's when we enter the "tricky zone", the period when they have both the girl and the money,' and me!, I thought, 'you've got to try and minimise that gap.'

That was true, I did, for the sake of everyone's health including my own.

'I'll talk to AB, see if there's any way, in the background and quietly, that we can get a reception committee waiting for Kerry-Anne that includes the help she might need.'

Such are the advantages of privilege, I thought.

'Anything else?'

'No,' I said, 'I think that's quite enough don't you?'

She was already ignoring me, I could hear her fingers rattling across the keyboard.

I put through the call to the States.

It was answered immediately.

'Yes.'

It was George.

'George, can you gather together everyone that you need and call me back,' I said.

'Sure,' said George, 'you got news?'

I could hear the concern in his voice. I wanted to alleviate it immediately.

'Yes,' I said, 'and it's all good.'

'We'll call you back,' he said.

It wasn't long before the phone rang.

'We're all here, Mr Carpenter,' said Andrews.

I didn't know whether they'd patched in a conference line or who the 'we' were and frankly I didn't care. If they were happy with the attendance then so was I.

'I've seen Kerry-Anne,' I said without preamble, 'considering what she's been through she's coping well. They've moved her into a much better place and she wants you to know that she's sorry.'

'Sorry for what?' the female voice.

'She thinks it's all her fault she got kidnapped.'

'You tell her it's not,' the male voice, 'you tell her those bastards...'

He trailed off. Hathos was right to be worried, I thought.

'There's only one thing,' I said.

'What's that?' asked Andrews.

'I didn't know I was going to have to come to Cusco, I thought Kerry-Anne would be held in Lima.'

By tracking my phone I knew they would already know I was in Cusco. It must have made them wonder what was going on.

'We thought so too,' said Andrews, 'but so what?'

'So I didn't make the right preparations. I was put on a plane and brought right here. Cusco is at an altitude of almost 12,000 feet, it's like jumping half way up Mount Everest and I've got altitude sickness.'

'So?'

'So I'm badly dehydrated after vomiting my guts out,' I said, deciding giving too much information was better at this stage, 'I can't walk more than five yards without collapsing from exhaustion and my heart is trying to beat itself out of my chest.'

There was silence for a few moments, then I continued.

'It's a bad dose but no worse than that. It's common so I've seen a doctor. I'm doing the right things and I'll be OK.'

'You want us to send a helicopter for Kerry-Anne?'

Thanks for being so concerned about me, I thought.

'I think that would be a really bad move,' I said, 'I don't know where Kerry-Anne is being kept. When they took me there they stripped me of my phone so I couldn't be tracked and the windows of the car they took me in were blacked out. The transfer is going well so I would strongly advise you not to do anything different now. If you did you've got to understand that you can't hold me responsible for the consequences. My altitude sickness is unfortunate, not terminal.'

'We want her back,' the female voice.

'We want her back now,' the male voice.

'I'll be ready to bring her back in 48 hours,' I said, 'maybe sooner. As soon as I'm physically capable of escorting her properly I'll do it. I don't want to be here any longer than I have to either.'

There was fevered muttering. I broke into it,

'I don't know how long it would take you to get somebody else here but they wouldn't know what to do, they wouldn't know where to go, they wouldn't have made the contacts I've made… all I'm asking is for a bit more time. I'm sorry I got slowed down like this but it's a delay it's not a cancellation.'

'And she's OK?' the female voice.

'She's holding up well. She's been here longer than me and she's got used to the altitude.'

'She's safe?' it was George.

'She's safe,' I said, sticking my neck out. I was taking risks here to. I was trusting in Hathos. I was hoping that trust wasn't misplaced.

'48 hours?' asked Andrews.

'Can we talk to her?' the female voice.

'No,' I said, 'not until we're on our way back.'

'You're telling us that we have to put our daughter's safety entirely into your hands and delay her return,' the male voice.

'You've already entrusted me with her safety,' I said, 'but yes I'm asking you to accept this enforced medical delay. I'm sorry.'

'You're s…!' the male voice began.

The female voice interrupted,

'So be it. Don't let us down.'

A pause.

'OK,' said the male voice.

'Oh, and she'd like to know how Emily is doing.'

'She's doing OK,' the female voice, 'but she's worried about Kerry-Anne like we all are.'

'She must be traumatised,' I said, 'has anyone offered her professional support?'

'We said she was OK,' the male voice, 'that's all you need to know and what you can tell Kerry-Anne, anything else is not your business. Understand?'

'I understand,' I said, 'The next time I talk to you I should have Kerry-Anne with me.'

Chapter Thirty

I took a slow shower, changed into a clean set of clothes and then started to get organised for the next steps.

The memory stick Hathos had given me went into my main luggage and I completed my packing so that I was ready for a quick getaway. I then packed an overnight bag making sure I had the "samples" I would be needing and that there was nothing metallic that would upset anybody.

I was already downstairs in the reception area sipping coca tea when Isabella returned. She seemed impressed that I wasn't going to keep her waiting.

'Good,' she said.

After she had completed her security checks and satisfied herself I wasn't trying anything foolish, she opened the back door of the limousine for me and closed and locked it after I was inside.

Once we were on the road Isabella spoke to me through the intercom.

'We are conscious that you have not eaten this evening. If you drop the seat back alongside you,

you can pull through the food and drink we have prepared for you. There is a hot bag with the main course and a cool bag for the drinks and dessert. Please drink the water, it's important that you keep hydrated.'

I was tired but not exhausted. I was giving the altitude huge respect and avoiding any significant exertion, walking slowly, taking it easy.

I used the folded down seat as a shelf and lowered the folded table that was in the back of the seat in front of me. It was like travelling Business Class.

The bags contained everything I needed; plates, glasses, cutlery, napkins. Suddenly I was hungry and I got stuck in.

The main course was predictably meat. It was roasted and tasted like rabbit but I had the strong suspicion it was guinea pig.

What's wrong with eating guinea pig anyway, I thought. We keep rabbits, we keep chickens, but as long as we don't know them by name we happily eat any number of them. I didn't know the name of this one, whatever it was, and although there was not much meat on the bone, served with potato and vegetables, it was very tasty.

I ate in silence and, as well as drinking some water as instructed, I washed it down with a Peruvian red.

I have to admit that I had not had a Peruvian wine before. This one was a blend of Malbec, Tannat and Petit Verdot that poured a deep crimson colour. The nose had ripe, black fruit, with a plummy depth. On the palate there was a lick of firm, liquoricy structure and a nicely tart and juicy black cherry acidity overlaid with much softer blackberry flavours. It was a nice easy drinking wine with very good balance. I liked it, and the second glass seemed even smoother than the first.

The dessert was fresh fruit and cream and there was even a small flask of Peruvian coffee.

I was careful not to over eat as I didn't want an overworked digestive system to slow me down.

Eating the meal usefully used up the travel time back to Hathos' place.

We stopped at the gatehouse where my overnight bag was checked and x-rayed and I was frisked. Although some of the contents of my overnight bag raised an eyebrow the guard was soon satisfied that I was neither radioactive nor carrying a bomb and so, under Isabella's guidance, I was allowed to get back into the limousine and the metal gates were opened allowing us to proceed once more to the house.

'I'll take you immediately to Hathos,' said Isabella.

'No,' I said, 'I want to see Kerry-Anne first, she needs to know I'm back as I promised and that I've spoken to her parents.'

Isabella baulked at this but I was insistent and eventually she led me inside and towards Kerry's room. On the way she introduced me to a tall, thin man with sunned skin that was stretched over his bones like parchment. If you'd told me he'd just been unwrapped from an Egyptian tomb then I would have believed you. His expression was set to morose. I missed his real name and immediately christened him "Happy".

After I'd shaken his bony hand, not too strongly as I feared I might pull it off, Isabella explained that he would remain outside Kerry's door and that if I needed anything all I had to do was knock on our side of the door and "Happy" would see to any reasonable request. I wondered what "reasonable" might mean but guessed I would find out if I pushed any request that little bit too far. However I was aiming at behaving myself, letting time pass as effortlessly as possible and then getting out of here, so hopefully this undefined limit would never be reached. From here on I would attempt to adopt the guise of a "Mr Nice Guy who plays along and doesn't cause any problems".

When the door was opened Kerry looked up astonished and alarmed. When she saw it was me she relaxed a little.

The door was locked behind me.

'Your parents are looking forward to having you home,' I said to Kerry as soon as we'd got settled, 'I asked about Emily like you wanted me to and they said she was doing OK but also wanting to see you back.'

I was trying to be reassuring but her reaction was to start crying.

I didn't know what to do so I just sat and let her emotions run their course. This reaction was more than a bit unsettling as her physical appearance was on our critical path to getting out of here. I didn't want to tell her that though because I thought it would just add to her stress. I just hoped all this crying wouldn't make things any worse.

After she'd stopped and dried her eyes they were red and puffy. I decided to try a bit of tough love. I had a daughter of my own and, right or wrong, I would have done the same for her in the same circumstances.

'Kerry,' I said, 'we're nearly there. You've had a hell of a shock and a hell of a time. I can't even begin to understand all that's happened to you but my priority is to get you home, that's why I'm here, it's the only reason I'm here, and I need you to be strong. I know it's a tough ask.'

I could see my words sinking in. I was asking if she could put on a protective skin to get her through these next hours and days. I was asking her to act stronger than she felt.

'Let's concentrate on getting you home,' I said, 'let's look forward and not back. Can you help me with that?'

I stopped there. I left her with her thoughts. As a distraction I knocked on the door and asked for two coffees and some food.

When it arrived the coffee was hot and the food was assorted meats, salads and fruit.

I got stuck in, I was hungry. Kerry joined me, initially picking at her food and then more enthusiastically.

'I don't want to be left alone,' she said.

I asked what she meant. She said she wanted me to stay with her not just for the evening but overnight. I was uncomfortable with this but again I thought of my daughter. I would do it for her without a second thought. I knocked at the door and asked for a camp bed and said that I was ready to speak to Hathos.

The camp bed was delivered and a space created for it in front of the windows.

Chapter Thirty One

'Have you seen the girl?' Hathos asked.

He knew that I had.

'Yes,' I said.

'And?'

'And we can proceed to transfer the money,' I said.

'Good.'

Hathos sat opposite me and watched as I lifted my small shoulder bag on to the table, unzipped the top and withdrew two toilet rolls, one pale blue, one pale pink, each with about one quarter of an inch thickness of toilet tissue wrapped around them. These were my "samples".

I placed them on the low table end up. They looked strangely phallic.

No longer items of jest the two toilet rolls took on the character of utilitarian business objects, message carriers. Although it had been cause for embarrassment for me I thought it was quite a clever idea to use these items as the keys to the ransom. Who would have thought that anybody would be so stupid as to hide information in a toilet roll.

'As you can see I have not tampered with them in any way,' I said, 'I am reliably informed by my clients that on the cardboard core of each sample is written all the information you need.'

He seemed surprised at the amount of trouble we'd gone to, to conceal the information.

'My clients have done exactly as you asked,' I said, 'there are five accounts; two in Switzerland, two in the Cayman Islands and one in the Bahamas. Each of these accounts contains $100,000. The information I have brought gives you the location, account details and withdrawal procedures.'

I should have added "I hope" because I hadn't seen it or tested it for myself. What I did know for sure was that if any of this had been fucked up there was only one guy who was going to be held responsible, and I didn't have to think too hard about who that unfortunate person might be.

'Thank you, Mr Carpenter.' He turned to an internal phone, dialed and spoke into the mouthpiece in Spanish.

'I have asked Isabella to join us,' he said.

Isabella arrived looking as attractively elegant as usual. Her glasses gave her a slightly academic look but they could not hide her piercingly green eyes. Her brown hair cascaded down, past her shoulders.

It was hard to remember that she was also streetwise beyond her years and on a shared mission with Hathos.

'Mr Carpenter,' said Isabella.

'Paul has provided us with information,' said Hathos, pointing to the toilet rolls.

'Really?' said Isabella.

'Please explain again to Isabella what you have told to me,' said Hathos.

I did so.

'It certainly is a unique method,' said Isabella.

I think she was quietly impressed.

'You know what needs to be done?' asked Hathos.

'Of course,' said Isabella.

I reached forward, picked up the two toilet rolls and handed them to her.

'Thank you,' she said.

'I will leave it in your capable hands,' said Hathos.

She smiled, not completely immune to flattery, turned and left us. I was sorry to see her go.

Hathos poured himself a tumbler of whisky and this time I said yes to his invitation to join him. So far, so good, as they say.

We sat once again facing each other across the coffee table, like adversaries at a chess tournament. A chess tournament were it was always his move.

The whisky was a comfortable malt and the ice cubes chinked as I swirled the glass tumbler around, the yellow liquid glinting red in the reflected glow of the log fire, like a sunset or a sunrise.

'Isabella is a genius at handling money,' said Hathos, 'if the information is clear and complete then she will transfer the money, move it around the planet a couple of times and then make it available to me. This should take much less than 24 hours. I don't understand the way this is done, Paul, but I trust Isabella.'

He paused.

'If there is a problem, if the information is not clear or complete then she will contact you directly and you will be given the opportunity to solve the problem. If, for example, she believes there are serious efforts being made to track her transactions then she will tell me. If she has found a problem and you can't solve it then she will tell me. Is that clear?'

Crystal, I thought.

'Yes,' I said.

'We have been assuming,' he said, 'that all will be well.'

I was certainly relying on that same assumption.

'Now, Paul, I have to tell you that if we have a problem with the money then we have a problem full stop.'

He got up, went over and poured himself another whisky. Offered me a top up. I declined.

He returned to his seat. The log fire behind him crackled.

'This is a bad situation,' he said, 'I did not sanction this kidnapping. I am sorry it happened. I am doing what I can to rectify the situation.'

Including finding a scapegoat and executing him, I thought.

'The ransom demand is a purely nominal amount. I know that Kerry-Anne's parents would and could pay a lot more. I have chosen to overlook the armed team that were sent to my country, their fingers on the trigger, but, Paul, if after all my generosity your clients decide to play, now at this late point in the game, by different rules then I must reconsider my position. You understand? I would have no other choice.'

He swirled the whisky around in his glass. I didn't like where this was headed.

'If my generosity is thrown back in my face then the girl will not be returned. There will be no second chances.'

'You'll kill her!' I said.

'This will not be the solution of my choosing,' he said.

'But, Hathos, she's only a young woman.'

'A young woman with powerful parents,' he said.

'But if you kill her they will hunt you down.'

He sighed.

'If they trace me through the money, if they find me through you or through Kerry-Anne, it all amounts to the same thing.'

He was probably right.

'I'm sorry Mr Carpenter but you should now understand a little more of the world in which I operate. If you show weakness or lack of control then there are always others ready to make their move. Discipline must be maintained at all costs. A mistake has been made, recompense is necessary and retribution is only of value if it is seen to be done. You have seen it. I trust you will communicate what you have seen when you return to your clients. I hope, if we get that far, that it will stifle any thoughts of further action on their part.'

'All actions have consequences, Paul, but at some point the equation must balance. I hope that balance has now been achieved.'

He lifted his glass and took a long pull, smacked his lips at the fiery bite of the liquid.

'I must add, Paul, that I am not accustomed to apologising and I hope that you can see that I have no choice. Should my efforts at goodwill not be respected or be wrongly interpreted as weakness then I must respond both ruthlessly and thoroughly.'

'It is the same principle that I have tried to explain to you, Paul, my response to being attacked is to attack back harder. For example, should anyone, Paul, take action against me or any member of my family then they will be hunted down, no matter where they may run, no matter where they may hide, no matter how long it may take, we will find them … and they will pay.'

It was said calmly, not as a threat but simply as a statement of fact.

'If you're a leader you can't show weakness, Paul. If I'm provoked I don't turn the other cheek. In this instance I would have to minimise the risk of being located too quickly. That means that I wouldn't be able to let anyone leave who might be a risk to me. That means Kerry-Anne and, Paul, it also means you…'

He looked me in the eye.

'But of course if everything is OK, if Isabella is happy with everything, then there's nothing to worry about.'

Great.

I decided not to dwell on it. After all I had some relatively good news for Hathos.

Chapter Thirty Two

'You have your delay,' I said.

'Good,' said Hathos, 'we would have delayed in any case but it is good that it will not now create any friction.'

'But you need to recognise that Kerry is young, she is very fragile and we must minimise the time you keep her here.'

'I agree,' said Hathos, 'as soon as my doctor gives me clearance that the marks are no longer visible then the girl is yours.'

'She is frightened to be alone,' I said, 'I will stay in her room with her tonight as she has asked me to.'

Hathos sighed.

'She is not at risk here but I have already heard that you asked for an additional bed. You can do whatever you want to keep her calm,' he said.

'And tomorrow,' I said, 'how can we pass the time? She needs some fresh air. Is there anything you can do to help the time pass more quickly?'

'You think on it,' said Hathos, 'no reasonable request will be turned down,' he paused, 'we have also provided you with your own room. It is adjacent to hers.'

I felt like a fish that was on the hook, had felt the pull, and had decided there was no point fighting it.

It was Happy who showed me to the room that had been allocated for my use. It was immediately adjacent to Kerry's room but was smaller. A single bed, bathroom, a table and two chairs was about all there was.

So this was it then. All that remained was for the transfer of monies to go smoothly, Kerry to pass the remaining time without losing it and me to then deliver her back into the bosom of her family. If all that happened then everyone could draw a veil over the whole affair, put it all behind them, just like Emily was in the process of doing.

Seemed all very straightforward to me. Maybe this was going to be an easy one after all.

I got washed and changed in my own room and then, with Happy's help, made my way back to Kerry's.

It was awkward, but it was what she wanted so I went along with it.

When I arrived she had already changed into her night dress. It had short sleeves and a low back and allowed me a greater opportunity to look her over. I tried to do this nonchalantly but it was difficult.

Suffice it to say that I could see some evidence of marks if I looked closely enough but as Doctor Alvarez had said they were fading. I didn't like to think about how Kerry had got them.

She was quiet and kind of curled up in herself.

'I'm not normally like this,' she said, 'I just…'

'It's OK,' I said, 'I understand. But don't worry you'll get through this.'

'Will I?'

'Yes, definitely,' I said.

We talked of nothing very much for a while and then I said,

'It's important you try and get some sleep.'

She took this seriously and settled down in her bed. I stretched out on the camp bed trying to avoid the hard, lumpy metal bits of the frame and quieten my mind enough to get some rest. I wanted to get out of here as soon as possible but I'd also been complicit in managing the delay. It was a very uncomfortable situation to be in.

Although the camp bed was uncomfortable I'd slept on worse. I'm a light sleeper anyway and was conscious that Kerry's sleep was, initially, a disturbed one. She woke after about an hour.

'Are you there?' she said.

'Yes, I'm here,' I said, 'everything's alright, try and get some sleep.'

'OK.'

I could hear her turn and twist but after a while her breathing became even and she slept better.

It was a strange situation for me. I was a man in a young woman's room. In any other circumstances it would, at the very least, have been frowned upon. I was a relative stranger to Kerry but she was so in need of support, to no longer feel like she was on her own, that she had chosen to first believe and then to rely on me. I felt the responsibility. It brought out my paternal instincts. I had to be careful. It is never good to get emotionally involved in an assignment.

In the morning I was shaken awake.

'Mr Carpenter…'

'Huh, oh, huh, oh yea, morning.'

I'm never at my total best first thing.

'I'm going to get cleaned up now,' said Kerry.

'Oh, right, I see.'

I dragged myself out of bed and to the door. I knocked and as there was no answer I knocked again.

Happy opened the door.

'Si?'

'I need to go to my room, to get washed,' I said.

I don't think he really understood but he got the gist.

Chapter Thirty Three

We breakfasted together in Kerry's room. We'd been provided cold meats, salads, croissants, fresh bread, butter and fruit. Kerry was surprisingly hungry. I was pleased. To drink we had fruit juice and coffee. I majored on the coffee, the bitterness and caffeine content shaking me awake.

After breakfast I asked Happy if we could go outside. After seeking and receiving permission he led us out to a swimming pool area and we took a lounger each. I sat in the shade because of the adverse effects of sunshine on my sensitive Scottish skin. Kerry sat in the morning sunshine.

I'd thought Kerry would have been glad to get out of her room and I think she was. Once we knew it was a swimming pool area however it had led to an awkward moment.

'You have a swimming costume with you don't you?' I'd asked.

She said that she had but she would rather not put it on. It took me another few moments to realise what an idiot I was.

Kerry was a shapely, attractive young woman but she had acted like she was embarrassed by her body. The reason we were still here was because we were waiting for marks on her face and arms to fade. I had not considered the rest of her body! I smacked myself on the forehead.

'I'm sorry Kerry, I'm an idiot,' I said.

She smiled slightly.

'It's OK, Mr Carpenter, but I'd rather stay covered up. I hope you understand.'

I was beginning to.

10 minutes or so later I glanced across at her stretched out on her lounger. Something had happened. Kerry's body-confidence had been shot to pieces. I knew it was not the right time to ask but I wanted to know. If Hathos was worried about retribution then right here would lie the source of it. If she were my daughter…

I tried not to think about it. Keep her calm, get her home, that was my job, and that was all I had to worry about.

We sat close enough together to talk privately and I noticed how fidgety Kerry was getting and how she was constantly scanning the perimeter fence that curved away from us in both directions, the three lines of barbed wire that topped it and the security cameras that looked both in and out at regular intervals.

'Do you think we could escape?' she said leaning in closer so that we could not be overheard.

Outside of the property, I would guess to the East from the position of the sun, the land rose precipitously into the foothills of the Andes mountains and to the north east was a sharp ridge that ran parallel to the property perimeter, on the side of which I could see animals grazing. On the top of the ridge was some kind of monument, a white cross which stood atop a three-layered plinth. It looked bedazzled in the bright sunshine.

Escape would be very difficult to impossible.

Happy was on sentry duty and he came towards us.

'Puedo ayudarle con algo?' he said.

I didn't know what that meant but from his expression I guessed he was asking if we wanted something or if something was wrong.

'Podemos tomar un vaso de jugo de frutas con hielo, por favor,' said Kerry, 'mucho hielo.'

'Si,' said Happy and called into the house for assistance.

'You speak Spanish?' I said.

'A little,' said Kerry, 'it is the US's second language after all and when you have people helping around the house and the gardens and driving you around,' she shrugged her shoulders, 'it's difficult not to pick some of it up.'

She was used to telling people what to do, people like Happy. I realised that issuing requests or orders must be second nature to her.

Within minutes two large glasses of juice clinking with ice were handed to us. I took a taste. Mango. Delicious.

'So,' said Kerry, 'could we?'

She looked at me imploringly.

'I've got to get out of here,' she said, 'this whole thing is surreal. On the one hand it feels like I'm in a holiday resort and on the other it's like I'm a lifer in a high security prison camp. Its driving me nuts. I just want to go home.'

I needed to buy time but I didn't want to draw attention to her injuries. If I did I couldn't predict her emotional reaction. Whatever memories she had were too fresh, too raw.

I decided to play along a little. It would help pass the time.

'How could we escape?' I asked.

'Well, we're not tied down. If I wanted to I could get up right now and make a run for it.'

'And where would you run to?'

'Hmm, good question.'

'Neither of us could climb the perimeter fence, it's too tall, too much barbed wire and with all those cameras we'd be seen and captured in seconds.'

'And I suppose we'd then be locked up, have even less license than we have now?'

'That's about the long and the short of it, and even if we did get out what would we do, we've no idea where we are?'

I looked at the monument. I guess with a landmark like that it wouldn't be impossible to find our bearings, but we'd really need our phones and a get-away car; an unlikely scenario.

'You've thought about this?' she said.

I nodded. Sussing out alternative routes to get out of a situation, just to have on stand-by, was what I did. Here however there was really only one solution.

'I'm here to help you get home,' I said, 'we need to just play along, there is nothing standing in our way except time.'

'Oh god, I can't wait,' she said.

'Drink your juice and enjoy the view,' I replied.

After a while she started talking about her backpacking trip. I was happy to listen.

'We'd laid our plans carefully,' she said, 'and came here buzzing to see Machu Picchu and Lake Titicaca; the floating islands, the Island of the Sun and all that. Then we were going to make our way to Bolivia, to experience the drive down into the huge crater that La Paz is built in and after that Argentina, Buenos Aires, the Iguazu Falls and finally to Brazil, to Rio de Janeiro and then north to the Amazon and home. We were going to do all that at our own pace and in our own way. We had the freedom to change our route if we wanted, when we wanted, and each day we'd be seeing new things, broadening our experience. But all that's been blown out the water. This wasn't the experience…'

She tailed off.

Scotland's great bard Robert Burns one wrote, "The best laid schemes o' mice an' men gang aft a-gley", but I don't think even he had this kind of contretemps in mind when he wrote that.

I felt for Kerry, she'd been flying high and expecting everything to go like a breeze but the world had come crashing down around her in an instant, one turn in the road had led her and Emily off-piste. Kerry was being tested in a way no father would ever like to see their daughter tested. It was difficult not to be protective but I could not afford to be emotionally invested in Kerry's predicament. It would not help. I needed to stay objective and do my job.

Chapter Thirty Four

We lunched back in Kerry's room. The food provided for us was a kind of crayfish chowder called "Chupe De Camarones" served with crusty fresh bread. Under different circumstances I would have said it was delicious but under current circumstances it was a chore to eat.

I needed to do something to lift Kerry's spirits.

'Do you play games?' I asked.

'Sorry?' she said.

'You know, when you're travelling, do you play any games to pass the time?'

Kerry went to the wardrobe, rummaged in her backpack for a bit and then came back.

'We play this,' she said.

In her hand was a travelling version of Scrabble. I took it and opened it up. The board was folded in two and when opened the playing surface was about 8 inches square and the lettered tiles about half an inch. There was also a bag for the tiles that you shook them up in and dipped into when you wanted to replenish your rack of seven. The spaces on the board were recessed so that the tiles were kept securely in place.

'OK,' I said, 'how about a game?'

After a bit of cajoling (a good word carrying a basic Scrabble score of 18 even without any letter or word multiplier squares it may cross) she agreed.

'I brought it to play on flights to stop us getting bored,' she said, 'Emily was very good at it,' her face brightening up a bit at the memory, 'I hardly ever beat her.'

She obviously saw me as an easier opponent and there were a few reasons why she was probably right. First, my spelling is atrocious. Second, the breadth of my vocabulary, beyond words that it would not be polite to use, was about that of an eight year old. And third, I was constantly distracted by thoughts of how I could speed Kerry's release and the number of things that could go wrong in the meantime.

As we played, we talked.

'No Latin words,' she said.

How unfortunate I thought as my Latin stretched all the way from 'caveat emptor' to 'cave canem' with nothing in between.

'I have a small dictionary,' she said, showing it to me. It was palm sized. 'It only contains about 90,000 words but if a word is not in here it doesn't count,' she looked at me, 'sorry.'

It was more than ten times what I needed, other than guesses.

'OK,' I said, 'any leniency on spelling?'

She thought about it.

'Three retries in a game,' she said, 'No looking up a word before you put it down.'

Harsh, I thought, watching my chances of even approaching a draw recede. She'd been privately educated for goodness sake. If money couldn't buy you a good score at Scrabble then you'd picked the wrong school. Anyway beating me hollow might give her a lift, although I would do my best to win. That was only fair. No point being given a false victory.

'English spellings or American?' I asked.

This is an important question when two people separated by a common language are setting out to play a word game.

'Hmm,' she said, 'we can accept either.'

She pronounced either as ee-ther, whereas I would have said eye-ther, but that was no reason to call the whole thing off. At least we spelt it the same way.

She shook the bag and we picked out one tile each.

'Closest to "A" starts,' she said.

I had an "M", Kerry had drawn a "D". Her start.

The game proceeded as expected. I got thrashed. Kerry would use words like "Quixotic" running through a triple-word square, the "Q" on a double letter square and using up all her tiles as well as 'stealing' the "X" from the end of my word "Box". I would manage words like "Humble" picking up a double word and with the "H" on a triple letter square if I was lucky. I was giving it a good go but I was generally outplayed and outmanoeuvred. Kerry was enjoying it.

Good.

We talked as we played.

'I feel like an idiot,' she said, looking at her letter tiles and not at me, 'this journey was all about me trying to prove that I didn't need to be looked after all the time, that I was old enough to look after myself,' she sighed and put down a five letter word I'd never heard of. I didn't challenge it.

'Don't blame yourself,' I said.

She seemed to ignore my comment.

'People have always told me who I am, and who I'm supposed to become but nobody has ever asked me. All those who work for my parents are always pleasant to me even if I'm rude to them, that's not real life is it?'

In my experience people can continue to be polite against provocation if the money is good enough or the personal consequences of reacting more naturally too severe. I didn't say this however, I didn't want to add to her belief that her existence took place within some kind of sterilised bubble. Although to be honest it probably did.

'Cooks, maids, bodyguards mostly they just do what I ask, and if I misbehave my parents get to know about it immediately and sanction me by cutting off my privileges. It sounds like classical conditioning doesn't it? I do the right thing I get rewarded, I do the wrong thing I get punished. So eventually I learn what to do to not get punished and I think I'm being clever, but I'm not, I'm learning to do what other people want me to do.'

I thought she might be distracted from the game but she put down a six letter word through a triple word square.

'That's 48 points, your go,' she said.

I looked at my tiles for a good riposte.

'Now I'm a woman,' she paused to see if I'd object. I didn't, 'I want more personal space. I want to work out for myself who I am and this was my first step towards more independence. I wanted to show I could be trusted… and look what happened! I'll never be trusted again.'

I put down a 4 letter word.

'That's 6 points,' I said.

'You've got to be more ambitious, Mr Carpenter, you're not going to beat me like that.'

There's not much you can do with 6 vowels on your rack, I thought, but I held my tongue. I was showing symptoms of the false politeness she'd been complaining about. But my excuse was that I was trying to get her spirits up. Sometimes unfiltered politeness can be a good thing.

'I'm due to go to Harvard,' I knew that, 'if I still go I know I'll be unobtrusively chaperoned the whole time. It is all so claustrophobic.'

She put down a 4 letter word.

See, I thought, you can't always use most of your letters.

Unfortunately the word was "Zoom" with the "Z" on a double letter square and the whole thing on a double word.

'That's 50 points. You don't always need long words, Mr Carpenter, it's also about seeing the best place to put them.'

That game ended in a thumping defeat for me. I tried to accept it graciously. Kerry rubbed it in.

'You really need to do better than that. Emily would wipe the floor with you,' she paused the memory of Emily brought her up short.

As she was shaking the bag full of tiles for the next game she said, 'I'm really sorry about Emily, I more or less forced her to come with me and it was me who thought I saw someone shadowing us in Lima airport. I was probably imagining things.'

No you weren't, I thought.

'So because of that we forgot everything we had been told about official and unofficial taxis and grabbed the first man who offered to help us. If I had just been more sensible, thought about what I was doing then none of this would have happened. It's all my fault and whatever happened to Emily when we were separated is my fault to!'

There was some truth in what she said about doing things in haste and repenting them at leisure but it wasn't going to help her mood to point that out.

We started a new game.

'It wasn't your fault,' I said.

I didn't want to tell her she was right about being shadowed as that might only cause her to blame her parents and that wasn't a healthy emotion right now when they were the ones desperate for me to bring her home. Let her find out later, I thought, then she can deal with it more calmly.

'I've seen Emily, I've talked to her.' I don't know why but I hadn't told her this before and she'd probably been frightened to ask.

She stopped playing the game immediately. She looked downwards at the floor and said, 'How is she?'

I could see she was fearing the answer.

'She's pretty good, considering,' I said, 'she's worried about you, wants you back home just like everybody does,' I paused, 'she thinks everything was her fault.'

The tears came quickly. I wasn't sure I'd done the right thing to tell her.

'What!?' she said fiercely, 'she thinks it was her fault when it was my fault, all mine…'

For the first time I reached out and touched her. Only on the shoulder but I could feel her body shaking.

'Emily is waiting for you,' I said, 'when you get back home you'll have all the time you need to talk to one another, to work things through.'

I hoped that that was true.

After a while she recovered her composure. She looked me straight in the eye and said,

'What do I need to do to get home?'

'You need to remain calm,' I said, 'you've been controlling your emotions very well, you have to keep doing that, it's very important,' I paused and then decided to take the risk, I was going to treat her like an adult, an adult with a strong personality, 'The only other thing is that we need to ensure that the marks you have, the scratches and bruises, are not visible. The people who have you now want you to get home safely but they don't want any reprisals.'

She thought about this for a while.

'So the people here just want this over with, just like we do?'

'Yes,' I said.

'And they are not the same people who took Emily and me?'

'No, they are not the same people,' I said.

I decided not to say they were connected or to tell her about Paulo's execution. Neither of those pieces of information were going to help matters.

She put her hands together in her lap and sat in silence for a few moments, then she looked up.

'I will not tell my parents about the marks,' she said, although there were tears in her eyes, 'I just want this over.'

We resumed the game. I lost heavily.

Chapter Thirty Five

Eventually we stopped playing. I think beating me had become boring for Kerry and even though she was doing her best I could see that she was starting to dwell on the clock. Her demeanour was starting to darken as the reality of the last few weeks came back to bite her. I had a feeling it would be some time before she would be able to fully deal with her experiences. She hadn't given the scratches and bruises to herself. My job was to keep her positive enough to safely get her home.

'I'll prepare the evening meal,' I said apropos of nothing in particular, 'why don't you help me.'

She pointed to the locked door.

'Really?' she said.

'I'll sort it out,' I said and went and knocked on the door. When it was opened by Mr Happy I said, 'tell Isabella I would like to talk to her.'

He closed the door without changing his expression. I just had to trust that he'd understood me.

He was back almost immediately.

'Come,' he said, looking at me, 'you only.'

I smiled reassuringly at Kerry.

Isabella was outside on the patio sitting in a wicker chair, Hathos was sitting alongside her. They sat at a circular glass table. Isabella had a glass of red wine, Hathos a tumbler of whisky.

'Paul,' said Hathos, 'please sit down. Would you like a drink?'

'A Scottish single malt, no ice,' I said.

I needed it and I think I deserved it. It was a stressful job trying to keep Kerry positive. She just wanted to leave and so did I.

Hathos nodded to Happy and he dutifully went and brought me a tumbler containing a generous quantity of an amber something.

'We have good news for you,' said Hathos.

The bite of the whisky gave me a kick.

'All of the money transfers have been completed successfully,' said Isabella.

I tried not to show the true extent of my personal relief. All that stuff about not letting Kerry or I go could now be forgotten. Hathos had to let us go to save his own skin.

While I was mentally celebrating Hathos said something about the money being put to good use but I didn't really catch it. I wasn't really listening anymore. I was keen to just get Kerry back home.

'And now, how can we help you, Mr Carpenter?' asked Isabella, 'after all it was you who asked to see us.'

I wondered when they would have volunteered the good news about the money transfers if I hadn't, but I let it pass. Good news is good news no matter how and when you receive it.

'Kerry-Anne is in a fragile state,' I said, 'the longer you keep her the higher the risk you're taking.'

Hathos sat up. I had his attention.

'You want her to go home without any physical marks and I understand that. You don't want any further repercussions, that's how tit-for-tat escalations start. But if she goes home in a feverish mental state the effect is the same.'

'I'm listening,' said Hathos.

'Well first she needs some mental stimulation, something to occupy her mind and to stop her dwelling on things that don't help.'

I felt like I was trying to manipulate Kerry. It was a very uncomfortable position to be in. My only excuse was that I had what I believed to be her best interests at heart.

'And second,' I continued, 'we need to leave tomorrow. You can't continue to delay and I can't continue to give excuses to her parents.'

Isabella looked worried.

'I'll get Doctor Alvarez to look at her again,' she said.

'OK,' said Hathos.

'And I want us to make our own meal this evening. It will give us something to do,' I said.

Isabella shifted uncomfortably.

'Kitchens are dangerous places,' she said, 'lots of hot and sharp things.'

This was true. There was risk. But everything has risk.

'I'll take responsibility,' I said, 'it will give her some personal responsibility back. It will start to prepare her mind for going home.'

The sun was setting, a red glow spreading from the horizon. I noted the direction.

'Drink your whisky, Mr Carpenter,' said Hathos, rising from his chair, 'I'll be back.'

After he'd disappeared back inside Isabella said,

'You are lucky Hathos gives you such leeway, Mr Carpenter, he is embarrassed by what has happened. But don't push him too hard.'

I didn't think I was pushing him, if anything I thought I was helping him. But egos are fragile too.

'Why do you do this?' I asked, I was getting tired, fed up and fractious, 'you're an intelligent woman, why do you do these things, kidnap, drugs, arms dealing, killing...'

She did not shirk from answering. She took my question seriously, as if it were something she had asked herself more than once.

'Do you believe in the greater good, Mr Carpenter?' She did not wait for an answer, 'my father was killed in street fighting,' she said, 'just another body on the road but the centre of my universe,' she paused, remembering him, 'we fought about things, about education, about boys, about what was a good life and what was a bad, but in the end I always listened to him even if I disagreed and do you know why, Mr Carpenter?'

Again it was a rhetorical question, 'It was because however fervently we fought I always knew he was looking after my best interests, he was trying to protect me from some of life's realities. That's why he wanted me to go to Europe. In his mind Europe was a peaceful, civilised place, the kind of place he wanted Peru to aspire to be. Of course when I was in Europe I could see that he was wrong. The streets were not paved with gold and although society was more stable, more ordered that stability and that order was only skin deep. You didn't have to scratch too deeply to find the same baseness of human behaviour, the stronger praying on the weaker, the rich ignoring the poor. I did not tell my father of this. I told him what he wanted to hear and he died believing he had saved me from a life like his.'

She swirled the wine in her glass, a Peruvian ruby red, to appreciate the texture and then took a sip, savouring it. She held the glass up to the darkening sky.

'This is a part of my land,' she said, 'the vines, the water, the grapes, the manual labour, the ageing, the bottling that all goes in to giving me this moment of pleasure. So much work for such a passing moment.'

'My life is like this wine, Mr Carpenter. I am a part of Peru, the soil, the rivers and just like any vineyard I suffer droughts and disease, the bad years are what makes the good years feel better. My country has made mistakes. I have made mistakes. But it is not a time to stop and lament. It is a journey, it is a time to continue to seek a better life. We have a rich heritage, skills, raw materials, labour, we can build on those.'

I'd listened very carefully. It all sounded very noble. Hathos' ambitions and strict requirements for loyalty on the one hand and swift retribution for wrongs on the other also had a core of principle in them. But Hathos had executed one of his own and filmed it, Kerry and Emily had been kidnapped on his watch even if it were without his sanction. This was not some movie were the good guys always win and the bad guys don't, this was dirty, grubby and complicated. This was one of the reasons I respected AB, this elevated world of seeking the greater good by making decisions that resulted in lives being saved and lives being lost was not for me. I had enough trouble deciding what to do next.

'Do you really believe Hathos is aiming for the greater good and not just his own aggrandisement?' I said.

Given that my job was to keep everything calm and on an even keel, to make no waves, to keep everyone sweet, this was not a sensible thing to say. But I was tired, I'd spent the day listening to and seeing the effect on one of the victims, so I couldn't stop myself.

Again, to her credit, Isabella did not react angrily. She considered the question, cupped her glass of wine in her hands, and then said,

'I have to believe in something and I choose to believe in Hathos,' she put down her glass, 'And now, Mr Carpenter, enough talking, the sun has set and it is getting cool, it is time to go inside.'

I finished my whisky and followed her in. As we entered the lounge Hathos emerged from the deeper interior.

'Ah, good,' he said, 'I have talked to Doctor Alvarez and he has said that as long as there are no new injuries it would be safe to let Kerry go home in two days.'

I opened my mouth to protest. Hathos held up his hand.

'I have discussed risks with the good Doctor. Like any physician he likes to play it safe. And I have listened to you, Paul, and I have decided that Kerry should leave tomorrow morning. One more night, Paul, just one more night.'

I could see there was no point in arguing, this was the best deal I was going to get.

'And cooking our meal?'

Hathos smiled, 'As long as Isabella agrees to accompany you at all times then that is also acceptable.'

We both looked at Isabella. She nodded.

'Good,' said Hathos, 'I have already warned Chef Martinez, he is not happy to have amateurs in his kitchen but he will go along with it.'

He turned to me.

'And remember, Paul, we do not need any new injuries.'

Kitchens, I thought, full of scorching heat and sharp things. No problem there then.

Chapter Thirty Six

When I told Kerry that we'd been granted permission to cook our own meal she was both surprised and apprehensive.

'We have people who do our cooking. I have no idea what to do,' she said.

'Don't worry,' I said, 'I'll take the lead, you can help.'

Now, to be fair, I am not a great cook. I was thinking on my feet, this was all about keeping Kerry active and not injuring her.

Isabella escorted us to the kitchen.

Chef Martinez was dressed in kitchen whites. He was short, plump and far from jolly. It was clear that this was his domain and he didn't want us anywhere near it.

'What do you want to cook?' asked Isabella.

Before we could answer Chef Martinez talked to Isabella in speedy, animated Spanish.

'Ah, si,' said Isabella, 'entiendo, mantenga la calma, momento.'

She turned to us,

'There are some dishes,' she said, 'that need preparations. Chef Martinez has already made the first preparations for Frito trujillano, a traditional Peruvian dish of pork ribs that are soaked in salted water overnight. He has done this and they are ready to cook.'

'Can we cook them,' I asked, 'it would be a shame to waste them.'

Isabella spoke to Chef Martinez. The conversation did not seem to be an easy one.

'The ribs need to be drained and fried in lard over a low heat until tender and then fully cooked by turning them up to a high heat and browning them on all sides. This is specialised work, the chef would not be happy to let you do it. However the ribs can be served with French Fries and a special Creole sauce. You could help with these.'

'That will do,' I said, 'Chef Martinez can also make the sauce. I'm an expert at making chips, we'll do those.'

'Chips?' said Kerry, 'what flavour, I only like cheese and onion.'

I laughed.

'Sorry my mistake, I meant that I'm an expert at making French Fries. In the UK we call French Fries, chips.'

'And what do you call chips?' asked Kerry.

'We call chips, crisps,' I said.

'Really?'

'Yes, really,' I said, aware of the vagaries of our common language, 'although French Fries should be called Scottish Fries, at least the way I make them.'

Out of the corner of my eye I watched Chef Martinez as he proceeded smoothly and expertly with his work.

There was a two basket deep fat frier in the kitchen. Chef Martinez had started to heat it up, the fat was already clear and sparkling. He was going to use one basket for the ribs and I was going to use the other for my own master class.

I only had one real hurdle to get over and that was that back in Scotland I only had to choose between a handful of potato varieties and always tried to get hold of either Maris Piper or King Edwards when I was preparing French Fries.

In Peru there are more than 4,000 varieties of potato to choose between! Peru is, after all, the birthplace of the potato and the first plants probably occurred somewhere close to where we were now around the banks of Lake Titicaca with domestication of the crop already in evidence 8000-5000 BC.

After a conversation with Chef Martinez mediated for me by Isabella I agreed to use the Papa

Perricholi variety. This is apparently a very popular choice for French Fries and is a new variety of white potato that does not change its colour or go grey/brownish after its been peeled. Super!

I chose four medium sized tubers which I knew would be more than enough for the two of us.

Telling Kerry to watch and learn I first cleaned the potatoes under running tap water. Then I got two potato peelers from Chef Martinez and gave two potatoes and a scraper to Kerry. She looked worried.

Isabella was watching us.

'I haven't done this before,' whispered Kerry, 'I don't want to look foolish.'

'Don't worry,' I said, 'just watch me. I'll show you what to do.'

I took one of the potatoes in the palm of my left hand and with the potato peeler scraped off the skin from the exposed surface watching the peelings curl away and fall onto the kitchen work surface. By rotating the potato I finished the job. With my last scrape I caught the tip of a finger but it didn't break the skin.

Isabella immediately interrupted Chef Martinez in his work and spoke to him quickly. He shook his head, went to a drawer and took out some kitchen gloves. Isabella gave them to Kerry.

'Please use these,' she said.

Kerry took them without question and put them on. Then she took a potato into one hand, the scraper in the other and set to work. The peelings were thick, irregular and haphazard but after a while a smaller residual potato free of skin emerged. She handed it to me proudly.

'It's not that difficult after all,' she said.

I'd finished the other three.

I then half-filled a deep glass bowl with water and put it on the work surface between us.

'Now,' I said, 'we need to slice these peeled potatoes into individual French Fries. Let me show you.'

This time I took up a sharp kitchen knife from a rack of sharp knives that sat in a wooden block on the kitchen work bench. Isabella went pale.

'Really?' she said.

'I'm sure Kerry can do a good job, can't you Kerry?'

She was still wearing the kitchen gloves but I wasn't sure they were cut proof.

'Of course,' she said.

I handed her a knife, smaller than the one I was using. I also placed two potatoes in front of her.

'We want to slice the potatoes quite thickly, watch me.'

As I cut away each slice I put it into the bowl of water.

'Got the idea?' I said.

'Got it,' she said, holding the knife in an awkward and dangerous manner.

'Take it easy,' I said, 'we're not in a rush.'

Watching Kerry I was worried that I'd gone too far. I cut some more slices as she watched and finished the first potato.

The water in the bowl started to go from clear to milky as more and more slices of potato were added to it. I finished the second potato and turned to help Kerry. She had managed to slice the small potato into pieces and added them to the bowl. Good.

She now took the remaining potato and as she tried to make the first cut it slipped out of her hand.

Isabella gasped.

Fortunately my reactions are fast and I caught the errant tuber before it hit the floor.

'Have another go,' I said handing it back to Kerry, 'hold it steady, put the point of the knife into it and then lower the knife as if you were cutting a cake.'

Kerry concentrated. She did as I suggested and low and behold the potato fell into roughly half.

'Now put the flat part down and slice long-ways like I did.'

She did it.

'Put the pieces in the water. And then repeat the process with the remaining half.'

Isabella was watching Kerry's every move. The knife was razor sharp.

What is life without taking a risk, I thought, although I did stand quite close to Kerry, ready to leap in if there were any sign of a slip.

Kerry finished with aplomb. She'd got more confident as she'd gone on.

'It's good to know how to feed yourself, it's one of life's basics,' I said.

'That was fun,' said Kerry.

Isabella took the knives away.

I turned to Chef Martinez.

'Is the temperature up to high in the deep fat fryer?' I asked.

Isabella translated for me.

'He says, yes,' she said.

'Now Kerry we take the potato slices out of the water and lightly pat them dry before putting them into the fryer.'

So the risk to Kerry had now moved from sharp edged metal to hot fat. Kitchens are just full of danger. I hadn't realised quite how much.

I took a handful of potato slices and using a kitchen towel patted them dry. Then I carried them to the fryer and dropped them in. There was a satisfying foaming as potatoes began to fry.

I did another couple of handfuls and then told Kerry to have a go.

'Stop!' said Isabella holding up a hand. She walked over to a row of pegs and took down an apron and handed it to Kerry.

'Put this on,' she said.

Kerry obeyed.

I reflected briefly on the fact that I had not been offered protection. Clearly me splashing myself with hot fat was not seen as an issue.

Kerry then did the last handful. She had obviously been watching closely as she did it flawlessly… and did not splash herself with hot fat.

I shook the basket the potatoes were frying in.

'Now we watch and wait,' I said, 'when they're done they'll rise to the surface and I want to see a bit of browning at the edges.'

Kerry listened intently. This was a new experience.

The meal finally came together and we sat around the kitchen table to eat it, Kerry having removed her protective clothing.

The ribs tasted good, the Creole sauce was the perfect accompaniment… but the chips… sorry French Fries … they were superb!

I'd got some "vinagre tinto" and natural sea salt from Chef Martinez's larder together with some fresh, crusty bread and butter.

With the acid edge of the vinegar, the bite of the salt, the crispy outside, the fluffy interior of the fried potatoes accompanied by the simplicity of the bread and butter it was nothing short of sublime. It was a meal in itself. I saw the enjoyment on Kerry's face. It had been worth all the trouble.

We invited Isabella to try one. She took it between her fingers in trepidation but finished it with relish.

After asking my permission she motioned Chef Martinez to taste. He broke open one of the fries and examined it first with his eyes and then with the chemical senses of taste and smell. He took his time and then he came towards me, smiled and patted me on the shoulder. This was praise indeed.

I smiled back.

'Thank you,' whispered Kerry.

Chapter Thirty Seven

After Kerry was back in her room I took Isabella to one side.

'I think we should go now,' I said.

'Tomorrow morning,' she said.

'But right now Kerry-Anne is in good spirits,' I said, 'I saw the way she slept last night, it was not good. You've got the money. Let her go. If she goes now you can see the mood she's in. If you wait until tomorrow you take another risk. She could fall out of bed, she could cut herself in the bathroom.'

Isabella thought about it.

'It is still possible to catch the last flight to Lima,' she said, 'come with me.

I followed her back into the lounge where Hathos was on the telephone. He cut the call short as we entered.

'Yes?' he said, 'is the girl injured?'

Isabella spoke to him in Spanish. At first his body language told me he was resistant but as Isabella continued to explain he asked questions, she answered, and he softened. Eventually he turned to me.

'I think our business is complete, Paul. As you

have seen I have done my best for Kerry-Anne in these difficult circumstances. You can go now,' he smiled, 'I do not think we will meet again.'

It felt like an instruction.

Hathos reached out his hand, his perfect white teeth shone against the bronze of his face. I took it, there was no reason to part on bad terms.

'Go and tell Kerry-Anne,' said Isabella, 'I'm sure she is as anxious to leave as you are. Pack quickly. I will have a car and driver waiting for you. You can buy your tickets at the airport.'

'Remember I need to go via my hotel,' I said, 'to pick up the rest of my things.'

'I will tell the driver and don't bother to pay the bill, we will do that for you.'

I appreciated the gesture but most of all I was thankful that it was time to go.

Kerry and I were guided into the back seat of the waiting limousine, its engine running.

'Is this really happening?' she said.

'Yes,' I said, 'it's really happening.'

She was trembling.

'Keep it together Kerry,' I said, 'you've done really well.'

She reached out for my hand.

'OK,' she said, 'OK.'

'Let's go,' I said to the driver through the

intercom. As we started to move off I felt Kerry relax, just a little, but enough.

I looked away, I needed to remember that this was not my daughter. I was here to dispassionately escort her home.

The limousine crawled down to the end of the drive, the sound of gravel crunching beneath its slowly turning wheels added a soundtrack to the sense of movement, the possibility of escape. The driver lowered his window, shouted something in Spanish to the gatekeeper and gave a single guttural laugh in response to the reply.

The gates opened and we passed through.

The stopover at the hotel was a brief one. My bags were already packed and I was delighted to be reunited with my phone and watch. It felt like I was re-entering the wider world.

Chapter Thirty Eight

Once at the airport the driver silently unloaded our belongings from the trunk of the limousine and, leaving them at our feet, got back into the driver's seat and drove off without a backward glance.

We sped into the airport each equally animated and I quickly booked and paid cash for seats on a LATAM Airbus A320 flight that was going to leave Cusco Alejandro Velasco Astete Airport at 20.35hrs and arrive in Lima Jorge Chavez International Airport at 21:55hrs, a 1 hour 20 minutes flight, 3minutes faster than the flight in the reverse direction that I'd originally taken with Isabella. It must be because we were going downhill.

While we were waiting I got online and booked us Business Class seats on an Airbus A321 American Airlines flight AA988 leaving Jorge Chavez International Airport at 23:45hrs arriving Miami International Airport at 06:42 local time, a +1hr time difference and a flight time of 5hrs 57minutes. In Miami we would change to a Boeing 787 American Airlines flight AA2675 leaving Miami at 09:12 hrs and arriving in Los Angeles International

Airport (LAX) at local time 11:24hrs, a flight time of 5hrs 12minutes and a time difference of -3hrs.

All in all it cost me around $8,000 but sod it, I had the money, spend it.

I texted the details to 'The Store' for onward transmission.

After I'd finished I offered Kerry the phone, hers had gone home a lot earlier with the armed retrieval unit. She looked at it and then she looked at me.

'Do they know we're on our way?' she asked.

'They will do,' I said.

She chewed at her bottom lip.

'Then I'll leave it for a while,' she said.

Kerry had been so focussed on surviving her capture that the fact that she'd done that and was now on the way home had come as a surprise. I've seen this a few times, kidnap victims do not just have to survive their captivity they have to survive their release as well.

We didn't have long to wait. Kerry was very subdued on the flight down to Lima, she just sat looking out of the window. I left her to her thoughts.

In Jorge Chavez airport I found the right desk, confirmed my bookings and got printed tickets. Call me old fashioned but I always prefer something you can hold rather than anything ethereal. I was impressed that Kerry, although not at all talkative, was keeping herself together and, with a little support from me, got through the Business Class check-in procedures. Her passport had been returned to her in Cusco and she removed it from the top pocket of her backpack as she checked that into the main baggage hold.

'Can I keep that for you?' I said.

She handed it over without a word, clearly seeing me as her guardian, placing herself in my hands and simply following my lead. It was a little unsettling for me to see her like this. Although she was doing all that was required of her she seemed to have switched to auto-pilot. It was better than having her shaking with anxiety, on the edge of losing control, but somehow it was just as troubling.

We shuffled through the security checks and on into the Business Class Lounge. Here she told me she wanted to freshen up and made her way to the washrooms.

I stood outside, pacing up and down like an expectant father, worried that she would somehow disappear, slip through my fingers, and vanish into thin air. That was my nightmare. It would be professional suicide. After all Kerry had a history of slipping her shadow and I didn't want that to happen to me. On the other hand I was her lifeline, the straw that she could grasp in order to haul herself back home and out of the quagmire she had slipped into so easily and so unintentionally; up to the neck. The likelihood that she would somehow decide to shun that opportunity was remote to say the least. But a man can worry. Stranger things have happened. Although looking forward to getting home I think she had also begun to think about the consequences of her return; the explanations, the interviews and was not looking forward to them. She was an intelligent young lady and mentally this journey could not be easy for her.

When Kerry finally reappeared she definitely looked better although there was darkness behind her eyes and her posture seemed forced. She was fighting the black dog. I respected her for that.

We took a seat at a small round table in the far corner of the lounge, by a window that overlooked the runway, so that we could watch the arrivals and departures of the aircraft. Kerry sat quiet and motionless. I know a little about young girls from my memories of my daughter and I thought I should offer her a dose of retail therapy.

'Kerry-Anne, we're on the way home now. You're doing a great job. We will board the plane soon and I will get you back to the States. In the meantime how about a look around the shops?'

'Is that really true?' she asked, ignoring my offer, 'I can't really believe it,' her eyes filled with tears. I wondered if they were of relief or of some unwelcome recollection of recent events. 'I was expecting to be freed soon but when it happened it was so fast. I even thought it might be a bad joke. It's not is it?'

'No, it's not a bad joke,' I said.

My phone beeped. It was a text. Kerry looked at me.

'It's confirmation that your parents will be there to meet you when we arrive in Los Angeles,' I said.

I had thought that this would be reassuring but I was wrong. Kerry's reaction was to cry. Maybe the "normal" Kerry was self-confident with a well-founded level of self-assurance bordering on arrogance but the Kerry in front of me now was simply a vulnerable young girl who was both looking forward to going home and at the same time fearful of people's reactions and judgments on what had happened to her. I reached out to hold her hand. She gripped it tightly and began to regain control.

'They'll never trust me again,' she said, 'this was my chance to show that I could look after myself,' she put her head down, gazing at the floor, 'what a mess.'

I felt for her. The only thing I could do was to repeat my offer.

'Kerry I have money with me. How about we go and do some shopping?'

This time she did hear me and, after taking a few more moments to compose herself, we set off.

Chapter Thirty Nine

Shopping is not one of my strengths. I lack the interest, the patience and normally the money, but it wasn't long before I saw that I was in the hands of an expert.

Kerry became more animated as she moved from store to store and was soon filling carry bags with her purchases. I followed in her wake, paying for them. I was pleased to see more colour return to her face and the partial re-emergence of some self-confidence as she scrutinised, questioned and chose her items. She even smiled at my obvious discomfort whilst she was choosing some new underwear.

To see this improvement was worth every cent of the money she spent and besides, she was only spending a part of the wadge of dollars that George and Richard had handed to me all those hours ago in New York. I was indebted to whoever it was that had had the foresight to provide this extra cash. I would have to admit that I wouldn't have been so casually open-handed if the money had been all my own.

The only unfortunate thing was that, whilst

reaching for a T-shirt on one of the higher shelves, a sleeve of her blouse slipped back and I could not help but be reminded of the fading marks on her skin. They were hardly noticeable now but I was sensitised to them. She had said nothing about how she came by them and I did not know if she wanted to talk about her ordeal. I rather hoped that she did not. In reality it was nothing to do with me, after all I was only the intermediary sent to bring her home, and that's what I was doing. It would probably make my life easier if we kept off the subject. The less I knew the more I could concentrate on just bringing her back.

I kept on following her around although I was increasingly feeling like a trained poodle. A trained poodle with money.

As soon as we boarded the plane the Business Class service kicked in. Champagne, fresh orange juice and hot towels eased us into our seats. Kerry had fallen back into silence and although she sat in the seat next to mine it was as if she were a million miles away, separated by barriers that cocooned her in her thoughts. To my questions she now only gave monosyllabic answers, a deadpan look in her eyes.

I tried to look beyond the subdued young lady that sat beside me and envisage her as she must have been when she and Emily set off on their search for independence; bright, well fed, well clothed and looking forward to new experiences. At that time she must have felt sure of herself, probably exuding a degree of that common American brashness known the world over that is especially the right of the children of the well-off. She would have felt confident that this trip would prove to all, particularly to her hyper-capable mother and mainly-absent father, that she was no longer a child. She would fulfill her ambition and show that she was now a free spirit and had outgrown the need for parental succouring. Her life experience up to that point may well have led her to believe that people would generally be nice to her, would listen to her requests and usually respond positively to her wishes. Her smoothed and preened looks were a badge of her class, her brightness the result of expensive private education, of her youth and of her youthful surety.

Unfortunately it had not worked out as planned and she would be forgiven if the difference between the dream and the reality sent her crashing. At least she was alive and free to tell the tale.

As I was being ignored I decided to put the time to good use and go through the messages that had downloaded on my mobile phone. Although she had lost her own smartphone Kerry had begun listlessly playing with a mini-tablet she had rescued from her hand baggage. All young people seem to have at least three alternative electronic devices to hand these days.

She glanced across at me and when she saw what I was doing it seemed to spark an interest and she asked if I would like to see something. I of course said 'Yes', as any form of interaction was a good thing, and she turned the screen to face me. It was displaying a photograph. A selfie. The background betrayed the location as being the inside of an aeroplane. Kerry was smiling broadly, Emily had her head alongside and was sticking her tongue out at the camera.

'I took this while we were waiting for our first takeoff and managed to Facebook it before we were told to switch off,' she said, 'we were so up for the trip.'

From the tone in her voice you would have thought she was talking about some long lost childhood event and, in a way, I suppose she was.

'Nice photo,' I said, 'it's after midnight for us now so try to get some rest and take it easy, you're doing just fine. The flight is about 6hours long so if you can grab some sleep before we arrive in Miami that would be good.'

She lay back, headphones on and eyes closed. I wasn't sure she was sleeping, just shutting out the outside world for a while.

It was not long before the meal was served. I waved it away. It was more important to sleep. Kerry had put on the black sleeping mask provided and reclined her seat. I didn't want to disturb her.

I find the engineering of these high-tech seats in Business Class to be fascinating. They have the ability to recline almost all the way to the horizontal forming a fairly comfortable, though short, bed to sleep on. The provision of an adjustable partition between the seats and the availability of an entertainment system that can be individually tailored to one's own preference of movies, TV shows, musicals, radio and so on almost makes you feel like you are on a private jet, in your own private compartment.

As we were on a nighttime flight I wanted Kerry to get some sleep while I stayed awake and kept an eye on her. To keep my eyes open I slipped on the headphones and started to peruse the catalogue of movies on offer. I made sure that the intervening screen between my seat and Kerry's was left down and soon I could see that she had fallen asleep, albeit a fitful and uneasy slumber. The constant drone of the powerful jet engines provided the familiar soundtrack to our flight and I started watching my first selected movie.

Every now and again Kerry squirmed as if she

were trying to physically turn in on herself, to make herself smaller, as if she were trying to find a place to hide.

It was about an hour later that she woke with a start and took off her sleeping mask. She had been increasingly animated and had begun to mumble in her sleep. Her green eyes suddenly wide and with sweat on her forehead she reached over to me. I leant in closely and whispered,

'Kerry, Kerry-Anne, its okay, its okay. You're safe.'

She looked at me uncomprehendingly at first and then I saw a glimmer of recognition and her breathing began to slow.

One of the air hostesses had seen the commotion and hurried over to see what was wrong.

'It's okay,' I said, 'she's my daughter and has just broken up with her boyfriend. I'm taking her home. She's very upset.' It was the best I could come up with on the spur of the moment. Using the word 'daughter' gave me jolt.

The stewardess nodded in apparent understanding and empathy.

'Is there anything I can bring her?' she asked.

'Maybe a glass of water,' I said.

Kerry was agitated. I spoke to her again. Gently. Softly.

'We're on an aeroplane. We're going home. You

are safe.'

She blinked away tears.

'You are going home,' I said again, 'I am here to look after you.'

As I repeated the words her breathing eased. Steadily she was recovering her control.

The stewardess brought a glass of ice-cold water and I got Kerry to take small sips. After five or ten minutes she said,

"Oh god! I'm so sorry. It was such a vivid nightmare. I thought it was all happening again.'

I didn't want to hear about her nightmare but I couldn't help it. Once she started to speak I couldn't stop her, it would have been wrong. She held my hand, leaned in close and let it all out. I simply listened, said nothing. Between the tears and the cooling sips of water I listened to her recount her story. She spared me no details. It was the story that I had hoped not to hear. This at least explained why Hathos was so reticent about the marks.

I knew at that moment it did not matter to Kerry who she was speaking to, it could have been anyone, it just happened to be me. She was talking out loud to herself, hoping for some kind of self-therapy in the telling. It was just my misfortune that I was the one there to listen.

When Kerry had finished telling of the events; haphazardly, repeating things, questioning herself, revisiting the moment, I knew I had a problem.

The problem was that I knew.

I took myself to the toilet for a moment and prepared a measured quantity of the sedative I had previously tested on an earlier flight. Returning to my seat I took Kerry's hand and surreptitiously administered the drug. She needed to sleep and I could help her do that.

Despite all of their aggravation I greatly preferred the memory of my recent Economy Class flights to the reality of this one.

Chapter Forty

With Kerry asleep I now had time to think and reflect.

Kerry was a young woman, not that many years younger than my own daughter. If I were honest with myself I probably would not have taken to the Kerry-Anne that had started out on this journey. But whatever my past view might have been what was certain was that she did not deserve what had been done to her. It was wrong.

Why, oh why, did her idiot captors need to take it on another step, to take such savage advantage of the situation? What the hell did they gain by it? Did they think it was okay, that it could be overlooked, that it was without consequences? Once done it could not be undone.

Of course it was idiotic and what was worse was that I couldn't prevent myself from wondering whether Kerry was the first to be treated in this way or whether she would be the last.

Paulo was at best the taxi driver who took the girls from the airport, he wasn't either of the main perpetrators. Somehow or other Carlos and Diego, in my view alias Matias and Hugo, had managed to make him the scapegoat and I'd had to be complicit in his execution.

But it wasn't up to me to care. My job was to get Kerry home and complete the transfer. That was it, no less, no more. Those were the terms of the assignment, the limits and the boundaries. If I did what I was told all would be well, everybody who mattered would be happy.

When Kerry awoke she seemed refreshed. Taking the unfathomable mixture of toiletries and make-up she had bought at the airport with here she disappeared into the washroom. She was away so long I began to wonder if she had found a parachute and managed to jump out.

Returning at last I hardly recognised her. The mask that she wore now was very convincing as long as you didn't look too deeply into the shadows of her eyes.

She had also changed her clothes. The bright red, yellow and green patterned silk blouse and cream slacks gave the impression of a casual tourist and you would have to look very closely indeed to notice any vestiges of scratches or bruising. She smiled at my reaction.

'You look great,' I said, both in truth and in encouragement.

I had clearly underestimated her resilience. She knew she would soon be reunited with her parents with all the possible consequences that entailed and she was determined to put on a brave face.

'Thanks,' she said and returned to her seat, put on the world-excluding headphones, leaned back with a heavy exhalation of breath and closed her eyes.

When we landed in Miami we were met off the plane and shepherded through Immigration and Customs. By the time we were clear it was 07:30hrs and we found a place to have breakfast. Kerry had crab cakes with a side of French fries.

'They're not as good as yours,' she said, as she dipped them into mayonnaise and ate them anyway.

I had a pile of pancakes with maple syrup and two or three mugs of strong black coffee.

As I was paying I noticed a familiar face browsing a magazine rack. George Landers had joined us as our shadow. I smiled. Although Kerry had not spotted him this was already evidence of a return to normality.

The flight to Los Angeles left on time at 09:12hrs and we spent the next 5hrs talking about nothing much in particular, eating and playing with the entertainment system. Just as we started to prepare for landing Kerry said,

'Thank you, Mr Carpenter.'

'It's OK,' I said, 'it's my job.'

She smiled.

'There were times I thought I'd never get home,' she said.

There were times I shared that view, I thought. But what I said was,

'Well, we're almost there now.'

'I want to do something to try and make sure this is really the end of this,' she said.

'What do you mean' I said, a bit worried about what she might have in mind.

'I know why they kept hold of me even after you arrived, even after they had their money.'

I didn't say anything.

'So I'm going to try and ensure that all this ends here and I can concentrate on getting on with my life.'

I was full of respect for her presence of mind.

'What are you going to do?'

'Just don't walk too close to me when we're at the airport,' she said, 'and trust me.'

She smiled. Now it was my turn to trust her.

'And oh, by the way,' she said, 'don't let George get too close either.'

I had also underestimated her powers of observation.

Chapter Forty One

The flight landed at Los Angeles International Airport (LAX) just 5 minutes behind schedule at 11:29hrs local time, 3hrs behind Miami, 2hrs behind Lima. We were met as we disembarked by a uniformed airline representative and fast-tracked through baggage collection and again through the Green customs channel. I mean really fast tracked. Anyone who has arrived at any American airport will know the pain of queues, the seemingly endless waiting and the need to be polite at all times to avoid upsetting any of the various officials. But not this time, I could have been wearing a belt full of smuggled sovereigns or a colon full of hard drugs and it would have made no difference.

I was walking just behind Kerry as we came out of Arrivals and approached the public concourse area. Before we had taken enough steps to pass the barrier that separated us from the rest of humanity, and in view of anybody that was interested, Kerry seemed to get her feet tangled up and went sprawling to the floor. I lept forward determined to be the first to help her. She was already on her knees when I reached her.

'I'm OK,' she said loud enough for everyone to hear and with her arms outstretched to fend off any unnecessary physical assistance including mine.

She got back to her feet and dusted herself off. The tide of passengers swept around us. Panic over, I helped her right her bags. Only to me she said,

'How did I do? Was that convincing enough?'

She rubbed her arm and stretched her back.

'Wouldn't be surprised if I wasn't a bit battered and bruised after that. But no real harm done.'

Nothing like making a dramatic entrance, I thought. At least if she was examined she could plead past and present clumsiness as the cause.

I looked at the alarmed faces only a few feet away. Other hands took hold of her, George approaching from behind us, Richard from the front. They paused just long enough to give me a kind of non-committal nod and then transferred their entire attention to Kerry, fussing around her, taking her bags and leading her away.

She did not look back.

Further away I could see a very well dressed lady in dark glasses and a hat clearly designed to shade her identity. Kerry-Anne was shepherded in her direction and she stepped forward and wrapped Kerry in her arms. Kerry appeared to be embarrassed by this unexpected and exuberant public show of affection and tried to pull away.

I looked on, a bag over one shoulder, dragging another behind me.

George extracted himself from the reunion, walked over to me and handed me a phone. Putting it to my ear I heard Samantha's voice,

'You've handed over Kerry-Anne to her parents?'

'Yes,' I said.

'Good.'

The line went dead and I handed the phone back to George.

'Thanks,' I said.

George reached into an inside pocket of his neatly tailored jacket and pulled out a fat brown envelope and handed it to me.

'Ah'm glad we meet agin under happy circumstances,' he said, 'her people'r very happy to have her back.'

He turned and walked away.

At a distance I overheard the woman speaking to Richard,

'Let's get her out of here. You see any paparazzi, you deal with them, you hear. I don't want any attention. We'll deal with this our way…in private.'

And then turning to Kerry-Anne,

'It's OK poppet, you're home now. Everything will be OK, you'll see, you'll see.'

I hoped so.

I would never see Kerry again. Our time together was over. I stood watching her retreating back until she was swallowed up by the crowd. That's why you must never get emotionally invested in an assignment, when they're over you need to walk away and get on with your life.

However as far as this assignment was concerned I still had a bit of tidying up to do.

In the room was Andrews, George, Richard and two other guys who kept their distance and stayed silent. I wondered if they were FBI or CIA or one of each.

It was Andrews who led the conversation.

'We're delighted to have Kerry-Anne back, Mr Carpenter, well done.'

It felt like I was getting my report card marked. I just said,

'Thanks.'

'There are just a couple of things I'd like to ask.'

'OK,' I said, 'ask away.'

'The memory stick you brought back has been viewed,' he said, the silent guys glanced across, it wasn't difficult to guess who'd done the viewing, 'I do have to ask if you were a witness to the events and can validate the reality of what it appears to show.'

'I can validate it,' I said.

The two guys nodded.

'Good enough,' said Andrews, 'and the person involved, as far as you know, he was the kidnapper?'

'That's what I was told,' I said.

'And you didn't see anything to contradict that conclusion.'

Now we were in the world of untruths. I did not know how much Emily or Kerry-Anne had revealed or whether my initial interview with Emily had been recorded and scrutinised. I'd built up a degree of credibility and I didn't want to cash it in unwisely. I decided to do some fishing first.

'It's been traumatic for the girls,' I said, 'I hope they'll be given help to re-adjust.'

'You can rest assured of that,' said Andrews, 'their parents have also insisted they not be questioned too closely. That's very frustrating for some of us,' he looked meaningfully towards the quiet two, 'we obviously have a duty to deter those who believe they can take advantage of travelling Americans. With all due deference to Emily I mean especially someone like Kerry-Anne. The question, Mr Carpenter, is whether a further deterrent is needed in this case. There are those who are keen to ensure that the message that this kidnapping was and is intolerable is received very loud and very clear.'

George was shifting uncomfortably in his seat. Richard sat placidly gazing into space.

So Hathos was right to be worried, I thought. I bore no allegiance to him but neither did I see the value in precipitating a string of tit-for-tat exchanges into an unknown future. As far as I was concerned it was better that it ended here.

'I guess I know as much as you do,' I said.

The silent types looked at each other, shrugged their shoulders and left the room without a backward glance.

'Well, Mr Carpenter, I think that's all,' said Andrews, 'thanks again.'

George looked at me questioningly.

I also called into 'The Store' using my "Agaricus" moniker and gave Samantha a summary of events and outcomes, the only things I omitted were my suspicions about Carlos and Diego and the contents of the envelope George had handed to me.

'Good,' she said, 'we've also received satisfactory client feedback.'

She didn't ask about Kerry's mental or physical health. It may as well have been a can of beans or a diamond necklace I'd been charged to bring back rather than a human being with all the complexities that that involves. For Samantha it was just another assignment, a cargo satisfactorily paid for and delivered. I wished I could see it so dispassionately. I was thinking that maybe I'd come back to work too early when she said,

'We know this assignment was an easy one but it was your first for a while. You completed it successfully and we know you've got family in the States so AB has authorised me to tell you, you can take 5 days paid leave.'

It hadn't seemed that easy to me, but I was grateful that AB had remembered his promise about the leave.

'Thanks,' I said.

'Don't thank me,' she said, 'it was AB's decision.'

'I'll start it immediately,' I said.

'OK, but remember to write up this assignment in the usual way as soon as you can.'

'Will do,' I said.

Chapter Forty Two

My daughter lived in California. It was time for the promised visit.

When I stepped out of the taxi I thought I'd come to the wrong place. The driveway was a litter of boxes, rolled up rugs and chairs, some upright, some tipped on their backs. The garage door was raised and the inside looked in no less of a turmoil. I was still taking it all in when I saw my daughter running towards me. She flung her arms around my neck and squeezed me so tight I began to feel dizzy. When she let me go I said,

'Have you had a raid? It's a good job it's not raining.'

'It's not going to rain,' she said.

I looked up at the sky. It was blue from horizon to horizon except for a few cotton wool wisps of white. I pointed.

'See rain clouds,' I said.

She laughed.

'This isn't Scotland, Dad,' she said, 'some weeks it doesn't rain here at all.'

I tried to digest this information. How could anybody cope without the certainty of a forthcoming downpour, the knowledge that if it wasn't raining at the moment then that was only because it was just about to start.

'We thought if we put some of our things out then it would help create some space inside so we could see what we were doing,' she saw my face, 'the mess is only temporary,' she said, 'and nothing will get stolen because we're keeping an eye on everything, I saw you arrive didn't I?'

She said this last as if it were cast iron proof of all that had gone before. It was good to see her so animated and happy even though the dark blue boiler suit she was wearing did nothing for her appearance. She'd tied her hair back out of the way and I'd felt the wetness of work generated sweat when she'd hugged me. It wasn't unpleasant, I'm just saying…

Brett walked down the drive with his hand outstretched. I took it. He had a firm grip, apparently the sign of an honest man. I hoped so.

'Hello Mr Wilson,' he said, 'it's good to see you. We had hoped to have all this cleared away before you got here but I guess we're running late.'

Yep, I thought, I guess you are.

The long and the short of it is this; I took off my jacket, found somewhere indoors it was still safe to hang it, rolled up my sleeves and got stuck in.

The idea of creating space wasn't a completely stupid one and I lost count of the number of boxes we filled and stacked, the miles of bubble wrap we used, the rolls of sticky tape. On each box my daughter used a thick black marker pen to note the contents and the room.

After a couple of hours we'd become a good team and I'd enjoyed the exercise. When the outside was back inside again and the garage door was closed my daughter said,

'Time for a coffee break, unless we've already packed it.'

We retreated to what was left of the kitchen.

'You sit,' said Brett, 'I'll make the coffee. Mr Wilson how'd ya take yours.'

His American accent was not strong. Just every now and again he would lose a syllable or a coupla vowels here and there.

'Just black,' I said, 'no milk, no sugar.'

Sitting on some as yet unpacked metal chairs around a kitchen island we sipped our coffees and nibbled our way through a bag of chocolate chip cookies my daughter had rescued from one of the dark recesses of a cupboard. The cupboard was a fixture and wasn't going anywhere, the contents were to be scrutinised, eaten, packed or discarded. I felt like I was helping the cookies find a favourable end.

'How long before you move?' I asked.

'A week, ten days,' said Brett, 'we haven't booked the van yet but most of the papers are signed and we're waiting to know when we git the keys.'

'Is the house empty?'

'No,' said my daughter.

'So I can't look around,' I said. I had a suspicion my daughter knew where I'd been heading.

'No,' she said, 'you can't.'

'We can drive past it,' said Brett helpfully, 'and maybe stop outside.'

'We can drive past it,' said my daughter, 'and not stop, and not get out and not go knocking at the door and asking to look around.'

As if I would do such a thing!

It seemed like the best deal I was going to get so I decided not to fight it.

'That would be good,' I said.

In the event I had an unfortunate episode as we were slowly passing their prospective new home and Brett, who was driving, stopped the car despite my daughter's protestations, to allow me to get some air. Somehow I found myself at the door of the property which was opened by a nice lady who after hearing that I'd travelled all the way over the Atlantic from Scotland and didn't know when I might be able get back, left Brett and my daughter on the doorstep and gave me a quick tour of the place. I was back in 5 minutes, well 10 at the most, and I thanked the lady profusely as I was leaving and said that if she were ever in Scotland she should look me up. We parted on really good terms, she even waved when I was back in the car and we were pulling away.

'Nice house,' I said.

My daughter did not even turn around.

'You're impossible,' she said.

To try and recover my position I took them out for a meal at a restaurant of their choosing. Brett winced when my daughter announced her preference. It was expensive. It was my penance. As a Scot I'm not a big fan of parting with my money but on this occasion I opened my wallet wide and let the dollars flow out unmolested. It was a great evening, my daughter and I shared memories, Brett listened politely and seemed to be interested. By the end of the meal my daughter had forgiven me my earlier misdemeanour and we parted with a hug. Brett offered his hand, as I took it I said,

'You can drop the Mr Wilson, my name's Mark.'

My daughter beamed.

'Thank you, sir,' said Brett

I was sure he'd get the hang of it eventually.

When I got back to my hotel I was still on a high. The whole experience had been like a shot in the arm. It was only when I tried to sleep that my anxieties returned…

Chapter Forty Three

Back in the hotel, sitting in a standard room, I was staring at CNN. I had just zoned out. The reason for this is that I had opened the brown envelope that George had handed me and found $100,000 cash inside. I had counted it three times just to be sure. It was a very pleasant surprise but somehow also an added responsibility.

I didn't like what had happened to Kerry, but I'd done my job and I was both physically and mentally tired.

She was back in her version of civilisation and would no doubt get the best rehabilitation that her parent's money could buy. I would never see her again and I didn't want to. The damage would take some time to repair and, even so, was likely to leave a residue. Our experiences change us, it is part of being alive, we can't prevent that and Kerry had had some powerful experiences that could never be completely expunged. I was confident that she would learn to cope and to look forward. Even after such a brief encounter I could see that she had a strong enough personality for me to believe that.

'Just go with the flow you idiot' I told myself. But

I couldn't stop the thoughts circling around in my head, repeating themselves over and over, annoying the hell out of me.

I had to let it go. Some things you can't change and you have to find a way to accept them and a way to carry on. It's not the same as forgetting, some things you can never forget. It's more that you have to carry them with you but not let the load pin you to the ground.

Like my wife.

I will never forget her. My god I don't want to. What I have to do is to carry on. Was it possible for me to love someone else without negating the love I had had for my wife? She told me to and maybe it is. I know we have the ability to love more than one thing. I love my daughter, although I might not tell her very often, and I loved my wife and I carry the love I had for my mother. Those loves are not contradictory, they are complimentary. Yes, we have the ability to love more than once and more than one thing. Love is not mutually exclusive, you don't have to forget the one you had before, before you can invest in another. But it takes time. Loss is like a wound. Open and raw at first, sewn and healing to a scar over time.

I had to work out how to restart my own life in a world that was full of other people's traumas.

Even though I had my own problems my thoughts kept returning to Kerry and what she'd told me. They settled into an uncomfortable loop.

The long term effect of all this on her life would remain a mystery to me. **Repeating**. Yet I couldn't help feeling that somehow it wasn't fair. **Repeating**. She was from a society I would not normally meet. Did that matter? How did that effect my own behaviour? **Repeating**. Sure she had been foolish, but she had also been vulnerable and had been taken advantage of. **Repeating**. It didn't feel fair. **Repeating**. What was it to do with me? What did it matter? Why not just enjoy the rewards and get over it! **Repeating over and over ...**

Unlike my own daughter this girl had nothing to do with me. Who would care enough to consider further retribution?

Eventually an uneasy sleep came.

It was the wee small hours.

There was a knock on the door.

I thought I'd dreamt it at first but it's volume and persistence persuaded me it was real.

I switched on the room light, got out of bed, went to the door and peered through the spy hole.

George Landers was on the other side.

I opened the door and he immediately pushed past me, his eyes flashing.

'We'all need to talk,' he said.

I was only in boxer shorts.

'For god's sake put some damn clothes on,' he said.

I went to the bathroom and splashed my hands and face in cold water. Whatever George wanted to say I wanted to be awake enough to understand it. After I'd pulled on some clothes I joined him in the seating area.

'Yous'all's not been completely straight, Mr Carpenter. Ah'm here to tell you it was me'n Richard taped you'n Emily's li'll chat'n all. Ah've also looked at all the footage on that ol'memory stick of your'n,' he shook his grey head, 'it jus' don't look right, nope, it jus' ain't right.'

He looked at me. He seemed to be expecting an answer.

'What do you want me to say?' I said.

'Ah'm figuring you'all owes me a little truth. What is goin' on here, Mr Carpenter, what is goin' on?'

I wanted things to end, I didn't want to tell him anything.

My silence riled him.

'Yo'all'd better unnerstan' ah'm not fer lettin' this rest! If'n you want FBI an' CIA guys involved then you jes leave that to me. Ah sure as hell bet they'll know what to do!'

I thought about the abortive armed retrieval team. I wasn't sure that getting others involved was the best solution. Sometimes the best solution is to do nothing, but I could see George wasn't up for that either.

'Emily talked about two guys,' said George, 'one called Matias, the other called Hugo. The guy on the memory stick was called Paulo.'

'What's in a name,' I said.

George looked at me disbelievingly and then he said,

'An' he don't match either of them descriptions Emily gave,' he said.

One thing was for sure, and I knew it, Hathos had got the wrong man. Paulo might have been the original taxi driver, the guy who hung around the airport looking for victims, but he wasn't either of the men Emily had described. I'm not saying he was blameless but he'd managed to find himself chosen as scapegoat, a choice orchestrated by Carlos and Diego. Hathos was impetuous, I don't think he'd looked any further than he thought he needed to. But his behaviour had indicated that not even he was sure that he'd got it completely right.

I could have made Carlos' and Diego's lives very uncomfortable but I had decided not to. It was fairly obvious they were involved in Kerry's kidnap. I didn't have absolute proof but it would have to be a huge coincidence if there were two other men that both matched Emily's description so closely and were also a part of Hathos' "extended family" in Lima.

My decision had been the expedient thing to do at the time. I didn't need the complicated distraction that would have resulted from implicating them. My focus had been on Kerry and getting her home. But had I done the right thing? By avoiding the problem had I created another one for somebody else? Would Carlos and Diego have learned their lesson or because they'd got away with it would they try again? Was I willing to just forget about it and just let happen whatever happened? And if something did happen, if another girl was kidnapped and was not as lucky as Emily and Kerry was I culpable, would it be partially my fault?

'If I tell you anything what are you going to do with it?'

'Ah'm only willing' to promise that if ya'all tell me something it stays between you'n me. If you don't I tell Kerry's parents an' my friends in the FBI about my concerns. How's them eggs?'

Hathos had wanted to avoid any reprisals. It seemed that all his efforts may well have been in vain.

I didn't see anywhere else that this discussion with George was going to go so I chose what I thought was the lesser of two evils and decided to tell him about Carlos and Diego and my suspicions that their alter egos were Matias and Hugo.

After I'd finished I could see his mind working. I had no idea how much more he knew and some of the information I still held back was incendiary. I needed to find out why he was here, how much more he actually knew and take it from there. I wanted to do it as gently as possible.

'You've just woken me up,' I said, 'it's god knows what hour in the morning and I've answered your questions. Is that it? Can I go back to bed now?'

He snarled, he actually snarled. I could see that his fists were clenched. He was on the verge of violence and it was clear who would be the recipient of it.

'Don't,' he said slowly and through clenched teeth, 'don't shit wi' me. What happened to Kerry-Anne?'

So he didn't know. I thought it best to keep it that way.

'She was kept in a pretty bad place,' I said, 'damp, cold and was fed only enough to keep her alive. She's had a rough time. It's going to take her a while to get over it, but with the right help …'

'Ya'll know what ah mean,' he said, 'Ah know there's more'n that. Ah saw her. Ah know her as good as her parents do. Ah saw she was puttin' up a front.'

'Have you spoken to her?'

I needed to know.

'Ah was gonna, Ah was on ma way to her room. When ah was passin' a washroom an' ah heerd a noise. Ah got'n close and ah could hear somethin',' he paused, 'Ah heerd her crying, Mr Carpenter. She was talkin' to herself, tellin' herself it would be OK, sayin'...'

He stopped, his face furious, he asked me again.

'What happened?' and then added as an incentive, 'Ah kin make sure Emily's interview tape goes missin'... forever ... if you'all understan' me. Richard will go along with it for sure, he knows who butters his bread.'

I was tired. If George did as he threatened to do this could all stretch a long way into the future. We'd all be looking over our shoulders, there'd be action, successful or abortive, reprisals, successful or abortive, and it was difficult to predict at what point everybody would have had enough and it would finally stop. I'd be in that mix somewhere. It would be uncomfortable. George was offering me a way to end it if I believed him, if I did what he asked.

You have to believe something. I chose to believe that George would do what he threatened to do if I didn't help him. He was too personally and emotionally invested in Kerry-Anne and her parents to do anything else. And I believed Hathos. He was too obsessed in his calling to go down without a fight and I believed him when he said that his response to being attacked was to attack back harder. If anyone took action against him or any member of his "family", which included Carlos and Diego, then they would be hunted down, no matter where they were, no matter how long it took. That was not a threat I took lightly and I didn't want to live the rest of my life with one eye constantly looking over my shoulder. But at the same time I reckoned that if I didn't tell George he would just guess or find a way to get it out of Kerry-Anne, and then I would have no control over his actions.

I felt like it was all about damage limitation, so slowly and calmly and without keeping eye contact I told him what I knew. After all a problem shared is a problem doubled. But I didn't think I had a choice. As I spoke he calmed down, asked questions. I answered them as well as I could. I told him there were huge gaps in what I knew and that I wasn't going to guess. He nodded and seemed to accept that. After I'd finished I leaned back. The silence that filled the room was palpable.

Eventually he got up and started pacing about.
'You got a minibar?' he said.

I pointed towards it.

After he'd opened it he took out all the alcohol; whisky, bourbon, gin, vodka, beer…

'What do'ya want?' he said.

I asked for the whisky miniatures, found a glass tumbler and emptied all of them into it.

'Cheers,' I said.

He cracked open a beer with a side of gin.

'Cheers,' he said.

We sat and drank for a while. We sat and drank until there was no more alcohol left. Then I called room service and we drank some more.

We talked about anything and everything other than Kerry-Anne and the kidnapping. I told him a select little about my days in the Services. He told me something of his FBI days. We talked about families in general, skirting around personal stuff. I told him about how I'd met my wife. How we'd dated. He told me about his first and second wives and how he'd met his third, which he thought might be his last. They were no spring chickens and he thought neither of them had the energy to jump ship and start again. We bonded just enough but not too much. We each knew what we were doing.

The alcohol didn't seem to touch either of us and when daylight began streaming through the gaps in the curtains we reckoned it was time for breakfast.

He left me alone to wash and shower and I met him down in the hotel restaurant.

He was already shovelling pancakes, fruit and maple syrup into his mouth, a steaming cup of coffee within reach. I went to the buffet and filled a plate with two fried eggs, over easy, bacon, sausage and beans, ordered some toast and coffee to be brought to the table.

We ate in silence for a while and then he said,

'What if'n it were your daughter?'

Coming out of nowhere it hit me like a stone between the eyes. If it were my daughter… I knew what I would do. I have a vengeful streak I'm not proud of. It would come out. Just like in the military. Make safe first then retaliate.

I'd made Kerry-Anne safe.

George let the question hang.

'Well,' he said at last.

'Well what?' I said.

'Will ya take me along to meet these fellas. You know where they are, ah don't.'

'Why do you want to meet them,' I said.

He smiled.

'I jus wanna have a little talk,' he said.

I was stuck between a rock and a hard place.

'Finish your breakfast,' I said.

Chapter Forty Four

What had somebody asked me? Did I believe that out of bad can come some good?

I had a notion that I wanted to try. It was pretty crazy, but it might come off. It might be a disaster, but I felt it was worth a try. It might just be a notion but there was nothing frivolous about it. It was serious.

If I was going to go back to Peru then I would need help. It would be very important that no-one at 'The Store' knew what I was doing.

I flew to New York.

I had a proposition to make to Teresa, the Costa Rican bartender, assuming she was still around.

The idea was a simple one. She took my phone and watch, by which my location was monitored, and took it with her on a Cooks tour of New York over the next day or two. She would then check me out of the hotel, get on an aeroplane to Paris, together with the rest of my luggage, and meet me there. I would have a second phone that all calls and messages would be forwarded to and she was only to answer calls or messages that came directly from me. I would provide a recognition code and register my second phone under a different assumed name in the contacts list so that she could have no doubt that it was me that was calling.

As an additional precaution I would add settings to my burner phone so that I would be sent a notice of alarm if my "works" phone were inactivated or was stationary for too long during daylight hours. The same kind of thing that would arouse interest in 'The Store'.

For carrying out this less than arduous set of tasks I would pay Teresa all her expenses, give her $5,000 upfront and a further $45,000 when we met in Paris. She had said she wanted capital to start her own business. In return for helping me I was going to offer it to her.

The risk was all mine. I had to trust her. She could, I suppose, simply take the money, dispose of my phone and sell all my belongings. The problem for her was that I would be tracking my phone regularly so I would know very quickly that something had gone wrong. If that happened she would have to consider the possibility that I would return, unhappy, and find her, which I didn't think would be that difficult. No, if she went for it, I thought there was a fair chance that I could rely on her seeing it through. That is, if I had made an accurate assessment of her character and personality. We'd see.

The cumulative effect of constantly swapping time zones, not to mention the altitude and the lack of sleep, was making me feel sluggish. As soon as I got to my hotel room I collapsed onto the bed and slept for six hours straight. When I awoke I felt much better and it was with a revitalised spring in my step that I made my way down to the lobby.

Teresa was in her customary spot behind the bar. She looked up and said 'Hi'. So at least she remembered me. That was a start.

'Hi, Teresa,' I said.

After a few pleasantries I ordered a regular burger and fries and a Bud. It was the mid afternoon lull and the bar was very quiet. This was perfect for me as I had Teresa almost to myself.

The burger and fries arrived and I squirted an unhealthy mix of ketchup, mayonnaise and American yellow mustard across the plate. I know that this probably does not constitute the healthiest of diets but sometimes you just can't beat it. This was one of those times.

As I gulped down my second Bud out of the bottle, the only way to properly drink Bud, my mind was working overtime trying to think of a way of making the offer to Teresa in a smooth and convincing manner. I supposed that if I were American I would just come straight out with it, a frontal attack, all guns blazing. But we Brits are peculiar critters, our strange view of manners and politeness is inbred and we need to have a 'hook' that somehow allows us to introduce the subject subtly.

Being clumsy I managed to splash a streak of ketchup onto the counter and this had the unforeseen benefit of bringing Teresa over to help clean it up. I engaged her in idle conversation, asked her about herself, tried to find the 'hook'.

As she was speaking I looked at her more closely. In addition to a fascinating cleavage Teresa had dark brown eyes, a beautiful tanned complexion and dark hair that cascaded well over her shoulders. Her wide mouth and smooth skin hinted at an inner sensuousness. Her voice was smooth, calm and she smiled often and attractively. She wore the light blue hotel uniform well and her choice of jewellery was neither brash nor showy. This was one attractive lady. I wondered why I'd never noticed all these things before.

I was conscious that whilst my brain had been engaged in making these observations I had completely switched off from listening to what she was saying. I'm not good at multitasking. Before I'd tuned out I had picked up that it was her mother that had moved to the land of opportunity from Costa Rica and that Teresa had followed her a few years later, leaving behind whatever schooling she had and starting over again. Her mother had since gone back and now she was here, making her own way. She was doing all right she thought (I think I nodded encouragement at this point - I hoped I had) and was always looking for new opportunities, ways to improve herself. My brain finally caught back up with reality.

Eureka!

I think she had stopped talking but whatever the case I just blurted out, 'Teresa I think you're doing really well but I wonder, would $50,000 help you out at all?'

Her mouth fell open and she just stared at me.

'Oh, and a free trip to Paris… er, Paris France I mean.'

There was another customer at the bar and he called her over. She went to see what he needed and when she returned she said,

'I don't understand, is this a joke?'

'No, no,' I said, 'I need somebody to do some work for me and although I hardly know you, I think you're an honest person and if it also helps you out, then why not?'

I shrugged.

She looked at me very suspiciously. She had not survived the life she had without learning that if something seemed too good to be true it probably was.

'Let me explain what I need,' I said, 'I promise there is nothing illegal about it, nothing that's going to get you sent back to Costa Rica.'

She flinched.

'You said you were open to opportunities when they came along, so I think I can offer you one.'

'Right out of the blue!' she said.

'Right out of the blue.'

She wandered off again, there were now two other customers in the bar and she went to serve them; a drink, some food? When she returned she was smiling wryly.

'Okay, you got me, shoot. I can at least listen to what you've got to say.'

I explained my proposition, speaking slowly and carefully. She listened very attentively, asked me to repeat some parts to make sure she understood and then she shook her head disbelievingly.

'It's crazy,' she said, 'just crazy. But if I go along with this, you give me $5,000 tonight?'

'$5,000 in cash,' I said.

She whistled softly.

'You've got to tell me why,' she said, 'you just got to tell me why me?'

Why her! I hadn't thought about that. I'd simply considered that the offer was so good that Teresa would simply jump at it. I needed to buy some time.

'You would like to travel to Europe wouldn't you?' I said.

'Oh yes, I've always wanted to see Europe,' she said, 'it would be like a dream come true.'

Thank god for that, I thought. Then why would she care what my reasons were? I was presenting her with the golden egg, why question the goose? However, she had asked me a question and now I thought I'd better have a go at answering it.

'When we had that meal together I was really interested in what you said about starting your own business,' she leaned forward, 'and when I had this need for help I thought we could help each other out.'

Honesty is always the best policy, I thought.

'So it's nothing personal,' she said, moving closer and putting her hand on my arm.

I started to sweat. I hadn't really thought about that. She was attractive that was for sure but what I had remembered was her enthusiasm and drive.

'Why should it be personal,' I said, 'I just need some help and I thought you'd be interested.'

She drew her hand back.

'Hmm,' she said.

She went away and served a couple of other people. Then she returned.

'I'd have to organise leave and I'd have to know

exactly what you want me to do, but in principle it's a yes… I could do with the money… and a trip to Paris, wow!'

'There is just one other thing,' I said.

'Yeeees?'

'You have to help me to dye my hair brown.'

Chapter Forty Five

I started to make my preparations for reluctantly returning to Peru.

From my range of available alternative passports, that I'd picked up from a "friend" in London, I had chosen Doctor Julian Craddock, university lecturer from Canada, originally an English immigrant, specialist subject Astrophysics and Cosmology. That should frighten most people off, I thought. At least I'd left "Sales Executive" and toilet rolls behind me.

Looking at the photograph I needed to ditch my glasses and dye my hair brown. My hair was still shorter than in the photo but in the unlikely event of anyone questioning me about that I was sure I could come up with a reasonable explanation like, I'd just had a haircut, for example. What was more important was that the details embedded in the passport's chip matched mine, so there should be no problem with electronic verification of my new identity.

I bought a new phone, made all the connections necessary and then called George.

'OK,' I said.

'Good,' he said, 'that's a fine choice.'

'I'll text you arrangements when I've made them. We'll meet up in Lima airport.'

'OK bah me,' said George.

I also visited a pharmacist and bought some Sorojchi and Gravol pills. This was because although this trip should only take me to Lima and not to altitude I didn't want to be caught wrong footed if Carlos and Diego had been called back to Cusco for any reason. I knew George was not the kind of guy to start over again once we were underway so it was better to be prepared. Also I booked a hire car to be picked up at Lima airport. I'd paid the maximum damage waiver and gone for the unlimited mileage option. I'd booked it for 4 days which should be far too long. I booked it under the name of Julian Craddock.

Finally I booked my flight online, Business Class, to be collected at JFK airport the next day. I texted George the details. How he got to Lima was his affair.

Teresa had agreed to come up to my room after her shift had finished so that I could give her my phone, watch, the money and sort out any other details she was still vague about. Being a thoughtful kind of a guy and not knowing how long she might stay I called Room Service and got a bottle of champagne delivered, which rattled enticingly in its ice bucket, together with two chilled champagne glasses and a simple cold selection; King prawns, steak Tata, stuffed mushrooms, that kind of thing. I was just being sociable.

When it came I answered the soft knock at the door at lightning speed. Teresa had changed out of the logofied blue livery of the bar staff and into a silky green blouse open at the neck and a medium length skirt. I realised that I had not actually seen her legs before and was pleased to note they provided a shapely path down to a pair of neat ankles encased in sensibly heeled shoes.

I tried to quickly dispense with the business side of our meeting. Teresa took the fat bundle of bills and put them into her handbag. I answered and repeated again the parts of the planned actions that she asked about. She certainly wanted to be clear on every point, and we tried one or two test calls and messages between the phones just to make sure everything worked well.

She then helped me dye my hair. She didn't ask why I was doing it which I found somehow reassuring. The feel of her hands on my head and through my hair was exhilarating.

I broke open the bottle of champagne and we sat huddled together around my tablet, choosing and booking online a flexible ticket to Paris. Glasses were refilled, nibbles were nibbled. I tried to insist that the ticket should be Business Class, she wore me down through many and repeated protestations to an agreement on Premium Economy. I organised it so that she could pick up the ticket from JFK whenever she wanted. She said she would add her passport details later, and I wondered idly how much of the $5,000 that would cost her. And that was that.

I lifted my glass to toast our agreement but instead she leaned forward and kissed me.

It was like an electric shock ran through me. I realised in an instant how all my arrangements must have looked to her. What an idiot I was! I liked Teresa, there was no doubt about that. I thought maybe we could be friends. She was attractive. But my head was all mixed up. I still loved my wife. It had happened too fast.

I pulled back.

She smiled.

'Good,' she said.

'Good what?' I said.

'Just good.'

'See you in Paris,' she said as she left the room, closing the door softly behind her.

After she left I took a cold shower and collapsed naked onto the bed. What had I started? Had I started anything?

I turned over and went to sleep.

I slept like a baby, not waking until the shrill shriek of the bedside alarm called me reluctantly back into consciousness.

Chapter Forty Six

The kidnappers must have thought they had a good thing going. They'd laid out their plan; a man at the airport looking out for the right kind of victim, a basement room prepared for the captivity, false names, masks. It was a simple, well-trodden path. Set a ransom, negotiate if necessary, use a bit of bravado, collect the spoils and then leave the victim at the side of a road somewhere. The victim, if interviewed afterwards, could be of little use because he, she or they had no idea where they'd been held or by who. They would probably be so pleased to be home that the last thing they would want to do would be to relive any of their recent experience through detailed questioning.

So their plan on the face of it must have seemed perfect. What could possibly go wrong?

Unfortunately three things transpired that went against them. Without initially knowing it they took too big a prize. The power they had over their captives went to their heads. And thirdly, their boss somehow found out that there was a kidnapping in progress, on his watch, by his people, and without his permission.

Once they knew they were in trouble all their attention changed from riches to self preservation. They needed to find an escape route… and that's were Paulo came in.

It didn't take a genius to guess that Carlos and Diego, and Matias and Hugo were most likely the same people. For some reason Hathos had engineered it so that the two of them had to show themselves to me. It would have been much better for them to simply keep out of the way.

I couldn't believe that they would be so arrogant, or so stupid, as to believe that their appearance would not arouse suspicion in someone who had probably interviewed Emily and was acting on behalf of rich and aggrieved parents. So my guess was that Hathos had his own suspicions, but in the end I effectively cleared them.

Whatever the truth of these matters it was now time to roll the dice, to see what would happen. I picked up my mobile phone and texted to Carlos' number.

"I know what you did Matias. Suggest we meet 5p.m. tomorrow or H will hear. You pick the location. Confirm."

I hoped his English would be good enough to get the gist.

It wasn't revenge I was after. I was acting as a vehicle to get George Landers in front of these guys. But if I was honest with myself what they had done had interfered with my fragile equilibrium and that's why I'd agreed to help George. I needed to find out what happened next. I was just a guy who needed to sleep at night.

It wasn't long before I got a text back giving a location. The fact I'd used his false name, Matias, in my message told Carlos everything he needed to know. It was his turn to be blackmailed and he had no choice but to find out what terms I was offering. I knew I was putting myself in harm's way but if I was to help George there was no other option.

I quickly tidied up the hotel room, took the one bag I would be travelling with and left the hotel promising the taxi driver a $30 tip if he took me the short distance to the airport without dawdling.

At the airport I checked I still had enough Peruvian currency, the Nuevo Sol, left over and then proceeded to the gate.

I caught the 05:35 hours Boeing 787 Avianca flight out of JFK to Bogotá and then onwards to Lima, about nine hours flying time with a one-hour stopover, due to land in Lima at 14:35 hours local time.

The flights were uneventful. I drank, I slept, I ate, I bought a change of clothes in Bogotá airport and it didn't seem long before I was disembarking again at Lima's Jorge Chavez airport.

Here I met George and picked up the hire car, paying in cash.

He looked at me strangely but did not comment on my change of hair colour.

Before we started off I restarted my mobile phone and opened the tracking app. I could see that both Carlos/Matais and Diego/Hugo were in the same place. Then I put the meeting location into the car's Satnav and was pleased that it coincided.

With me driving and George seated in the back we left the airport. I drove warily through the Lima traffic and noticed that I was increasingly in what I would call one of the less salubrious parts of town. When I finally got to the correct street I needed to find the right house. This didn't prove too difficult as atop a short flight of stone steps to one of them there was an open door and two familiar shapes; one short and fat, the other long and thin.

I pulled up outside. It looked downtrodden even though the sunlight was streaming down from a cloudless sky. George lay in the back of the car, out of sight. As I leant back to pick a suitcase from the back seat I whispered,

'You stay here like you promised. Wait for me to come out and then it'll be your turn.'

'Sure thing' he said.

I got out of the car and walked up the steps.

'Good evening Mr Carpenter,' said Carlos/Matias, 'your message disturb me. Pleez come in.'

'After you,' I replied.

I did not want these two guys behind me, it was too risky.

'Okay,' said Carlos. Diego simply nodded.

Turning on their heels they led me through a series of corridors and stairways, through a room full of guns and on into one that had a sink to one side of the door, a bed in the corner and a table and chairs in the centre.

I was in the right place.

The mis-matched duo walked past the table and turned so that we were standing facing each other.

'You like to sit?' said Carlos, gesturing with his arm to the seat on my side of the table.

'Not immediately,' I said, 'let's just stand and talk.'

I put the case I'd brought in with me on the table between us.

'You look different,' said Carlos, 'ah yes, your hair.'

'I fancied a change,' I said.

Carlos shrugged.

'Okay,' Diego spoke for the first time, 'it not matter. What you want? Why you come back?'

'It appears Hathos does not know what you two have been up to,' I said, 'you've been bad you know and I was wondering whether I should tell him or not.'

If I had needed any reassurance their culpability

then their nervous reaction to my words was proof enough.

I'd got the right men. The next move was up to them.

'How you know this?' Diego asked.

'Emily,' I said and then, just in case they'd forgotten who that was, 'the girl you let go first. She told me about the people she remembered. It was clever of you to use false names and wear masks.' I tried not to sound too facetious.

'So why you not tell Hathos when we up at house?' asked Diego.

'Because I didn't know at that stage everything you'd done,' I said calmly, 'I was hoping that everything would be settled.'

They then talked briefly together in Spanish. Once they'd reached a decision it was Carlos who spoke.

'You don't have gun,' he said, 'foolish, Mr Carpenter. Blackmail useless. We have no money. So maybe you don't go home. So sorry.'

These were really not nice people, I thought.

Diego grinned as he reached inside his jacket, took out a handgun, and pointed it at me.

'Adios Mr Carpenter,' he said.

I raised my hand.

'Maybe there's another way. Tell me what happened and I'll leave,' I said, 'you'll never see me again.'

Carlos laughed.

'Why we believe?' he said.

'Because I have a message timed to be sent to Hathos at 6pm if I don't stop it. You don't think I'd have come in here without having insurance do you?'

Disbelief, shock and fear mingled together and fear won.

'We talk you go?' said Carlos.

'Yes, then it's all over as far as I'm concerned. And,' I said with emphasis, pointing at the suitcase, 'I've brought $25,000 for you if you do what I say.'

Their eyes lit up at the prospect of money.

Carlos looked at Diego. Diego nodded then lowered the gun.

'We tell,' said Carlos, 'why you want know?'

'I just need to know,' I said, 'that's got to be good enough for you.'

'OK, OK,' said Carlos.

He stopped to gather his thoughts.

'It not meant be like this,' he said, 'we need money, we have bad luck, must pay gambling debt or big trouble. We buy time but need more money. If Hathos know then big trouble also. We need cash. Paulo happy to be driver. We have this place for guns. It all easy. We pick up few tourists before, not enough. We bring them here, scare them a little, get some cash. Masks are Diego's idea and they work good. After we get cash we dump them. Everybody happy again.'

He spread his arms out like a performer taking the applause of an appreciative audience. Diego smiled in agreement.

'But this time?' I said.

His arms dropped listlessly to his sides, his voice dropped in volume.

'It all going normal with first girl. She scared and we get $1000 in cash from backpack. But second girl, she scream at us, "Do you realise who I am?" and on. To begin it funny, she think she frighten us. But then I check out passport and took away for conversation. Just her and me.'

'After, we google a lot of things and talk and drink, Diego and I. We think a gift is dropped to our hands from the sky. Our luck turn. We must take it.'

He shrugged, as if fate had been mean to them, as if they had been led astray through no fault of their own.

Diego looked downcast.

'Now first girl not important. We get rid with message. Then we phone parents. We expect negotiate so start high. They go yes so we very happy. They get daughter back. We get big, big money. All simple. Our problems over.'

'But we very smart,' he said, tapping the side of his nose with a finger, 'We think if girl important then parents try rescue. Save money. It normal to think. We guess she tracked with phone. Here in basement no signal. I tell her write note then we hide phone far away. We keep watch.' he smiled, 'Ha, we right! We watch men with guns attack skip full of rubbish. Ha, ha, the way they look...'

'Si,' said Diego, 'clever, they not.'

'Where did it all go wrong?' I asked.

His smile faded. He seemed as if he wished that he could go back in time and do it over, but no-one can do that.

'We very confident now. We celebrate, we three, me, Diego and Paulo. Now I see we make mistake, we think everything under control, money in our pockets already.'

He looked at me with puppy-dog eyes. If he was looking for sympathy he wasn't going to get any from me.

'After big lot drink,' he continued, 'in the other room with guns we play cards, we start argue. Paulo want more share in money. But he only drive. Not fair Diego, me do hard work. So we start push each other around. Diego pull out gun. Paulo not stupid so leave cursing. The girl next door shout for food. She should not...'

He stopped.

'Go on,' I said.

'Idiot Paulo try drive car too drunk. He crash. He come off road. In ditch. Even in Cusco Hathos hears. Tracks story back here, finds girl. He mad. Paulo say sorry, big mistake, forgive. We close family. Next day Hathos ask me and Diego question Paulo! By miracle we saved. We make deal with Paulo. He keep quiet we get him off. He keep his promise. I tell him gun has blanks. It not. Poor Paulo.'

So Paulo had thought there would be an escape route did he? The act, if it was an act, that he had put on out in the courtyard seemed very convincing to me. However, Carlos' story did appear to loosely hang together and he seemed relieved to tell it, to get it off his chest. It was a series of escalating calamities, one thing leading inexorably to another, leading them away from the original intent.

From his gestures he implied that some greater force had been at work, he himself had had little choice in the matter. Fate had determined the state of affairs, against his wishes and his best intentions. He, Diego and Paulo were simply flotsam carried along in the stream, powerless to counteract the current of events.

I begged to differ. But no matter, there was one part of the tale that he had glossed over.

'What did you and Diego do with the girl?' I

asked, purposely de-personalising the question to try and make it easier for him.

He shuffled his feet, looked away evasively, and said nothing. I decided to take a different tack.

'Young blonde American girls are so attractive aren't they? Do you like blondes? So difficult to resist.'

It was Diego who spoke now.

'Young girls,' he said, 'special blondes,' he shrugged, 'me mucho drunk, we argue, me not happy, girl shout…' that shrug again.

'And'?

'Stupido Paulo,' said Diego, 'he upset me… the girl she nice…'

He had a half-smile on his face unsure which way to go now. Crowing or apologetic. I could see I wasn't going to get anything else of value. But it was enough.

'And when he was finished? What happened next?'

Carlos' lips were dry, his tongue protruded to lick them moist. Carlos had had the chance to stop Diego but he hadn't. They were both culpable.

Suddenly there was a tension in the room. The atmosphere changed.

Carlos moved over and took the gun from Diego. He toyed with it for a moment, then he spoke,

'I change mind,' he said, 'Mr Carpenter, we tell

too much. Not good.'

'But if you do anything to me Hathos will get my message,' I said, even in my own ears I sounded a little desperate.

Diego said something in Spanish to Carlos. Carlos nodded.

'We take chance,' he said, 'who Hathos believe, strange message or us?'

This was not a good. It looked like I'd misjudged the situation. I knew I was taking a big risk. There was no timed message ready to go to Hathos. Maybe there should have been but there wasn't. I don't know why but for my own sanity I needed to know the truth, as far as it is ever possible to know it. I hadn't pushed the conversation as far as I wanted to, but I'd obviously pushed it too far for Carlos and Diego. I now knew too much. I was a danger to them.

I could see that in their minds the idea of taking the money, shooting the courier, disposing of the body and taking their chances was now Plan A. Any possible complications brought about by Hathos' reaction to my message or any repercussions my loss may or may not bring down upon their heads were now seen as minor considerations compared to the certainty of a quick cash windfall and a bullet in my head.

They must have thought that fate had made one more opportune twist.

'Pleez,' said Carlos waving the gun barrel in my direction, 'open case.'

This was actually a smart move. It was possible that the case was empty, or booby-trapped, or needed a unique combination to open it safely. To me it had the advantage of prolonging my usefulness and therefore extending the time I was likely to remain breathing.

I bent towards the case and moved it around so that the catches were facing me.

I was thinking rapidly, looking for a way out.

Coming here was always a risk and now it had become an impossible one. Maybe George would find a way to avenge my death when he heard the shots but I wouldn't be around to enjoy it.

I looked at the gun in Carlos' hand. Even in the dim glow of the underpowered light bulb that dangled from the ceiling I could see that it had a silencer fitted.

The room was probably soundproofed anyway, I thought. My hope that George might hear the shots evaporated.

'No,' I said, 'you open it.'

Carlos smiled. I was playing up to his idea that there was something about opening the case that needed to be worried about. He must have thought how smart he had been to realise it.

'No, oh no, Mr Carpenter. After you pleez.'

Carlos turned to Diego while keeping the gun unerringly pointed at me.

'Diego, go to car out back. Make sure place ready to burn.'

He spoke in his broken English, presumably he wanted me to know how good their preparations had been.

'Mr Carpenter, kerosene lamp dangerous, easy to fall, smash and start fire, so sorry.'

Diego threw a box of matches on the table.

'You leave now,' Carlos said to Diego, 'wait in car. I come quick.'

Of the two of them it was clear who was more the mastermind and who more the lackey. As he had lied to Paulo, I wondered whether Carlos had future plans not to share this windfall with Diego. But that was for them to work out. Right now I had more pressing problems. There was a gun pointing at me and there was nowhere to run.

Chapter Forty Seven

'Open case' said Carlos again, this time more aggressively.

This time I did as I was bid, I couldn't delay forever. I turned the open case towards him.

Carlos frowned.

'No money,' he said.

'No money,' I repeated, 'just a change of clothes and a toothbrush.'

He gritted his teeth. Fate was not playing fair… again. But he'd already crossed the line. He had to go through with the rest of the plan.

There was a shot.

I instinctively flinched.

But then I stood surprised.

I did not seem to be dead. I didn't even seem to be bleeding.

But Carlos was.

A bullet had entered his right eye. The deadly projectile had passed through his skull, shattering bone and exiting from the back of his head with a fair proportion of his grey matter. The impact propelled him backwards and he landed in a sitting position, a large splash of dripping red on the wall behind him.

Over my shoulder someone said,

'Thought you'all might need a little help.'

I turned to see George standing in the doorway, a silenced handgun in his hand.

I was pleased to see him.

'How long have you been there?' I asked.

'Plenty long enough,' he said.

'And Diego?'

'Fella's out cold,' he said.

I went over to Carlos' body and examined it. He was definitely dead.

This was a dead human being. Seconds ago he was alive. Did he deserve to die? Does anyone? These questions were too big for me. I salved my conscience with two facts; if George had not been there it would be me lying on my back lifeless, and it was more than likely that he and Diego would have plied their ransom trade on more unsuspecting victims at who knows what physical and mental cost to them.

'Don't touch the gun,' said George, 'Ah might be usin' it.'

I looked at him quizzically.

'Now, Mr Carpenter, you'all jus' go an sit in the car a mite. Ah'm jus' goin' to finish a conversation with Diego after ah wakes him up.'

The first thing I saw when I entered the adjacent room was Diego lying on the floor unconscious. Beside him was a kerosene lamp, its contents leaking onto the floor like flammable blood. Emily's description of this room had been good, although she didn't do the contents justice!

It was definitely an armoury. I let my eyes float along the cases of handguns, the racks of rifles, the wooden or composite stocks, the polished gunmetal grey barrels, hard and cold.

The firearms came from all over the world; a number from North America, but also guns from Germany, Russia, and even Italy. However, it was when I spotted the British made L115A3 super Magnum sniper rifle that I could not suppress a nod of recognition.

It is a beautiful weapon. Fitted with a stainless steel, fluted, 686 mm (27 inch) barrel it is accurate over ranges in excess of 1000m (1094 yards). With a detachable single stack removable box magazine for five rounds of .338 Lapua Magnum it packs a big punch and this one was also fitted with a set of Schmidt & Bender 10x42 day or night telescopic sights to ensure 24hr utility. It is a deadly weapon and compared to most other sniper rifles has considerably less weight, recoil, muzzle flash, smoke and report.

I took the gun.

The devil mask balaclavas that Carlos and Diego had used to hide their faces were also there. I took one of those as well.

Outside it was already dark. I put the gun in the trunk and climbed into the front seat to wait for George. He'd saved my life so I should have felt relieved and grateful but instead I felt tense and anxious.

Chapter Forty Eight

We drove away in the dark. The street was not well lit. Looking in my rear view mirror I could see flickers of light in the windows of the building we were leaving behind. The fire seemed to be growing and spreading rapidly.

'That there kerosene's a good fire starter,' said George looking over at me from the front passenger seat, 'ah wonder how long afore the fire department gits here?'

Too long, I thought.

'Diego?' I asked.

'Got him to talk a mite more'n he had to you,' he said.

'And?'

'An' he ain't goin' to be talkin' to nobody no more.' said George, 'that idea'rn of their's to burn the place down was a pretty fine good one. It'll git rid of the evidence anyways.'

In an area of the city like this most people would probably prefer to mind their own business, I thought, but if someone didn't act fast the fire could easily spread.

As we drove on I saw a woman walking on her own. I pulled over. She seemed interested.

'Fuego!' I shouted pointing, 'Fuego!'

The woman's face became concerned.

'Teléfono!' I yelled, I'd just about reached the limit of my knowledge of Spanish.

George leant across me, 'Consigue ayuda! Rápido! Inmediatamente!'

The woman started scrabbling around in her bag. She pulled out a phone, dialled and put it to her ear. The fire was becoming more obvious and she was gazing at it. I gave her a $20 bill. She took it and started speaking into the phone in fast Spanish.

'OK,' said George, 'Ah reckon that's yer conscience cleared. Drive.'

I drove. If only clearing my conscience were that easy, I thought.

George looked over his shoulder. Turned back and smiled.

I complimented him on his Spanish.

'North America's second language,' he said, 'some say won't be long 'til it's the first.'

'We've just left two dead men behind us,' I said, still shell-shocked.

'What did you'all expect?' he said, 'this'n here is a big boy's game, you know that.'

'But…'

'But nuthin', those guys had it coming. We jus' saved some other young girl from the same fate as our'n… or worse'n that,' he said, then added, 'we're the good guys.'

I was wishing I hadn't brought him here.

'Listen, ah'll take any rap fer this,' he continued, 't'aint your responsibility OK, those guys ain't breathing no more. I'll clear it all up back home or take the damn consequences. Not anything for you'n worry about.'

If only choosing to take responsibility was so easy. If it was I'd have taken responsibility for my wife's tumour. In fact I'd have taken the tumour and just said, 'Don't you worry about this, I've got it.' But I couldn't do that. Instead I had to watch. Feeling absolutely helpless.

'I appreciate the thought,' I said to George, 'but country enforcement agencies are one thing, Hathos is quite another.'

He was listening.

'Hathos doesn't even know you exist,' I said, 'but he's met me. He's not an idiot and he's extremely likely to put two and two together when he hears about this. He told me that he does not believe in an eye for an eye… he goes for the whole head.'

George thought for a while.

'Anythin' ah kin do?' he said.

'You can go home,' I said, 'do what you can for Kerry-Anne and Emily. They're going to need help coming to terms with what's happened to them. Emily probably has an unhealthy dose of survivor syndrome and Kerry-Anne something close to PTSD.'

'Ah'm a bit player,' said George, 'nuthin' but a paid employee. Mah voice don't mean nuthin'.'

'I'll take you back to the airport,' I said.

'Good enough,' said George.

I relied on the Satnav to get me through the night-time streets of Lima. I drove slowly, annoying most of the other city drivers.

When I'd pulled into the drop-off zone outside Lima's Jorge Chávez International Airport George got out and retrieved his bag from the trunk. If he saw the rifle he didn't comment. We shook hands.

'Ah guess ah've given y'all a problem,' he said.

'Yes,' I said. There was no point sugarcoating it.

'What you gonna do?'

'I don't know yet,' I lied, 'maybe nothing, maybe something.'

'Good luck,' he said, 'maybe y'all shuddn't ha listened to me tho ah'm glad that yer did. It's over fer me now and for the folks back home.'

'Yes, it's done now,' I said, 'the milk's out of the bottle. Safe journey home.'

Chapter Forty Nine

I had a problem. If I believed Hathos, which I did, I had just transgressed the golden rule of "family" and should expect to be punished. This was not an overwhelmingly pleasant prospect. It would not be too long before Carlos and Diego were missed.

Before I did anything I briefly took stock.

Two human beings were dead. I hadn't killed them but I'd led the killer to them. One of them had tried to killed me, but it was me who had engineered the meet. I could have let the whole thing go.

I stopped in my thinking. I knew that last point was self-deception. I'd decided I couldn't leave things alone. I couldn't let them prey on someone else's daughter. I had a daughter. I'd lost a wife. I couldn't let it go. I don't know what I had expected to happen. Did I think that we could frighten them enough for them to change their plans? Unlikely. They'd been found out but had put it on a scapegoat and had got away with it. They'd have tried again. I was sure of it. So I must have known that coming back had only two possible outcomes; their blood on our hands or our blood on theirs. I was fooling myself to believe anything else.

Now that it had unfolded as it had I had to deal with the consequences. It was a bonus that Carlos and Diego had planned to burn down the house, presumably to destroy any incriminating evidence including bodies, like mine, that they might leave in there. As it had worked out they had actually designed their own funeral pyre. So now the important question was: Did I really have anything to worry about? Could I rely on Hathos simply believing that there had been a nasty but unfortunate accident? Could I simply leave Peru with the confidence that I would not be hunted down?

Hathos had said that he would not let any slight lie, anything that he saw as an insult or a threat he would not let pass. Did I believe that or was it bravado? Could I rely on it not being true? What should I do if I did believe it?

George was anonymous as far as Hathos was concerned. I wasn't. I was very prominent as the only link between the mystery of Carlos and Diego and there untimely deaths. I could claim that I did not know what George was going to do. But that would be self-deceit.

If I was going to act it had to be now while there

might still be uncertainty in Hathos' mind. I would have to stop him before he became determined to get me.

I had to act.

It's fair to say that finding myself in this situation had not come as a complete surprise.

I had decided beforehand and included in my preparations the possibility that in order to not be constantly looking over my shoulder, I would have to try and nip Hathos' vengeful tendencies in the bud.

I had a L115A3 in the back of my hire car. I had 4,000soles in my pocket, and as there was no way I was going to get the gun through airport security my only option of getting it to Cusco was to drive it there.

Driving from Lima to Cusco is not a popular option. The roads can be rough and the distance is over 1000 kilometres and takes somewhere around 18 hours at best. Luckily I had two things in my favour; I'd learnt in the military how to survive without sleep and it was not the rainy season.

My choice of the petrol driven Toyota RAV 4 2.0L 4WD as my hire vehicle was not haphazard. I needed something that could cope with the distance and the terrain. I had also got the hire company to put three 20L cans of petrol in the back for me. I didn't want to run out of fuel at some inopportune moment.

Before I left the airport I parked up long enough to go for a shower and a change clothes. I also dispensed with the tortoiseshell glasses. It was Paul Carpenter who went in to the washrooms but it was Dr Julian Craddock who came out.

To complete my preparation I had something to eat and drink and bought some sandwiches and drinks I could use on the way. I was going to be climbing over 3,300 metres and knew that I needed to keep hydrated to help manage the effects of the altitude. For the same reason I also took the Sorojchi and Gravol pills I'd brought with me from the States although I noticed that I needn't have bothered bringing them all that way because I could have bought them at the airport.

An aerosol canister of oxygen completed my "altitude kit".

I packed everything I was taking with me into the back of the RAV and took a glance at the cause of all this trouble, the L115A3 rifle. It was still there.

I knew I would be totally reliant on the Satnav, which worried me even though it spoke to me in English, so after selecting the route I wrote down some of the key checkpoints so that if I did lose connectivity, which was almost inevitable driving through the type of terrain I was going to be driving through, I could keep going and not have to stop and ask for directions in a language I didn't speak.

It was about 9pm by the time I left. I had more than 18hrs of driving ahead of me but as they say the longest journey starts with taking the handbrake off and starting the engine.

Getting out of Lima was a hassle. Although I'd done it earlier I found it no easier driving through this strange city at night. Thankfully I soon happened upon the PE-1N and turned south where it quickly became the PE-1S. I stuck to this like glue. Whatever signs I passed, whatever the Satnav told me to do, I followed PE-1S as if it were a safety line.

In this way I escaped the city limits and drove down the coast road sandwiched as it is between the moonlit waters of the Pacific Ocean on my right and the artificial lights sprinkled about the burgeoning foothills of the Andes on my left.

After about 3 hours I reached Chincha Alta and just kept going, passing through Ica 2 hours later and reaching Nazca 2 and a half hours after that. By that time I'd been driving non stop for 7 and a half hours and had put 450km behind me.

Both the RAV and it's driver needed a break.

As it was around 5am there wasn't much traffic or sign of movement. It was therefore easy to find a dark and convenient place to relieve myself. It was cold and I was glad to get back into the relative warmth of the car. The RAV had become my safety blanket in this strange land, and I sat and ate a couple of sandwiches and took a drink of water. I then ventured out into the night chill once more and filled up the petrol tank from the 20L cans. I was exceptionally pleased when I found that someone at the hire company had had the foresight to provide a funnel.

Nazca is one of the most arid regions in the world, with an average precipitation of only 4 millimetres. You can't even call it rain because the weather is controlled by the Humboldt Current which carries water from Antarctica up the west coast of South America. As the cold water moves northwards it cools the air limiting the ability of moisture to evaporate and accumulate into rainclouds. As a result although hazy clouds, mist and fog are able to form, there is little real rain. For someone like me used to the lochs and rivers of Scotland this was a difficult concept to grasp.

This shortage of fresh water drove the ancient inhabitants of Nazca to construct a system of underground aqueducts. With construction dating back to before and during the time of the Incas it is interesting to note that they are still used to irrigate farmland and provide domestic needs. So some things are built to last!

Across the arid plains in the vicinity of Nazca the Earth's surface has been used as a canvas to carry enormous and complex line drawings, the so-called "Nazca Lines". These lines and figures, the most famous of which are the hummingbird, the condor, and the monkey, were constructed sometime between 500 BC and AD 500 and can be seen from the surrounding foothills as well as from the air. As far as I know they are not landing sites for aliens as some people have suggested.

Chapter Fifty

At Nazca I made a critical turning, leaving the relative flatness of the PE-1S and joining the PE-30A to travel eastwards and start to weave my way up.

This was the beginning of the most arduous part of the journey. The sun rose red in front of me as a new dawn cracked its light through the shards of mountain that I wove between and across. With the light came new energy and I ate ham and tomato sandwiches as I drove along, keeping an eye on the edge of the road, the drop, the traffic and always on the lookout for unexpected potholes.

The RAV drove faultlessly, the female SatNav voice was nice to me and I actually began to enjoy the challenge of the ascent and the scenery.

Part way up I drove across the River Pachachaca and joined the PE-3S. This was another critical manoeuvre and I was glad when I'd passed this checkpoint as this was the road, with all its windings of ascent, that I would follow all the way to Cusco.

At 10:30hrs I entered Abancay, whose 50,000 strong population resides at an elevation of 2,377 metres (7,799 ft). With the morning, the temperature had risen to a much more pleasant 18C.

Here I refuelled the RAV, made good use of the restrooms and found myself some early lunch. My battle with Spanish continued with a combination of gesticulations, 'Si's' and 'No's'. It felt inadequate but it got me through.

Back on the road I drove on to Izcuchaca. I was taking more frequent stops now in order to test how I was reacting to the increasing altitude. I walked slowly and felt the same tiredness that I'd felt the first time, but nothing worse. I even found somewhere that had Coca Tea on tap and enjoyed its rejuvenating effects.

At around 15:30hrs I left Izcuchaca and although it had been a very long and challenging drive and I had gone a night without sleep, I felt OK. I was running on adrenaline.

En route to my final destination I visited Cusco Alejandro Velasco Astete Airport to suss out where I would later drop off the RAV and check out the flight times back to Lima. Taking a chance I bought a ticket.

I'd now travelled over 1100km in a little over 19hrs.

Chapter Fifty One

Before leaving the States I'd done my homework and found Hathos' place by searching the google Earth satellite view for properties with a circular perimeter, a nearby monument, and within 40mins drive of Cusco.

It didn't take long and confirmed Hathos' apprehension that if anybody was determined to find him, even with all the precautions he'd taken, it wouldn't be that difficult. I'd also found a spot where I thought I could safely park the RAV and I'd put the reference into the Satnav.

By 17:00 hrs I was outside of the RAV and lifting the L115A3 rifle out of the back.

The sun was lowering as I crawled slowly up the bank on the side of the ridge away from the perimeter wall. I moved slowly, the sheep seemed more amused than upset and largely ignored me as they continued to feed on the close cropped greenery.

I was pleased it wasn't alpaca in the field as I had it on good authority that they could be more temperamental and this wasn't a good time to be spat at.

As the light dimmed I began to lose colour vision,

greens became grey, and the sheep became indistinct white ghostly woolly lumps. I lay on my stomach and pulled the devil mask balaclava, that I'd taken from the armoury, over my head to reduce the reflection from my otherwise white face. Then, with the rifle alongside me, I slithered forward.

It was exactly as I remembered. I had a clear view over the perimeter wall and across the patio at the front of the house. There were one or two people moving around the grounds but I could not identify any one individually.

I was conscious that one of the unknowns in this evening's equation was how good the CCTV coverage was of my position. There was nothing I could do about that except blend into the twilight as best I could and be as careful as possible in all the movements I made. Bearing this in mind I inched the gun into position and set the sites to the distance I'd estimated from the contoured location map I'd scrutinised back in the States.

Slowly and deliberately I scraped away some of the stony ground from the crest, creating a groove to take the weight of the gun and steady my aim. I got into position and waited, becoming aware of each sight and sound around me, the grazing sheep as they tore at the grass, the more distant sounds of car engines, their lights streaming down far off roadways.

The most important thing for anyone in a position like this is to be still and not let the waiting, which is inevitably boring, lead to lethargy or loss of concentration. I dug my fingernails into the palms of my hands every now and again to remind myself to stay focused and kept my eyes mainly on the target area to ensure the best possible level of dark adaptation.

As I lay in wait I kept thinking 'What choice did I have?'

I wanted to get back in the game so when I was offered this assignment I took it - what choice did I have?

When I let my well founded suspicions of Carlos and Diego take second place to my need to get Kerry-Anne home as quickly and as smoothly as possible - what choice did I have?

When George convinced me he would not let things lie if I didn't help him - what choice did I have?

And now, if I took Hathos at his word, and I wanted to survive - what choice did I have?

I had to act before he did.

As the lower edge of the orange Sun grazed the horizon I heard the metallic click of a door opening and a familiar outline emerged into the twilight. He moved slowly to the edge of the patio, raised his eyes to the heavens and opened his arms wide.

I took careful aim, centred the target in the crosshairs and pulled the trigger.

Chapter Fifty Two

I slid back from the edge and out of view of the property as quickly as possible. I didn't need to see that I had hit the target. I knew that I had.

In contrast to the careful, stealthy way I had slithered up the slope my egress was a chaotic avalanche of stones, feet and disturbed wildlife. I ripped the devil mask from my head and dove into the car, grateful that it was still where I'd left it and that it still had all four wheels.

Slowly I pulled away, sweat streaming down my forehead as thick as blood, the gun and the mask on the passenger seat beside me.

Gasping lungfuls of air I tried to steady my trembling hands, focus my vision and drive away slowly, normally, and not like I was leaving a Formula One starting grid. I struggled to avoid the urge to leave burned rubber smeared blackly across the road in parallel lines of adrenaline.

The choices I had for disposing of the gun were few. I could bury it or throw it away. If I were to bury it the obvious problem was that I would need to dig a hole and that would need a spade and, more importantly, precious time. 20 minutes drive away from the house I stopped half way across a bridge and threw both rifle and balaclava into the foaming rapids below. That would have to do. Back up the road I could see lights. I had to move quickly.

When I got to Alejandro Velasco Astete Cusco International Airport I returned the hire car. It was like saying farewell to an old friend. The young man who checked it back in gave me a strange look.

'The car is very dirty, sir,' he said, 'but there appears to be no damage other than a few scratches. I will have to charge you for those.'

I was pleased his English was so fluent.

'That's OK,' I said, 'I understand.'

He scratched his head.

'You've done a lot of mileage in a short space of time. Is the computer wrong about the day you picked the vehicle up, sir?'

He showed me a printout.

'No,' I said, 'that's right. I've done a whirlwind tour.'

He grinned.

'Yes,' he said.

He finished his checks, there was also something to pay for replenishing the fuel back to full and the three 20Litre cans.

I settled up readily, paying cash. I was hoping that in his mind I was just one more, maybe a bit more crazy than most, but only one more in the long line of faceless tourists he had to deal with every day.

I was also hoping that I had enough of a head start on any pursuers. Now that I had brown hair and no glasses I should be less recognizable. That should help. Lastly I hoped that the guys who had rushed in to catch the same flight as me were just normal last minute passengers and not any of Hathos' people.

The LATAM Airlines A320 Airbus left Cusco at 8pm. The flight lasted only 80 minutes but I was asleep as soon as my bum hit the seat and was shaken awake when the plane had already landed and taxied to its disembarkation gate.

Right now the only thing I was thinking about was getting out of Peru. I did not want to look back, it wasn't good for the soul nor the conscience. What was done was done. Let the self-recriminations wait until later and then they could add to the catalogue of memories that already woke me sweating and shaking in the wee small hours.

One of the many mistakes Carlos had made was to turn his nose up at the contents of my case. If he had dug a little deeper, down under the socks and the boxer shorts, he'd have found two 3 inch thick envelopes stuffed with $100 bills. In total about $140,000's worth of cash.

In the melee of people at the airport I thought I glimpsed someone who might have been Isabella. It was disquieting but nothing more. Nevertheless I hurried through security and into the relative safety of the Departures area.

When you've got that much money hanging around it starts to burn a hole in your pocket so before boarding my next flight I visited the airport shops where I perused the quality watches and bought myself a Rolex GMT Master II at a tax free price.

It was a beautiful watch with a black face and bicoloured black/blue cerachrom bezel, capable of showing the time in three different time zones and held on the wrist by a finely polished stainless steel strap. I put it on immediately and threw away the box and its contents. I didn't care about the paperwork, I couldn't ever see myself parting with it.

I had been keeping an eye open for pursuers. I did spot a couple potential candidates but thought I was probably being over-sensitive. In any case I now kept as low a profile as possible in the hope that if there were anyone looking for me they would be disappointed.

I'd checked in as Dr Julian Craddock, the

university lecturer from Canada, I'd checked in for the 01:40hrs LAN Boeing 787 flight of just under 9hours to Los Angeles. I was no longer flying Economy and with time still to wait I made my way to the Business Class lounge where I found a secluded spot and sampled the whisky. I tried to calm the adrenaline still coursing through my veins but was interrupted in my search for solitude by a mechanical engineer from Boston who wanted to talk.

I couldn't stop him.

Over the course of several refills of our whisky tumblers he insisted on explaining to me the many possible causes of mechanical failure on commercial aircraft.

'Flying,' he said, 'is wrong. If man had been meant to fly he would have been born with wings. The skin of these plastic lined metal cylinders we sit in are incredibly thin you know. It's amazing to me that we rush to get onboard, eager to get into this high risk container and sit there for hours submissively believing in its safety and solidity.'

'To make matters worse the massively heavy jet engines that push us along are suspended from the wings by the most fragile web of metal. Do you know that the wings are attached to the fuselage by only a few welds and bolts and we have to hope that none of the engineers who built the damned thing, or any of the hundreds of others who have tampered with it in the name of maintenance, were having a bad day. It's imperative that these welds have no cracks and that the bolts don't shear as we rattle our way through the sky whilst the vibrational stresses and strains compete to pull us apart,' he paused to take a long pull from his whisky glass.

'The one thing you can rely on,' he continued, 'is that once you're up you will definitely be coming down. It's only a matter of when, where and how quickly.'

I smiled at this gravity-driven reassurance and asked if he would like another drink. He glowered at me. This promise of probable disaster had not had the desired effect on me.

I supplied the refill and then asked,

'You seem to know a lot about aircraft, what do you do for a living?'

'I work in Insurance,' he said 'I fly all over the world assessing the risks for the various airlines, giving them alternative ways of reducing their premiums.'

Maybe it was the whisky but this duplicity of occupation versus conduct just made me smile. He had offered me a timely distraction from my immediate problems and I was thankful for that although I did keep glancing around fearing the touch of a hand on my shoulder.

Chapter Fifty Three

I was extremely relieved when I eventually boarded the aeroplane. As I stepped onboard a young, blonde and attractively uniformed air hostess held out her hand for my ticket and directed me towards the Business Class area. I stowed my hand luggage in the overhead locker, sat down, closed my eyes for a moment and sighed. Here we go again, I thought. I was beginning to spend more time in the air than most birds.

After a very pleasant braised steak accompanied by a Chilean Malbec and an after-dinner Drambuie I thought I would be ready to sleep. My body knew I needed sleep, my mind knew it too, but I could not settle. Too many thoughts fought for attention. Jumbled images flashed through my mind in need of ordering, processing for storage or queuing for disposal.

Was what I had done right or was it wrong? I had no idea, I just knew that if I thought about it it would be circular, debilitating and without conclusion. I felt like I'd had no choice - but of course I had had a choice. I made a choice. I took action. Like all action that had consequences. If I had my time over again would I make the same choices?… fortunately you don't get your time over again.

I got another drink and snacked on some salted peanuts.

What else was there to do?

The passengers on the plane obviously included a fair number of South Americans. I was suspicious of all of them.

There were lots of uncomfortable minutes available for me to ruminate and one of the thoughts that I forced into my head as a distraction to others was "How true is it that a person is not defined by their name but by their actions?". It was better for me to try and think about things that had no clear answer than worry about those whose answer may be both clear and uncomfortable.

Diego was no less dangerous than when he was Hugo. Carlos' English was no better or worse than when he was Matias. I on the other hand did behave differently, I was more polite as Dr Julian Craddock than I was as plain old Mr Paul Carpenter for example. Maybe it was because I felt more erudite as a Doctor in Astrophysics than as a purveyor of toilet rolls. Maybe it was because I was travelling Business Class and was subconsciously trying to fit into the mould. I didn't know, but the thoughts and conjectures occupied my mind and blocked out those I was determined to ignore.

If you have thoughts and you want to avoid them then you need to think about something else, less serious. Don't leave a vacuum, don't leave your mind idle, don't leave any space, any cracks. Fill your mind to the brim with something else, delve into inconsequential minutiae, keep every synapse occupied.

So I thought about the meaning of identity and tried to recall every facet of the biographies of my alternate aliases. I put them mentally into different scenarios and considered how they would behave, how they would act and react to the situational stimuli. It didn't help me find sleep but it did while away the time.

I didn't want to talk to anybody and I couldn't concentrate on any of the proffered entertainment. If I did sleep I didn't want to dream. That was a way for the wrong thoughts to surface in the subconscious, to creep through in the form of macabre images, colours and textures, to create bizarre manifestations of the things I didn't want to think about.

It was a long flight, a very long flight, but slowly the time passed and as the distance from Peru increased my residual noradrenalin levels, that had biochemically fuelled my recent actions, subsided. I felt mental fatigue slowly overwhelm the internal turmoil and I began to relax.

Chapter Fifty Four

There's something I haven't told you yet.

There was good reason for me to worry and it wasn't to do with guilt or remorse or anything like that. It was because I had chosen not to kill Hathos and I wasn't sure that that, in hindsight, had been the right decision or whether it had irrevocably compromised my longevity.

I had not killed Hathos.

I had purposely diverted my aim so that the shot took off the head of the wooden statue of the Aztec Sun God that I knew he favoured. I had decapitated it just below the spot that Hathos habitually placed his hand. If the statue was intended to bring him luck it had fulfilled its obligation.

I'd driven over 19hrs and 1100 kilometres in order to put a bullet into a piece of wood!

Hathos was an intelligent man and I was pretty sure that he would have understood the message, "I could have killed you if I'd wanted to", as well as being a bit upset about the damage to his irreplaceable antique statue.

I'm not a monster. I'm keen on self preservation

but not on cold blooded murder, this seemed a good compromise. I definitely believed him when he told me that anyone taking unilateral action against any member of his "family" would be hunted down and executed. I'd been left in no doubt that he was capable of doing that.

In the sights of the L115A3 he was a defenceless target but his level of complicity in the original kidnap and maltreatment of Kerry-Anne was in all probability low to zero. The way I saw it, and maybe this was rationalising after the fact, he had actually acted to expedite Kerry-Anne's release once he had found out about it and had made it scorchingly clear that he was not happy that it had happened at all.

When I was stalking up the steep treacherous side of the ridge in the dark, with only the sheep for company, I had contemplated changing my mind and directing the gun on him. But I couldn't do it.

I was aware I'd taken a big risk to send a simple message, "Please leave me alone, let's end it here", and now I had to live, or not, with the consequences.

When we were finally on approach to LAX airport I peered out of the window determined to catch sight of the iconic Hollywood sign situated on Mount Lee in the Hollywood Hills area of the Santa

Monica Mountains. The white capital letters, 45-foot-tall (14m), spell out the word "Hollywood" across a span of 350 feet (110m).

The morning was clear and the achievement of this minor and inconsequential ambition gave me a bit of a lift, a lift that was soon negated by having to stand in line at Los Angeles Immigration for what felt like a day and a half and then be grittingly polite to a humourless immigration official who asked,

'Have you got any explosive devices in your luggage?'

I answered 'No' with a straight face.

I wasn't going to stop in Los Angeles. The thought of changing my plans and paying my daughter another visit flitted through my mind but if I were being followed this would only draw attention to her and that would be catastrophic. No, my idea was to assume I might be being followed and shake them off by leading them a merry dance.

It was now about 8am local time.

I was full but not overfull of alcohol and my body and mind were only loosely in contact. I was exhausted. My plane had landed at the Tom Bradley International Terminal of LAX and after I cleared Immigration and Customs I made my way to Terminal 5 Gate 52A for my onward flight to

Tokyo.

I had travelled via LAX before and was on autopilot as I made my way to the Lower/Arrivals Level and stood obediently under the "LAX Shuttle & Airline Connections" blue sign awaiting the arrival of the next "A Route" courtesy shuttle service.

Fortunately I was just about awake enough to avoid stepping onto a "C" or a "G" Route shuttle that would have landed me either in the LAX parking lots or the Metro Rail Green Line Station, neither of which would have helped me.

The "A Route" shuttle buses were scheduled to run every 10 minutes, 24 hours a day, seven days a week. I had to wait 20 minutes for mine but was nonetheless relieved when it showed up.

Once in Terminal 5 I immediately checked in and made my way through to the Departure area. It was a quiet time of day and, in contrast to the slowness of the disembarkation process, there was no delay for Dr Julian Craddock either at Passport Control or at Security.

Although a black coffee was desperately needed I stopped for a few moments at the magazine and books store and after a quick look around bought a collection of poetry; "The Oxford Book of American Poetry". This gave me the prospect of distracting myself by revisiting the dark tragicomic world of Poe's Raven, the fatalistic prophesying of Walt Whitman's "Crossing Brooklyn Ferry" and much more besides. It also gave me the opportunity to look around and see if I detected any familiar faces. I didn't.

Chapter Fifty Five

My Business Class tickets gave me entry to the Delta Airlines Sky Club Lounge which was situated between Gates 53 and 55, up on the mezzanine floor one level above the concourse. I lugged my weary way up the required flight of stairs in order to gain access and after walking up to the reception desk and having my ticket checked I entered the Lounge.

I needed refreshing and when I found that the Lounge had showers available I decided to put off the strong black coffee for a few minutes more. The hot water flowed rejuvenatingly over my tired skin and to complete the experience I lowered the temperature to ice cold for 10 seconds or so at the end before jumping out and vigorously towelling myself dry.

Back in the Lounge I was now on the hunt for that long awaited black coffee. There are many types of coffee, some bitter, some smooth and full bodied, but amongst them all the Kenyan Peaberry bean, in my opinion, rules supreme. They may have the same consistency as sheep droppings, they may be dry and tasteless in the raw, but when ground and infused the resulting thick black liquid is the nectar of the coffee world. Like the very best whiskies it should be drunk as it comes, undiluted by cream or milk, unadulterated by sugar. The taste is round and robust and at first tickles the very tip of your tongue before flowing to the back of the mouth where it hits you with the smoothly bitter impact of the African savannah before cascading, with satisfying warmth, down your throat.

The Delta Airlines Sky Club Lounge had a regular coffee machine. I hit the "black" button and drank the first cup of raw bitterness as soon as the temperature had dropped below boiling point. It was not the best I'd ever had but it would have to do. I poured another cup.

Ignoring the morning food offering of oatmeal and bagels I tried to distance myself from the ranting of a guy who had decided to pay $50 to gain entry to the Lounge and was clearly expecting more for his money.

I moved into the Quiet Area, situated in a far corner near to the windows that overlooked the concourse. Here there were five study booths separated by short glass dividers. I took possession of one of these and settled into it's armless faux black leather office chair. I rested my elbows on the varnished surface of the desk and noted that the area was amply supplied with power points. Fuelled by the caffeine and reinvigorated by the shower I set about the few things I needed to do.

The 9 to 10 hours that had elapsed whilst I was fretting my way through the sky was more than enough time for the chaotic scenes of destruction that I had left behind me to be found and thoroughly investigated and I felt like there was a loaded gun scouring the planet, its barrel slowly moving from place to place, trying to get me in its sights.

The first job I took on was to set my new Rolex, a beautiful thing whose design and function were in perfect harmony. I chose the three time zones that were most important to me; local, New York and London. I was relieved that I would no longer have to confuse myself with the mental arithmetical gymnastics of time conversion.

I then checked my phone to see what had been bounced across from my "business" phone that Teresa had in New York. There were a number of missed calls, including a couple from my daughter, and texts, again one from my daughter asking if I'd noticed the missed calls. There was also one from the office that read, "*Agaricus* - Please confirm when you will get back to London, S", so either Samantha actually cared or was using this apparently innocuous message to check that I and my phone were still together. I bounced back a reply giving the expected day and date and the codeword "Parasite" and hoped that that would keep her happy for a while.

Checking through the emails that were mainly junk and inconsequential, I noted that there was one from my daughter asking if I had noticed the missed calls and read the text and reminding me of my promise to keep in touch. I will, I will, I thought.

The last thing I needed to do was to see how Teresa was doing. I looked first at the traces that she had left as she moved around New York. I assumed that she would still be working her shifts at the hotel bar late afternoon and evening, so she really only had half a day to act the tourist for me. With this in mind I was delighted to see that she had already traversed the ravine-like depths of 42nd Street where the buildings are so tall that only a small slice of sky can be seen and there can only ever be one sunny side of the street. She had also visited the green-lunged acres of Central Park and the lights of Broadway.

I placed a video call and waited for her to answer. It took a while.

When she finally picked up the call her 'Hello' was in a distinctly sleepy voice and I could see that her eyes were only half open, her hair dishevelled.

'Did I wake you?, I said. I'm well versed in the blindingly obvious.

'Yes you did! It's might be mid-morning here but I was up late last night.'

Doing what I wondered, but she read my mind.

'I was online looking at where next to go and booking tickets.'

'What have you decided?' I asked.

'I'm going to make my way through lower Manhattan and take the ferry from Battery Park to Liberty Island and take a good look at the Statue of Liberty. I've never done that so it should be fun. I've booked all the tickets.'

'That's great, have a good time. I'll give you a call in a day or so to let you know when I'll arrive in Paris. Oh by the way, will you be anywhere near Brooklyn Bridge?'

'Yes I'll go right by it, why?'

'There's a poem by Walt Whitman called "Brooklyn Bridge",' I said, 'it just popped into my mind.'

'Who's he,' she said, 'never heard of it.'

I spelt out the name and repeated the title of the poem.

'Root it out,' I said, 'You never know, you might like it.'

'Sounds crazy to me, but you're the one paying so maybe I'll give it a try.'

I smiled, 'Thanks Teresa, you're doing a great job. See you in Paris soon.'

'Sure thing boss,' she grinned.

Chapter Fifty Six

I was ticketed on an American Boeing 777 flight to Tokyo leaving Los Angeles at 11:30 hours. It was a 12 hour flight that crossed the International Dateline, which always makes things more complicated. I was scheduled to arrive the following day at about 4pm in the afternoon local time, an apparent time difference of 16 hours.

I enjoyed Business Class travel and my Plan A was to get to sleep as soon as possible by distracting and soothing my brain through the delights provided by poetry. I would fill my mind with words exploring, seeking and untangling what layers of meaning I could. It would be both emotionally stimulating and intellectually challenging as well as mentally exhausting. With my mind filled I hoped that other, less conducive thoughts would be squeezed to the periphery and sleep would come.

I like to read poetry. For example Poe's hallucinogenic, almost comic, darkness in "The Raven". The line "each separate dying ember wrought its ghost upon the floor," aptly captured my present mood, whilst Walt Whitman's observation from "Brooklyn Bridge" that "it is not upon you alone the dark patches fall" at least gave a me some kind of dark comfort.

I was looking forward to re-reading these and others.

But to start with I had to slow my mind down, it was running too fast and to help it decelerate I knew from experience that it was best just to let my thoughts flow for a while in a kind of internal stream of consciousness. Once I'd boarded and I was settled into my seat I let it go,

"…the best thing about poetry, compared to all other forms of literature is… its short. You don't have to remember where you left off, you don't even have to understand it. The best poetry is like a song, like a head massage, you just allow yourself to be immersed in the flow of it. Poetry should soothe and replenish, none of that dreary stuff designed to make you feel even more suicidal than you were before you started, you can keep that - or burn it. No, it's best to find some poetry where the rhythm takes you out of yourself, for a moment, just for a moment. Poetry can leave you on a high, it's there when you want or need it. It doesn't chase you or ring, text, email, Tweet, message or Facebook you. It just waits patiently for you and is there when you're ready, when you're in the right mood. Poetry does not sulk if you stop halfway through, does not ask 'Do you love me?' does not demand, does not control, does not…

Take a breath. Take a moment.

I like opera too, but with poetry you can make your own music, in your own head. You can kick off a beat, you can go back and try a different rift, you can play with it. And it's yours. It can be warm, cold, angry or demure. You decide. The same poem on different occasions can conjure opposing emotions. You take the poem off the poet, it becomes yours, you don't have to return it, and nobody else needs to agree, disagree or even know about the music it makes in your head. It's just yours.

I like poetry better than opera."

The unfortunate thing was that I'd left my poetry book in the airport Lounge! It had probably been nicked by now by someone who wouldn't know a good poem if it bit them and now I had nothing to read and a long time to do it in.

My only alternative was to use other forms of distraction and after lowering my seat to the horizontal I put my headphones on and chose from the eclectic selection of music stored in the in-flight entertainment system. I tried the blues, and found Big Mamma Thornton's superb version of "Hound Dog", the dulcet tones of BB King's "The Thrill Is Gone". I tried Opera, the high C's of Pavarotti's Nessum Dorma, the unique voice of the ill-fated Maria Callas singing the aria "Casta diva" as Norma, "Vissi d'arte" from Tosca and then I switched genres and times to listen to Mark

Knopfler and the extended live version of
"Brothers in Arms" and so it went on, hopping
between genre and generations, choosing what I
liked and finally … in some alchemic way
my brain slowed,
my body relaxed,
and I fell asleep.

Chapter Fifty Seven

We landed at Terminal 2 of Tokyo's Narita International airport where, after a fairly speedy clearance through Immigration and Customs, I changed a couple of hundred dollars into Japanese yen and made my way to the only hotel actually within the airport precinct; the Narita Airport Rest House adjacent to Terminal 1. I had booked a room.

The uniformed male receptionist was extremely polite.

'Welcome to Tokyo, Dr Craddock,' he said in perfect English, 'Have we had the pleasure of you staying with us before?'

I wondered if the pleasure was due to me splashing out on a Luxury Room for the princely sum of $250 for the night, a sum that would hardly get you a broom cupboard in central London.

'No I'm afraid not, this is my first time in Japan,' I lied.

'In that case please allow us to be of any service to you should you need assistance.'

I wasn't sure what this meant but it was said with a smile and I thanked him for the offer. Accepting the keycard and declining help with my baggage I made my way to the room.

I hadn't noticed anyone interested in me in the airport so I was becoming increasingly confident that either my fears of being followed were groundless or I had managed to shake off any pursuit.

On inspection the room was definitely worth the money. When I'd booked it on the internet I had noted that the floor area was 58 m² compared to a Standard Room at 23 m² which had meant nothing to me at the time. Now that I was in the room I could appreciate that this meant big with twin beds, a lounge area with writing desk, two settees, a glass topped coffee table, a large marble floored bathroom and toilet, a walk-in shower that was big enough for four. And, as an added bonus, breakfast was included in the price of the room.

After a delicious shower, incorporating the use of all available toiletries, and a complete change of clothes, I opened a small bottle of gin that I had pocketed on the flight.

I wondered whether Hathos had purposely put Carlos and Diego in my path and whether he had his own suspicions? Or was it just serendipity? I knew I would never know the answers and it would gnaw at me for a while, but I would have to learn to live with it.

I have always appreciated the industry and the technological and engineering intelligence and application that you see in Japan. There seems to be an attention to detail that is extraordinary and made even more exceptional by its consistent repetition. The consequence is a deserved national reputation for reliability and quality.

I decided as I was here I may as well explore at least a small part of the city.

I took the sleek Keisei skyliner train and completed the 51.4 km journey from the airport to Nippori station in 36 minutes. Now in central Tokyo I took a taxi to Shibaura-Futo station, enjoying the clean and pothole-free drive through the concrete grey city. I wondered how people could live en masse in such an apparently ordered and disciplined way. It contrasted markedly with the haphazard, chaotic urban jungle that is London or the manic dynamism of New York.

My intended destination was Tokyo's 798m long Rainbow Bridge, a suspension bridge crossing northern Tokyo Bay between Shibaura pier and the Odaiba waterfront development. The towers supporting the bridge are white in colour, designed to harmonise with the skyline of central Tokyo. There are red, white, and green lamps all along the supporting wires that are powered by stored solar energy, and these illuminate the bridge each evening. The bridge carries three transportation lines on two decks. The upper deck carries the Shuto expressway, whilst the lower deck carries the Yurikamome rapid transit system, a driverless train which runs on a guided path, with the Tokyo 482 road and walkways on the outer sides.

I was heading to the south side walkway to look out across Tokyo Bay and onwards in the direction of an invisible Mount Fuji.

The walkway closes at night and the daylight was already failing as I took my first steps along it. There were not many people about although I expected that there would be CCTV surveillance of every inch or millimetre.

I walked along until I was well out over the water and had come to a point where the walkway purposely widened to include a viewing platform, a photo spot. I took out my mobile phone and took a few photographs. In such an exposed position I could look to left and right across the bridge. No one showed any interest in me and I did not notice anyone that stood out as South American.

I approached the railing and looked over. The water was a long way below. I wondered how many phones, or rings or other detritus lay at the bottom. Hopefully there were no bodies.

It was good to get out and about a little but as it

was getting dark I thought it best to get back to the hotel so I got off the bridge and caught a taxi. The driver was happy to accept American dollars and understood enough English to get me there safely.

Back in my Luxury Room I texted Teresa. I had consulted my Rolex and had seen that it was about 8am in New York and I didn't want to wake her again. On checking her movements I could see that she had indeed visited both the Statue of Liberty and crossed the Brooklyn Bridge, dallying for a while in Brooklyn Bridge Park.

I was pleased with this and thought that she was going above and beyond the call of duty. Maybe I could pay her back in Paris with an afternoon's shopping along the Champs Elysee.

In the text I told her when I expected to arrive in Paris and suggested she catch a flight to join me there the following day.

There was only one further thing to do before settling down to more sleep. Even though I was more and more confident that Hathos was not trying to track me down I thought I should continue with my plan.

For this reason it was goodbye to Dr Julian Craddock and hello to plain old Mr Gordon Glaister, an IT specialist from Peterborough, England. The idea of being an IT specialist sounded fine but I would have to make sure that I didn't get into conversation with any real IT specialists as I knew I would soon find myself completely out of my depth.

As I had not shaved for a while a growth of stubble helped give me a slight change of appearance. That would have to do, the passport photo and bio details would again see me through and, in any case, I was not in the business of false noses or wigs.

Once all the correct documents were dispersed about my clothing and the previous passport and other documents secreted, I was done for the night. Sleep without dreams was what I needed now.

Unfortunately unconsciousness would not come. Maybe I had eventually slept too well on the flight from Los Angeles, maybe my body clock was shot to hell and it was just letting me know it wasn't happy. It was 11pm in Tokyo, 9am in New York, 2pm in London. Sometimes even the mechanical exactitude of a Rolex is of no comfort - my body was just saying "help!".

I continued to toss and turn and could not settle. Finally I had had enough and it occurred to me that there was a way I could guarantee a few hours of peaceful oblivion. My father used to tell me that a good law to live by was "be willing to do unto yourself as you would do unto others". I had already successfully experimented with the appropriate levels of sedative for differing body mass, but it is strange how much more attention you give to the preparation of the correct dosage when the patient is yourself. I checked it over several times and finally overcame my reticence, rolled up my sleeve, splashed some whisky onto my lower left arm and gritted my teeth against the forthcoming, self inflicted pain. I felt the prick of the needle as it pierced my skin followed by the spreading of a kind of comfortable warmth as I drifted off…

…and then nothing for eight hours.

Heaven must be like this, but I was in no great hurry to find out.

Chapter Fifty Eight

When I woke up I was ravenous. I felt great. If this was the after effects of the sedative then I had done my "guinea pigs" a good turn. It was as if I had not eaten for a week.

Fortunately the buffet breakfast was of a lavish all-you-can-eat style with a mix of more than 30 different Western and Japanese foods; scrambled eggs, sausage, crispy bacon, fish, fruit, cold meats, yoghurt, dips, sauces and even what looked like small rectangular chocolate cakes.

Although everything was tempting, I stuck with the British staple of eggs, bacon, mushroom, sausage and toast, orange juice and black coffee. There was also a rowdy gaggle of holiday-making teenagers there and I noted with satisfaction that I may not have outdone them on the noise front but I certainly did on food consumption.

Over the years there have been a number of incidents at Narita airport including a few explosions and a midair collision. Consequently the airport is the only airport in Japan, and the only airport in the world as far as I know, where visitors have to show ID before they're allowed entry. I was able to pass myself off as Mr Gordon Glaister without difficulty.

I was flying from Terminal 1N and the check-in was on the fourth floor.

After receiving my boarding card I went immediately through Immigration Control and down to the Departure Area on the third floor.

My Air France Boeing 777 flight to Paris was scheduled to leave from Gate 16. The flight duration would be approximately 13 hours, arriving in Charles de Gaulle airport sometime around 16:55 hours local time. It was entirely a daylight flight and I would try to stay awake throughout. Unaccountably the cost of a return Business Class ticket was cheaper than the one-way fare so I'd bought that knowing full well that I would not be returning. Even so, due to the Scottish blood that courses through my veins, I could not bring myself to unnecessarily waste money;

I was on a bit of a high now that I was on my way back to Europe. Like a re-energised Scrooge I felt lightheaded. Obnoxious fellow travellers that pushed past me without apology would only make me smile and I nodded at their retreating backs saying, 'Oops, sorry', as if it were my fault. It might be a British trait to apologise for something you haven't done but it's not normal for me.

In less than two hours I was sitting back in my multifunctional Business Class recliner looking out of the window and watching our steep ascent. People, cars, buildings and trees receded into specks and then became completely indistinguishable as we rose through the clouds.

I chose to forget the complexity of time zones and jetlag and allowed my body to choose what time of day it thought that it was. Relaxed and pampered I allowed the flight to wash over and around me in a kind of meditative state.

It was when I was enjoying an after dinner airline-sized bottle of red French Merlot that the accident happened.

I was gazing absentmindedly out of the window at the ever changing silver-edged cloudscape that was lit white beneath a dazzling blue. Having already watched two of the available movies, including an excellent one called "The Hurt Locker", I was reflectively peering into space. Outside of my notice one of the stewardesses was leaning over me to clear away some of my debris but only succeeded in accidentally knocking over the half drunk bottle of red wine. My reactions were not fast enough to prevent the crimson liquid splashing into my lap, wetting my crotch and colouring my cream slacks an unattractive pink.

'I'm so sorry,' she said, 'how could I have been so

clumsy?'

She instinctively picked up my napkin and began dabbing at the wet patch. I had to grit my teeth.

'It's okay,' I said, 'I have a spare pair of trousers in my hand luggage. I'll go along to the toilet and change.'

I could see by her nametag that she was called Marijke, which I guessed was a Dutch name.

'I'll get you a cloth and some cleaning fluid,' she said, and took off up the aisle in a rather flushed state.

I retrieved my small bag from the overhead locker and held it in front of the offending damp patch as I waddled towards the toilets.

Fortunately one of the larger cubicles was vacant and I crammed myself inside resting the bag on the toilet seat. Halfway through my dressing contortions there was a polite knock on the door.

'Mr Glaister, we have some cleaning fluid for you.'

It was a male voice. Marijke had obviously reported the incident and the cabin crew must have checked for my name against the seat number. I assumed the voice must belong to some more senior member of the team. Opening the concertina door a crack I took in the offered materials.

'Thank you,' I said.

Trying to clean the stain from my trousers was an

unmitigated disaster. It didn't take long for me to increase the size of the problem to insurmountable proportions. I gave up in frustration and rolled the trousers into a soggy ball. When I eased myself out of the toilet wearing a clean pair of trousers there were two people waiting for me, Marijke and a male steward.

'Could you do me a favour?' I asked.

'Of course,' answered Marijke.

'Could you dispose of these trousers for me? They're too wet to put back into my case.'

'Are you sure you wouldn't like us to try and dry them for you? We have a few hours of flying time left and we could hang them in one of our cupboards. They might be alright.' It was the male steward speaking and from the look on his face I could see that he offered this alternative more out of politeness than conviction.

'No it's okay,' I said, 'I don't have any special memories attached to them, they're not heirlooms or anything, I'd rather just get rid of them and move on.'

I was doing my best to lighten the mood, to show that I wasn't aiming to sue Air France for millions. Marijke smiled. I glanced at the male steward's name tag, his name was Michael, and I handed him the rolled up and soiled trousers.

'Thank you,' he said, 'and our real apologies again

for this.'

I was interested that their apologies were now real, presumably compared to their earlier ones. I nodded, smiled and returned to my seat.

About 20 minutes later Marijke came by and held out a plastic carrier bag.

'Please accept this,' she said.

I peeked inside, the gold foil top of a 750ml bottle of Moët & Chandon Impérial champagne glinted back at me. Marijke was a natural blonde, slim, and attractive. It would have been rude not to accept her gift.

'Thank you,' I said, smiling, 'but it really isn't necessary.'

'And there's something else,' she said, 'we would like you to choose a gift from our on-board duty-free magazine, with our compliments.'

I was impressed. Maybe being accidentally showered with red wine was turning out to be a good thing. I thought of my coming rendezvous with Teresa, the champagne would be a great start and now I had the opportunity of adding a gift. But I needed help, I wasn't good at buying the right gift for a woman.

'I would love to buy something for my sister,' I lied, 'but I have no idea what she would like. Could you help me choose something?'

'I would love to,' said Marijke.

The easiest way to do this, without disturbing any of the other passengers, was for me to leave my seat and go to the small open bar and snacks area so that we could browse the magazine together and consider the choices. Marijke had an easy going personality and a dry sense of humour and made it fun. She crinkled up her nose at my suggestion of a teddy bear wearing a faux leather sheepskin hat and pilot goggles and steered me in the direction of jewellery. After a long and whispered conspiratorial conversation I settled on a silver Pandora bracelet and Marijke went to find it for me from amongst the stock of in-flight duty-free goods.

The accompanying paperwork was a bit convoluted as we had to agree on an explanation for the free issue and I had to sign for the bracelet.

It turned out that Marijke was indeed Dutch and originally hailed from Rotterdam. She had always wanted to travel and becoming a stewardess seemed a good way of achieving her ambitions. Having travelled around the world several times she was reaching the point where clearing up other people's mess and being nice to all and sundry was too high a price to pay and she was wondering what to do with the rest of her life. She was not the only one.

I didn't want to get Marijke into any trouble over what had clearly been an accident and asked if there was anything I could do or say that would help her.

'That's really nice of you,' she said, 'but it really, really isn't a problem. These things happen.'

Michael, the male steward, was passing by as we talked and I caught his attention.

'Michael,' I said, 'I just wanted to say how impressed I am with the way you and your team handled my little accident.'

I could see that Michael was a little taken aback, presumably unused to being complemented by passengers rather than abused.

'Well thank you very much, Mr Glaister,' he said and smiled what seemed to me to be a surprisingly real smile.

The rest of the flight was uneventful and as I was disembarking at Paris Charles de Gaulle airport Marijke smiled me a farewell.

The egress from Charles de Gaulle Terminal 2 has got to be one of the most convoluted of any airport on the planet. If you are not French or familiar with its peculiarities I am sure that you can become marooned Ben Gunn-like, endlessly lost on a series of ascending and descending escalators.

However I had passed through CDG many times and escaped through the rigmarole of Passport Control and Customs fairly quickly, proceeding to a Currency Exchange counter to change a few hundred dollars into Euros whilst marvelling at the daylight robbery of the exchange rate. If anyone other than the taxman, the rest of the banking industry and the energy companies were doing this to us there would be an uproar, the general populace, me included, are just too easy going.

Chapter Fifty Nine

Once in the Arrivals area it was into the washrooms and goodbye to the short lived Gordon Glaister and welcome back to Mr Paul Carpenter and his tortoiseshell rimmed glasses. My hair colour no longer matched but I thought I, and the authorities, could cope with that.

Getting to the centre of Paris was my next challenge and I hunted for the blue overhead signs pointing me to "Paris par Train / Paris by Train". It wasn't completely straightforward to follow these signs, the series of arrows signalled many changes of direction and I knew from past experience that if you missed one you were done for. The moving sidewalks at least made it a bit easier and I eventually arrived at the CDG Terminal 2 train station, on Level 4, and took the escalators down to the level for the Paris city trains, the RER B.

Wandering around like a lost soul I finally picked out the right ticket office for the Paris RER train which was, of course, at the extreme end of the concourse. After an embarrassingly inefficient conversation with the ticket attendant I emerged, through sheer willpower and perseverance, with a one-way train ticket to the centre of the city in my hand.

The next stage was to discover the right platform and to do this I needed to descend another set of escalators onto Level 1. By this time I had no idea where I was or how I got there. The platform sign read Aeroport Charles de Gaulle 2 TGV, which is not what I wanted at all, but rather than retrace my steps and start all over again I decided to ignore this and follow the advice on my ticket to find "voie" or "platform" 11. This platform reassuringly proclaimed itself as being for the "RER B Paris par Train", in other words the Regional Express Network that operates between Roissy-Charles de Gaulle and Paris city centre. Eureka!

The train arrived about 10 minutes later and once aboard the journey was relatively pain-free. After about half an hour we stopped at the Gare du Nord station followed by Chatelet Les Halles, St. Michel-Notre Dame, Luxembourg, and Port Royal where I got off. As far as I could see this was the closest station to my hotel and I made my way through the turnstiles and into the sultry early evening sunshine. It was not raining and it felt warm.

I had done my customary checks and was now utterly convinced I was home free, there was no possibility that anyone could be following me.

Instead of switching to the Metro I decided to

take a taxi the rest of the way. I had overestimated the distance still to be travelled to the hotel, the strangely named 4-star "Pullman Paris Tour Eiffel", and the Parisian taxi driver was none too pleased to have such a comparatively short fare. I didn't understand what he was muttering but I knew it wasn't complimentary and, although he didn't deserve it, I tipped him €20 and was rewarded by a shrug of the shoulders. You just can't please some people.

I like Paris. I even like the fact that the general populace probably don't much like me. It's a complicated place for a non-French speaking visitor. Not all Parisians are keen to help rescue a lost tourist. Some even seem to rather resent their presence. The driving is mad and the French owners of most cafes that line the Champs Elysee have successfully majored in "rudeness to Brits" as part of their school education. But the place is alive and once visited Paris is hard to forget.

The reason I had chosen this particular hotel was because of its location at the foot of the Eiffel Tower itself. I thought that this would impress Teresa in what may be her first and only visit to Paris. In addition I had booked two expensive rooms that each had a balcony with a view of the Tower as well as a panoramic view over the wider

Paris skyline. I thought Teresa deserved it for helping me and, to be honest, I thought I did too.

I checked in enthusiastically and prowled around all 72 m² of my room, much bigger than even the "Luxury Room" that I'd had in Tokyo.

The living area contained sofas and a coffee table, a writing desk, 2 flat-screen TVs and a Nespresso coffee machine. The bathroom had both a bathtub and a walk-in shower with all the obligatory free toiletries, bathrobes and slippers. There were two beds, one single and one extra-large double. It was enough to make you want to move in permanently.

Teresa's room was just down the corridor and to the same design.

Having checked my watch I could see that it was 1pm in New York and I hoped that Teresa would have left work, organised her leave and now be getting ready for her flight. I decided to give her a video call just to see how things were going. Once I established a connection on my tablet I dialled her number through Skype. She answered almost immediately and from her evident animation I could tell she was excited.

'Hello,' I said, 'is everything going to plan?'

'I've taken a few days off work,' she answered, 'I'm almost finished packing but I don't know what to bring, I keep changing my mind.'

This was foreign territory for me and to be avoided. I just hoped she would not ask my advice.

'What do you think I should bring?'

Oh dear!

'Just bring what you'd like. If there's anything you forget I'm sure we can get it here.' I answered, in what I intended to be both a helpful and a noncommittal way.

'You're no help at all,' she said.

I quickly changed the subject.

'Were there any problems booking me out of the hotel and have you got my luggage ready to bring across with you?' I asked, all professional and business-like.

You could tell from her face that she realised it was pointless trying to press me on the previous topic.

'No problem with anything,' she said, 'I just told them that you had had to leave in a hurry and, because no one had been at reception at the time, you had told me and they should just charge your card for the room. I had taken your bags out earlier and the guys on reception were not keen to let management know that they had missed a check out. They're well-known for disappearing out the back for a smoke whenever they can.'

'Sounds good to me. See you in Paris tomorrow. I'll meet you at the airport.'

'Looking forward to it,' she said.
I surprised myself because I was looking forward to it too.

Chapter Sixty

I awoke late and showered and shaved, removing the growth of stubble that I wasn't sure Teresa would like, and dressed carefully, deciding to discard the glasses. I then went down to the hotel restaurant for a petit déjeuner of croissants, strawberry preserve and a black coffee that felt fat on the tongue with an edge almost of nutmeg.

Later, after doing some shopping and having lunch, I returned to the hotel and cleaned my teeth for the second time. When I exited the hotel the day had turned into a soft summer afternoon.

I had not wanted to be late for Teresa's arrival but soon realised I had started off too early and, to claw back a little of this over enthusiasm, I risked the Metro to Port Royal and thence back to Roissy-Charles De Gaulle airport.

After disembarking the train I found my way back through the airport labyrinth to Terminal 2 Arrivals and checked both on the Arrivals Board and from a friendly chap on the Information Desk that I was in the right place. There was no point waiting around only to be sideswiped by Teresa emerging from a different exit, one I wasn't at.

The airport was what I would call moderately busy. There were lots of people milling in all directions but it wasn't at the intensity of a football match crowd, you could actually move around without risk of collision. The Arrivals Board was full of due planes from all over the world, some landed, some late, some approaching, thankfully none cancelled or diverted. The problem with my master plan of arriving early was that it had worked and I now had more than an hour to kill.

Prowling around the shops I browsed through books I had no intention of buying and did a lap or two back and forward to the barrier that separated the greeters from the arriving greetees. The large automatic doors swished regularly open, like a pair of opaque glass stage curtains, to allow through weary passengers who stepped blinking into the light, their ears still buzzing from the constant rumble of aircraft engines. Some would look blearily around surveying the forest of waving arms until they finally identified their own particular loved ones, at which point their lethargy would be instantly shed and they would burst into a dangerous trolley dash towards an embracing rendezvous. Others, the business travellers for example, would be more matter-of-fact, slinking out, squinting about, trying to find a card with their name on it.

I'd been there for so long that I was beginning to recognise the faces of other got-here-too-early meeters and greeters. But rather than run the risk of an impromptu conversation breaking out I took myself off to a nearby cafe and sat pretending to drink a small cappuccino.

Looking at my Rolex I begged it to tick faster but its response was professionally aloof. Simply to pass the time. I began to wonder what Teresa's reaction would be when she saw me again. The time slithered by, like a snail on a go slow, but pass it inexorably did and finally I got up, left my stone cold coffee and moved, in some trepidation, towards the Arrivals door.

The Arrivals Board now showed that Teresa's plane had landed and I shuffled uncomfortably as the final aeon or two passed, waiting for Teresa to appear through the automatic doors. Maybe she had missed the plane, maybe she had changed her mind, or maybe she had been taken to one side by French Customs Officials and was at this moment being strip-searched.

Then suddenly she was there, emerging through the opening doors, pushing a trolley laden with cases and looking from side to side, seeking me out. I waved my arms high in the air, surprised at my own impulsive enthusiasm. She soon located my semaphore and made a speedy beeline towards me.

As she approached I was in fear of being mown down by her fast-moving trolley but she hauled on the reins at the last moment and, after she had brought it to an obedient standstill, ran around the side and leapt at me, throwing her arms around my neck. I love the Latin temperament, it completely overcomes our British reserve. I had no alternative but to hug her back and return her "hello" kiss. Rather reluctantly I let her go.

'Paul, it's good to see you again,' she beamed. It had only been a couple of days, I thought, albeit an eventful couple of days. But hey who was counting. I wished, probably for both the first and the last time, that I really was Paul Carpenter, it would have made things so much simpler.

'Have you been waiting long?' she asked.

'Only just got here,' I said, not completely accurately, 'Well done on finding your way out.'

'No specs?' she said.

I had my answer ready, 'Contact lenses,' I replied.

She pushed me away to arms length and looked at me, scrutinising my face. 'Yes,' she said, 'I prefer you without specs.'

Phew! Thank goodness for that. I looked down at the groaning trolley,

'You've got so much luggage let's not bother with the train, let's get a taxi,' I said, spotting my own case amongst the pile and realising that I was at least partly responsible for the overload.

'Whatever you say,' she replied, 'I'm in your hands.'

Something strange had happened. We had spoken a few times now and kept in touch while I was travelling but what I hadn't realised until now was that we'd become friends. It had just happened organically. Teresa seemed to now take it for granted and chatted away without reserve, without barriers. I could feel my own defences weakening.

Chapter Sixty One

After Teresa checked in to the hotel I went to see if she liked her room. She 'looooved' it - I was relieved. She was so full of energy and, amidst the flurry of returning my phone and luggage, throwing open her cases and starting to hang things up and put things into drawers whose existence I hadn't even registered, she told me that the flight was a dream, that actually she'd slept really well, but not to tell her the time difference because she'd met somebody before boarding the plane and he had said that the best thing to do was just to live by the sun, to follow its rhythm, and was I okay and did I have any idea where we should eat tonight and, oh by the way, she had made a list, only a short list really, of the things she would like to see and do during the few days she was here in Paris. She was like a whirlwind, I was exhausted just watching her. It was great.

I left her to her unpacking and showering and changing and went back to my own room. It seemed empty.

When she knocked on the door I let her in and we went out onto the balcony and took in the view of the Eiffel Tower and the adjacent skyline that flowed out and over the Seine. The day was warm with one or two white cotton wool clouds floating in an otherwise sea blue sky.

I supplied the coffee and she eventually stopped pacing up and down, restlessly looking over the balcony rail, taking in the view from every angle and recording the moment on her phone, and sat down opposite me sipping the deep black liquid, wrinkling her nose deliciously at its bitterness.

'Wow,' she said, 'Wow, Wow, Wow!'

I found myself smiling and tried to pull my expression back into order, there was some business to be done.

'Teresa can I just check a few things through with you,' I asked.

'If you must,' she said coquettishly.

'First, thanks for looking after my phone. Were there any problems, any calls other than mine that got through to you?'

She thought for a moment,

'None at all,' she said, 'although there was one time when the phone rang and I could see that it wasn't you so I simply let it ring, just like you said.'

Good.

'Second, did anyone comment on my room being empty or go near my luggage?'

'Nope,' she said confidently, 'I went in and ruffled your sheets so that the bed looked slept in and I took your luggage home with me early. Quite the little conspirator ain't I?'

Very good.

'And third and last,' I said, getting up and returning with a hotel envelope, 'I owe you this.'

She took the unsealed envelope, carefully opened the flap and withdrew the notes.

'$45,000 as promised,' I said, 'please count it.'

She let out a breath, 'I've never seen this much money before,' she said, and then, as she started to count, laying out piles of $1000 neatly on the table in front of her, 'Did your business go okay?'

Nice of you to ask, I thought.

'It all went fine,' I said.

'Oh good,' she said absentmindedly, not really caring, as she continued to count the money, her eyes wide.

We ate out at the 58 Tour Eiffel Restaurant which is situated on the first level of the Eiffel Tower. With a little bit of manoeuvring I had managed to reserve a table with a view overlooking the Trocadero and insisted she try the "Escargots à la Bourguignonne", snails in garlic-herb butter, and after token resistance she gave it a go. It was accompanied by fresh, crusty French bread and washed down with a Saint-Romain white wine, its mineral flavours a perfect accompaniment to the snails' garlic butter. What could be more quintessentially French?

Teresa told me, not too convincingly, that she loved it. It was a fun evening and after dinner we took a leisurely stroll in the open spaces of the Jardins Du Trocadéro trying to avoid being wetted by the cool spray from the fountains, although we didn't try too hard. She made me laugh. I asked her what was on her list of "must do's" and she said that that could wait until morning because she was busy living one of them right now and wanted to savour it.

As the daylight faded Paris lit up, the Eiffel Tower rising golden into the evening dark. Teresa took so many photos that I feared that the global Internet may crash if she tried to upload them all.

Back in my room I retrieved the champagne I'd been given by Marijke from the refrigerator. But before I could open it Teresa said I had to wait, she needed another shower. She went back to her room and I waited on the balcony wondering if she would come back. I was conscious that I wanted her to.

After an age there was a soft knock on my door.

'Now where's that champagne,' she said.

We talked late into the evening. The mixture of my relief at escaping Hathos' grasp, the good champagne and the ease of the conversation, loosened my tongue. This was probably the first woman I'd had this kind of evening with since I'd lost my wife. Who am I kidding? It definitely was the first! I decided to open up a little. I told Teresa about my wife. If that was going to scare her off then I may as well get it over with quickly.

It didn't scare her off. She was both suitably interested and sympathetic.

I was pleased and moved the conversation on to talking about her. It was late when she bade me a good night and went back to her room.

Chapter Sixty Two

When I woke I looked out over the park. The sun had not yet burnt off all the morning mist and it lay like a blanket over the shrubbery, the edges torn into wisps of white that waved themselves into nothingness.

I called Teresa's room and agreed to meet down in the hotel restaurant for breakfast. I was already on my second black coffee when she arrived.

I'm not generally a big fan of tick lists but when you have a someone like Teresa, who was showing such natural joy in the adventure and discovery of each new thing, you would have to be hard man not to soften a little and be carried along with the flow. Even so we had two days and I suggested we pace ourselves a little and not try to do everything on the first day. She looked a little peeved and handed me her list in a less than contented manner saying that she would happily leave it to me, but she would like to have at least seen all these places before she left. I wasn't really seeking this responsibility but she insisted. I seemed to have somehow let myself in for it.

Taking off on our adventure I might have been

physically in the lead but Teresa was very definitely the emotional lead. You've got to know when you've met your match.

We trooped through the Louvre (tick), joining the perpetually long line of people waiting to catch a glimpse of the Mona Lisa (tick). The Gioconda followed us around the room with her eyes, making Teresa uncomfortable in a what-is-she-looking-at-me-for kind of a way. I laughed and got a dig in the ribs for my trouble. We visited the Arc de Triomphe (tick) and, with Teresa's urging, I bought a small metal bust of Napoleon. We traipsed up and down the Champs Elysee (tick), Teresa shopping (tick), me going to a suit rental shop and trying to be patient even when she would not let me pay for anything, 'You've given me enough money,' she said and I replied with a I-wish-there-were-more-women-like-you type comment that had me ducking out of the way of her playfully swinging arm. We had lunch at one of the many street cafes and the waiter was actually efficient and nice to us whilst all the time eyeing up Teresa. I didn't leave a tip.

We finished the sightseeing early as I had booked tickets for the Opera which was also a splendid excuse to get dressed up and for Teresa to try out some of her new purchases. She looked magnificent in a tight fitting black dress and red high heels and after she had paraded provocatively around my room to ask if it was OK, I gave her the Pandora bracelet to add to her ensemble. She was soooo pleased that I neglected to mention that I had got it for free. She put it on immediately. It looked great. Even I was taken along by the spirit of the evening and wore the black dinner ensemble with a white winged collar dress shirt and a rather fetching tartan bow tie that I'd rented for the evening.

I'd booked a table at the Opera House Restaurant where we could eat before the performance and the taxi dropped us off outside in good time for a leisurely meal. I obviously had had no choice over the opera that we were going to see, it was whatever was on that evening. As it turned out it was Mozart's Don Giovanni, the story of a serial philanderer who eventually gets his just deserts. I was not sure that this was the ideal opera to be taking Teresa to but, as it was sung in German and I somehow failed to buy a program, I think I got away with it.

You did not need to understand a word to appreciate the colour and the passion that somehow succeeded in stirring the heart. The power and complexity of the music, the strength, range and humanity of the voices produced an overall spectacle that pierced through the surface to what it means to be human. Teresa was riveted and during the whole of the final act held my arm tightly. I didn't move, even when I felt it cramp.

The following morning we breakfasted early and hit more of the big city. I took Teresa to the very top of the Eiffel Tower with magnificent views across the city. At her pleading, I held her tightly around the waist as she moved as close as she dare to the edge, complaining that she had a fear of heights but handling it as if it were part of a rollercoaster ride, fear and fun, those two strange bedfellows, intermingling.

Notre Dame Cathedral, a truly iconic landmark with its flying buttresses and gargoyles, was another of Teresa's required stops and we explored the huge nave and climbed one of the towers for more protective waist holding whilst she videoed and photographed the stunning views along the Seine.

'Let's stay at ground level for the rest of the day,' she said, after we had climbed down.

'Your wish is my command,' I replied, 'Would my lady perhaps consider that the time is right for a light luncheon?'

She laughed. We kissed. It seemed the natural thing to do. Anyone watching us would have been forgiven for believing that we were close.

Our last tourist stop of the day was the cavernous and superlative Orsay Museum, its origins as a train station clearly evident, even to the presence of the original station clock.

The museum housed a mind blowing collection of sculpture and an array of the more modern masterpieces including the likes of Cézanne, Monet, Renoir and Van Gogh.

On such a whistle stop tour there are so many outstanding works of art assailing your senses one after another that the majority of it just doesn't stick. The one painting that did stick however was an oil canvas by Vincent Van Gogh called "The Siesta". It showed two French rural workers of the mid-19th century, one man and one woman, who lay together in the shade of a haystack, the man had taken off his shoes and his cap was over his eyes. Their reaping tools lay beside them and in the distance unharnessed oxen grazed peacefully. It was somehow both a simple as well as an inspirational scene. It would have been nice to step into that painting with Teresa and to lie alongside her in the shade. But this was just a daydream although Teresa seemed to be daydreaming it with me. She was leading me astray.

Back at the hotel we decided to order a room service dinner and sat together on the balcony, relaxed and satiated. It was a clear, cool evening. The bright shining stars of the Milky Way were mirrored by the multicoloured city lights that filled the earthen part of the vista as far as the eye could see. I have no recollection of what we ate or drank or what we talked about. I have only the knowledge that I didn't want it to end.

However, it was Teresa who broke the spell.

'I'd like to shower,' she said.

'Of course,' I said, 'Will I see you later?'

'I'd like to use your shower,' she said.

I decided not to weigh up the pros and cons.

'Sure,' I said.

I lay on the bed listening to the splashing water. A few moments after the showering noises stopped and Teresa walked back into the room. She was naked. Her body glistened as she finished patting herself dry with a fleecy white bathroom towel. She looked fantastic. 5'6" of sensuality. Her breasts firm, her nipples standing proud, her skin dark and smooth. She was totally confident in her own womanhood. I gawped like a teenager. She walked over to the bed.

Later we showered together and I looked at her adoringly. I was still in shock. It had been so easy to throw off our inhibitions. The walk-in shower had ample room for the two of us and immersed in the warm water cascade we washed each other's body, the stimulation re-arousing me. She smiled at me and we kissed.

After, we lay together in each other's arms, each contour of our different selves finding a home, skin to skin, the boundary between where one body began and the other ended blurred, completely comfortable, compatible.

'I don't want to go,' she whispered.

For the first time since my wife died I felt human. I wanted to say 'And I don't want you to go' but I didn't, I just lay there, our breathing in unison.

This wasn't rational was it. To meet someone for the first time in an hotel bar. To ask her to help you out. For it to become emotionally significant. I had paid her a large amount of money. She wouldn't even be here if it wasn't for payment and the promise of more. Was I being taken advantage of? Please no! But could I believe this was real? Life wasn't like this.

Maybe I'd been overcome by the moment. What would my wife think? She'd told me to live, is this what she meant? What would my daughter say? Maybe the best thing for everybody was to let it end here.

It was Teresa who broke the silence, she the more mature one.

'I have to go back of course. I need the job.'

Thanks Teresa, thanks for making it easy.

'What will you do with the money,' I asked, trying to move on to something else, anything else.

I felt her body squirm against mine.

'I'm going to use it to start the business I told you about.'

The United States is definitely the home of the entrepreneur. If I'd asked an English girl what she might do with this kind of windfall I would not have been surprised if she'd said that she would buy a car, or use it as a deposit on a house, a boob-job or to pay for a wedding.

'You've really thought about this,' I said.

'Oh yes. This is the opportunity of a lifetime,' she said.

I smiled. I might have unintentionally founded a dynasty. She deserved it.

Chapter Sixty Three

The rest of our time together passed in a kind of a fog. I wanted the clock to stop but it wouldn't. The more I got to know Teresa the more I liked her. She had a clear vision of what she wanted to achieve. I respected her strong and determined personality as well as her irrepressible energy and enthusiasm for life. With all these things in her favour who could doubt that she would achieve, and maybe even better, at least some of her dreams.

I told her my real name. I shouldn't have done but I got carried away. I didn't think it was fair for her not to know. I wanted her to know that although my name was false my actions weren't.

'You're Mark Wilson?' she said, 'not Paul Carpenter?'

'That's right,' I said, 'Oh, and I don't need glasses.'

She shook her head.

'And you used a false name because of the work you do?'

'Yes,' I said.

'And you can't tell me about the work you do?'

'Right again,' I said.

'You're full of surprises Paul … er, I mean Mark.'

'Sorry,' I said.

'I don't know what to say,' she said.

She stayed silent for a few seconds.

'My real name is Teresa,' she said.

'Nice name,' I said, and got a half smile as my reward.

Before I knew it I was standing in the Departure Hall of the airport. We'd traded numbers. I'd given her the number of my personal phone in exchange for hers. For safe keeping I'd put Teresa's number into the memory of the burner phone I'd been using. I'd transfer it over before I disposed of it. We probably wouldn't keep in touch but it was a nice thought.

With bags checked in Teresa stood facing me, her boarding card clasped in her hand.

'We didn't see absolutely everything on my list,' she said, pouting 'we didn't visit Versailles.'

'That's the thing about Paris,' I said, 'you always have to leave at least one thing that you haven't seen or haven't done.'

'Why's that.' she asked, knowing the answer.

'To make sure you come back,' I said.

As she turned to go she pressed a small piece of paper into my hand. I watched her manoeuvre her way through Passport Control and saw her look back, see me and blow a kiss. It was too far away but I thought there may have been a tear on her cheek. I waved back, forcing a smile, and in a moment she was gone, having disappeared behind the screens, heading towards security and the x-ray machines, on her way back home.

Chapter Sixty Four

When I returned to my hotel room I noticed a plain white envelope on my side of the bed, lying on the pillow. Knowing how efficient hotels can be when check-out looms I guessed that this was a copy of the bill and wondered idly what "extras" would be charged. Deciding however that scrutiny of their mathematical accuracy could wait, I made myself a coffee – I needed the caffeine more than I needed the practice at arithmetic.

Sitting on the balcony, a cup of the black stuff cradled in my hands, I gazed blankly at the view, inwardly focused.

My trusty Rolex seemed to have slowed down again. After the hurricane of activity of the last 48 hours time seemed to have taken a breather. When I looked back into the room through the double glazed glass of the sliding doors it appeared sterile, silent and empty. I felt impatient for the morning when I would complete the last leg of this journey, the one that would take me back to London.

I got up and as I walked back into the room I caught the smell of a perfume I recognised. It was as if a small part of Teresa's essence, a very small part, was still there. I took out the piece of paper Teresa had given me and smoothed it out - "Thanks for a wonderful time" it said. I folded the paper carefully back up again and put it in my pocket for safekeeping.

As I was about to start on my packing it suddenly occurred to me that I had not returned my daughter's calls, texts or emails and it was about time that I did. I sat in the room gazing out of the window at the Paris street-life. People were rushing hither and thither with unknown purpose. The sun was shining, glinting from the tops of the cars as they hooted their way onward. I reached for my phone.

My parenting was patchy to say the least, I think I was more reliant on her than she was on me. And I'd met Teresa. What should I say? I made the call. When she answered I couldn't speak.

'Hello.'

Silence.

'Hello.'

Come on you idiot say something, I thought, you're supposed to be an adult.

'Dad?'

How did she know?

'Yes, Hello,' I said.

'Good to talk to you, I'm pleased you called. How

are you?'

'Just fine,' I said. How often is this lie repeated between loved ones? We say it but we know it's not the truth. 'How are you?'

She avoided the question like a pro. She talked about what she was up to, the forthcoming house move, only days away, their house sold, belongings in storage, they in a short rental. It just seemed to me that there was something else. I know my daughter, she is so like my wife. I let her talk. Eventually she said,

'I miss her, Dad,' it was my daughter acting the parent, saying what I wanted to say but didn't know how. 'I miss Mum.'

I could hear the catch in her voice, her closeness to tears.

'I miss her to,' I said. Very much.

'Cancer is such a horrible thing. She fought it so hard, it just wouldn't go away.'

Before my eyes flashed memories of the before person, the chemo, the determined woman.

'Try to remember the times your Mom was singing those daft songs, dressing up for parties, having a good time,' I said, trying to remember them myself, trying to superimpose them on top of the other less positive memories that always tried to muscle their way to the top.

We talked for a few more minutes.

'Better go now,' I said.

'Okay Dad, good to talk to you. Keep well.'

This was her traditional sign-off phrase.

'Maybe we can try a video call next time, get into Skype?' I said.

She laughed, 'Yeah, why not. Pleased to see you're creeping slowly into the 21st century.'

Kids can be so cheeky.

'Look after yourself,' I said.

'You too.'

Afterwards I remembered all the things I should have said; 'I rang because I was thinking of you', 'I rang because I'm missing you', 'I rang because I love you and I just wanted you to know'. And I hadn't mentioned Teresa. I looked at my watch. It would have been too awkward to call back, maybe another time.

Chapter Sixty Five

My attention wandered back to the envelope lying on the pillow. I'd vaguely registered that there was something written on the front of it, but assumed that it would be my name, or room number, or something equally insignificant. It was only when I picked it up and looked at it properly that it grabbed my attention. There were only two words, written neatly and in the centre,

"Found You"

Startled, I swung round, as if I was suddenly expecting someone to be in the room, standing behind me. The room, unsurprisingly, hadn't changed. It was as empty as it had been. It was my mood that had changed. I sat down on the edge of the bed, it felt harder. All that convoluted journeying, the changes of identity, the vigilance of looking for shadows, the increasing confidence in success. It had all been useless!

I couldn't believe it. It was as if I'd been punched in the stomach.

Inside the envelope was a single sheet of crisp,

white paper, sharply folded into thirds.

It was with some trepidation that I teased the paper flat. I could see that there was a handwritten message. I started to read,

Dear Mr Carpenter,

I am a proud man and could not let you disappear from my thoughts without a demonstration of my reach.

I hope you remember what I said to you – that I feel like a Father to those who I take under my wing, the extended family that is my organization. Therefore if anyone in my family is wronged I feel it my duty to act and to correct or avenge that wrong.

You have acted against me. Your actions have caused me distress.

However your particular case is not so straightforward. I acknowledge that I owe you a debt. I understand all too well that you could have taken my life but you chose not to.

Also my men Carlos and Diego may not have been without fault. You must have thought you had good reason to return to Peru and do what you did. It was a big personal risk.

I asked you if you had more information than I did on who was involved in the kidnapping. You should have told me, Mr Carpenter, you should not have taken the law into your own hands. It is my family, I and only I am responsible for their discipline.

However, I have concluded that there have been wrongs on

all sides and that perpetuating a cycle of action and reaction, foolishness and retribution, would serve no just cause. Indeed my killing you may even invite a further act of foolishness against me and I have no time for this — I have more important things to do.

Therefore I want you to know that just like you could have taken my life then I could have taken yours. But I also will avert my aim and there will be no further action on my part. I trust I can rely on the same from you and your friends in the States.

There is only one thing that I ask - do not return to Peru. At least not until we are each of us old and grey and in the mood for reminiscing. This, on my side, will take some years to achieve.

Take my advice Mr Carpenter do not abuse the gift of life that I willing bestow on you and do not see in it any sense of weakness on my part.

Hathos

P.S. The girl you have with you in Paris is very attractive, I congratulate you. I am sure that she will have added to your enjoyment of such a romantic city.

Make sure you keep her safe.

I was not sure Teresa would have appreciated being referred to as "the girl" and I was conscious of the not-so-veiled threat that was implied in his words. It was an obvious attempt at ensuring that I didn't do anything "silly".

I was surprised at just how easily it provoked the desired gut reaction in me.

I refolded the paper and replaced it reverentially in the envelope.

After the first surge of relief I felt something more akin to humiliation.

How had I been so easily followed? The blood pounded at my temples, a shudder wound its way down my spine. It didn't bear thinking about.

The truth was that I had taken my eye off the ball. I'd been overconfident and distracted and was extremely fortunate to have gotten away with it. I had assumed a successful escape too easily, closed the door on a chapter too early. If I didn't sharpen my ideas up I wouldn't need to worry about putting in an order for next year's diary. I needed to remember that if I was to get back into this game then I had to buck my ideas up. This was a tough job and it didn't pay to underestimate anybody.

So now what should I do?

I could try and make complex and contorted movements around Europe trying to slip any tail that was on me, I could see if there was a way to get to Hathos or I could simply believe Hathos and just go home.

I considered the options over one or two glasses of whisky.

Trying to shake off a professional shadow in a way that I'd failed to do up until now would be both time consuming and probably impossible. It would also mean that I got back to the UK late and that would lead to difficult questions needing difficult explanations at 'The Store'. I could do without that. Trying to get to Hathos was an even worse idea. He was forewarned, it was his country, the chances of success were slim to zero. Also up until now I had completely underestimated him and his abilities. It wouldn't be a good idea to keep doing that. So l was left with one choice.

I would decide to believe him.

I shrugged. What else could I do.

As I was packing I slipped the envelope into one of my bags, nestled between layers of clothing. I could decide what to do with it later, a ritual burning perhaps, or maybe I would keep it as a reminder, should I ever need it, that I wasn't always as smart as I thought I was.

As my heart rate slowed towards normal l looked around the room and began to whisper my goodbyes.

Chapter Sixty Six

I'd had enough of aeroplanes for the time being so I'd booked a ticket on the Eurostar leaving Paris' Gare du Nord railway station and delivering me to London's St Pancras International station. My Scottish conscience had pricked me slightly so I'd only booked a Standard Class ticket online, putting my days of Business Class travel behind me, at least for the time being. And anyway I wanted to sit amongst the ordered chaos of families, students and the other un-suited, rowdy, no-frills people, hoping that their life force might be contagious.

My Paris hotel was only 600 metres from the Bir-Hakeim Metro Station so, after checking out, I decided to get to the Gare du Nord station the hard way and, ignoring the appeals of the taxi drivers that clustered around the hotel forecourt awaiting their next victim, I dragged my clumping bags behind me and trundled on my way.

The Gare du Nord is the busiest railway station in Europe. This was in evidence as I manoeuvred a body-swerving course across the main concourse looking for the signs to Platforms 3-6, the Paris terminus of the London Eurostar service.

I felt like I wanted to be jostled by other human beings, to be frustrated by having to wait in line and to see, hear and smell my fellow creatures, ear-wigging their conversations, immersed as they were in their own personal trials and tribulations. If that's what I wanted then it was immediately clear that I had come to the right place. Even if the conversations I overheard were mainly in French, a language I had perfected to a level of about one word in ten, it was still soothing to dive back into this sea of humanity and to be swept along haphazardly and uncontrollably.

The 13:31hours Eurostar to London left on time with me on it and was scheduled to take about 2½ hours. This would get me into London at approximately 17:00 hours local time because of the +1 hour time difference. This was nothing to be worried about compared to the body shattering time differences that I had already put myself through.

The beauty of this train journey is that it takes you through the Channel Tunnel, an historic feat of engineering and a monument to collaboration between the British and the French, something that would have been impossible to imagine for several hundreds of the years of our joint histories. The tunnelling began in 1988 and the 50.5kilometre

(31.4 mile) tunnel was officially opened in 1994. In 1996 it was identified as one of the "Seven Wonders of the Modern World" and the Eurostar service achieves line speeds of up to 300 kilometres per hour (186 mph), slowed to 160 kilometres per hour (100 mph) within the tunnel, for safety reasons.

As long as you avoid the occasional train cancellation, disruption or fire, it is a very comfortable service. I was now reaching the end of my round the world trip and by some strange alchemy the mixture of actions, sleep, alcohol and sedatives had left me feeling less groggy than I had expected. Fuelled by the excitement of Teresa's visit I had completely forgotten to think about my body's reaction to all the travelling I'd done. Even now, in the wake of her leaving, I didn't feel so bad.

Disembarking at London St Pancras International station Platform 8, I made my way through the Passport and Security to the main ground floor level concourse. Here there is a 9m tall bronze statue depicting two people standing close, embracing, a man and a woman, oblivious of all that is around them, conscious only of themselves, gazing into each other through their eyes. It is called "The Meeting Place" but is more colloquially known as "The Lovers". It is an enigmatic symbol as, partly due to its location, the embrace could equally be one of welcome or one of farewell and this tempts the observer into their own interpretation, each as valid as the next.

I slunk out of the main station and into the bowels of the underground. Everything was now familiar and I took the Bakerloo Line north, alighting only a short walk from my apartment and arriving outside my front door at 18:30 hours. It was an almost out of body experience to see my hand place the key in the lock and push the door slowly open.

As I entered I had to step over a pile of junk mail before I could look around. Nothing had changed. I had been around the world but this place had just slumbered, like a dog when its owner is away. Unlike a dog it did not leap to its feet and come charging towards me, jumping up to lick my face, demanding to be fed, wanting to be walked. Instead it just sat there, non-committal.

It was as if I had never been away. Not a book was out of place. The half drunk tumbler of whisky was still on the small table beside the settee. In the kitchen the only thing that had changed was that more of the food in the refrigerator was now past its sell by date.

I considered what I should have to eat. I could make myself beans on toast without the toast or I could go for a takeaway. It was a tough choice.

Before I could decide between Indian or Chinese there was a shrill ringing noise. It was the apartment phone, a landline, used for increased security. At least it allowed you a better idea of who might be listening in.

I picked it up, 'Agaric...'

'I think we know that,' said a female voice, 'no need to share it with the world.'

'I've only just...'

'We know.'

It was unmistakably Samantha's voice. Did everybody know what I was doing all of the time?

'I haven't even...'

'We know.'

On some assignments a chip is inserted under the skin either at the wrist, positioned where it would normally be covered by the wearing of a wristwatch, or at the back of the shoulder, the upper ankle or buried in the scalp. Because of the speed of departure required for this assignment and the fact that it was classified "easy" I had avoided this particular method of tracking in favour of the simple geographic positional tracking of my phone backed up by my watch and the assumption that I would always have at least one of them with me at all times.

If you step out of line alarms would sound, email warnings would be automatically generated, texts would beep their arrival at designated locations, actions would be considered and taken. As far as I knew I had avoided any suspicion, although my return home was clearly no secret.

'Then what can I do for you?' I asked compliantly, 'I was just about to call you anyway.'

'Yeah, right,' there was a slight whiff of sarcasm in her tone, 'He has an hour before his dinner engagement. Don't keep him waiting, best to get these things done quickly.'

I didn't have to ask who "He" was.

'So you mean right now then, as in immediately,' I said, 'and oh, by the way, did you miss me?'

Click.

Fair enough, I thought. I don't like unpacking anyway and I'd be able to pick up a takeaway on the way back. I'd probably pop into a family run Italian I knew, even though their slogan "Meatballs to Die for" was more reminiscent of the Mafia than of Milan.

As I stepped out of my front door I thought about Samantha, I could tell from her voice that she liked me. It's tough being irresistible to women. But I'll just have to live with it, I thought.

Chapter Sixty Seven

Sir Anthony Baxter sat behind his desk with a lilac-coloured file lying open on the desk in front of him. From the little I could see of it it seemed to contain only two or three sheets of A4.

'Our client appears to be satisfied,' he said, looking down, making no eye contact, his suit as perfectly tailored as always, 'Our fees have already been paid in full and nothing has been questioned. All very clean and tidy.' He looked up, directly at me. I preferred the lack of eye contact, 'Any questions?' he said.

Yes, lots of questions, I thought, but we both know that asking them would be a sign of weakness on my part, a sign of caring. Besides you either wouldn't or couldn't answer the kind of questions that I would want to ask.

'No questions,' I said.

His hand hovered above the file as if he were about to close it, 'Now is there anything else you wanted to tell me?'

That depends on how much you already know, I thought, there are the three deaths for example, and there is what actually happened to the girl whilst she was held captive. I decided to play coy but I had to say something. It's always best to be honest - incompletely honest.

'Yes, sir, I was given an envelope when I had completed the transfer in the Arrivals Hall at JFK.'

'And?'

'$50,000 in cash, sir,' I answered, feeling that it was reasonable to assume that the other $100,000+ that I'd accumulated was always meant to cover my additional, unforeseen expenses. Business Class aeroplane tickets, hotels, and of course other essentials, like my Rolex watch, didn't come cheap.

'And what has happened to the money?'

'I still have it, sir. I intend to donate the entire amount to the Macmillan charity for Cancer support.'

He looked at me in a professorial manner, over the rim of his gold-framed spectacles.

'A fine choice,' he said, tapping the end of his silver Schaefer pen impatiently on the mahogany surface of his desk, 'you will of course provide a receipt.'

'Yes, of course sir,' I said, trying to put a polite but vaguely insulted edge on my voice.

'Post a copy to Samantha and write up your report. The sooner the better.'

'Yes, sir.'

'Anything else for the file?'

I thought about Hathos and his organisation and decided it was best not to mention it.

'No sir, not that I can think of.'

He got up from his seat and walked around to where I was sitting. I rose to meet him and he put out his hand. I took it. He had a surprisingly strong handshake.

'Nice watch by the way,' a small frown rippled across his forehead, 'did you ever think about keeping the money?'

'Oh no, sir,' I said quickly, maybe too quickly.

I should have remembered the watch, AB was very observant.

'No, of course not, that would have been an abuse wouldn't it?'

'Yes sir.'

'An abuse of a kind that we would all disapprove of. Isn't that right?'

'Yes, sir, that's right,' I said.

He seemed satisfied.

'So, Mark, your first assignment for a while and successfully completed. Sorry to give you such a straightforward one first up but it was an urgent request, you were available, so there we are.'

'Yes, sir,' I said again.

I wondered whether I would ever see or hear of Emily or Kerry-Anne again. I doubted I would ever meet either of them again. I'd popped into their lives at a critical time and then I'd popped out again, it probably wouldn't take them long to forget what I looked or sounded like. If they did meet me again it probably wouldn't be a good thing anyway, I'd just be a reminder of something that they would rather not have surface in such an uncontrolled way. But I thought I might hear of either or both of them in the future. They were from privileged backgrounds, especially compared to my own, and there was a possibility that they would do something that would attract media attention. Who knew, it was possible.

'Now you're back in the fold,' said AB, 'it's time for your next assignment.'

He opened the upper right hand drawer of his desk and drew out a thin manila folder.

He handed it to me.

'A bit more to get your teeth into with this one. Go and read through the evidence and then Samantha will arrange the necessary briefings.'

I took the folder and got up to go.

'Thank you, sir,' I said.

'It is good to have you back, Mark, finding people willing to do what we do isn't easy you know. But it is necessary. It does make a difference.'

I wasn't sure whether he was trying to convince me or himself.

'Thank you, sir,' I said again. I couldn't think of a more suitable response.

Out in the ante-room I showed Samantha the file.

'Fine,' she said, 'let me know when you've read it through.'

'I have to say,' I said, 'you're looking particularly attractive today.'

She allowed herself the glimmer of a smile.

'Mark Wilson, you're so full of shit,' she paused before adding, 'welcome back.'

2 Weeks Later

Have you ever lost somebody's phone number? Written it down on a napkin or a beer mat or on your skin and then either lost it or washed it away? Well, I hadn't done it before, but I had now. I'd put Teresa's number on the burner phone I'd used on my travels back to Peru and around most of the rest of the world and then I'd trashed it and the number with it. I could have rung the hotel and got put through to the bar, or if I hit a shift she wasn't working I could have left a message. But that didn't seem right thing to do. In this age of total and intrusive connectivity I'd managed to lose contact. Maybe subconsciously I'd done it on purpose.

I liked Teresa and we'd had a good time in Paris or at least I'd had a good time, but it couldn't have been serious. When you've loved someone like I loved my wife it feels disloyal to their memory to find another woman attractive. So it was probably best just to forget about it, it had been nice to meet Teresa, but that would have to do.

When my phone rang I didn't recognise the number. I thought it was probably a scam call but I wasn't doing anything at that moment so I decided to answer it, maybe I'd play along for a while, pretend I was interested in buying life insurance, accessing a tax refund or rescuing the security of my computer.

'Hello.'

'Hello.'

It was only one word but I recognised the voice.

'Teresa?'

'Yes.'

How? And then it dawned on me. Of course. We'd traded numbers! Just because I'd lost her number didn't mean that Teresa would have been so irresponsible. I had just never imagined that Teresa would call me. It wasn't how it was supposed to happen was it?

'Erm, hello.'

I wasn't prepared for this. I was wrong footed.

'You don't want to talk to me?'

I must have sounded unenthusiastic. It wasn't that, it was shock.

'Oh, I do,' I said, 'I'm just surprised.'

'I got tired of waiting for you to call,' she said.

I thought honesty would be the best policy.

'I lost your number,' I said.

'You lost my number! Really!?'

'Yea, really,' I said.

'On purpose?' Phew, I felt like I was under pressure. If I said yes I was obviously not interested, if I said no I was just an idiot.

'No, no, definitely not,' I said, scrabbling for the right thing to say, 'I wanted to call you, I intended to call you, I was going to call you, I was, yes, that's what I was going to do.'

Too much.

She laughed.

I felt relief.

'You sound flustered,' she said, 'you OK?'

I took a deep breath. My heart rate slowed to only double normal.

'Yes,' I said, 'I'm just pleased to talk to you.'

When I said it I realised that I meant it.

'I enjoyed my visit to Europe,' said Teresa, 'I never thought I would ever get to travel like that,' she paused, 'and you looked after me. You made me feel safe. You were a gentleman.'

She was embarrassing me. I was pleased I'd told her about my wife, at least she could understand my peculiar behaviour a little. I was making it difficult for her and she'd still called me … hmm.

We talked about our time in Paris. I found it easy to talk to her although I wasn't sure were the conversation was going.

She took the lead.

'Look,' she said, 'I want to stay in touch. I like you.'

A bit forward, I thought, and extraordinary.

Before I could stop myself I said,

'I like you too.'

'So are you coming over to the States any time soon?'

I hadn't thought about it.

'I am,' I said, deciding on the spot. I'd promised to visit my daughter regularly so why not pop into New York on the way, it was only 3,000 miles out of my way.

'Let me know when,' she said, 'let's meet up, my treat this time. I'll show you some parts of New York you'll never have seen before.'

It sounded intriguing.

'OK,' I said, 'it's a deal.'

After the call I turned to my diary and the flight booking website.

May as well strike while the iron's hot, I thought.

I was looking forward to seeing Teresa again.

2 years later

Peruvian News Online

…here in the northern reaches of Peru, amidst the headwaters of the Amazon and the foothills of the mighty Andes mountain range, the people are far removed from the facilities that we take for granted in our big cities. Sanitation can be poor and life expectancy short, but communities are strongly bound together and, after decades of struggle, there are signs of resurgence.

We are here today to talk to the leaders of a recently inaugurated institution that certainly seems to justify some hope for a better future. "El Centro de Carpintero" ("The Carpenter centre") is not, as its name might imply, a trade establishment for skilled woodworkers but rather a community school and hospital complex …

3 years later

Transcript of blog interview between Michelle K of "Issues of Today" and Kerry-Anne of the "Accessing Help for Trauma Portal"

Michelle K (Blog Interviewer): In this interview I'm pleased to have with me Kerry-Anne who's own blog the "Accessing Help for Trauma Portal" has built itself a very positive reputation. Hello Kerry-Anne and welcome.

Kerry-Anne: Thank you Michelle and please call me Kerry. It's good to be here.

Michelle K: Thanks Kerry, perhaps I can jump straight in by asking you what the purpose of your blog is and what inspired you to start it.

Kerry: Thank you, Michelle, and I'd like to start with the second question first. I had a pretty sheltered and privileged upbringing so when I finally got out into the wider world and saw some of the terrible things that can happen and the effect it can have on people, derailing their lives, damaging their feelings of self-confidence and self-worth it really cut me deep and I felt that if I could do anything, however small, to help then I should.

Now moving on to your first question, what I noticed was that a lot of people keep their trauma locked away in their own mental closet, they feel ashamed of what has happened to them, as if it was their fault, and they just try and live with it. This can lead to long term problems and negative behaviours and they feel like they are then blamed for their own symptoms. It can be a viscous circle. So what my blog attempts to be is a portal to help. There is a lot of help out there and sometimes one of the biggest hurdles is asking for it. It's a big thing to ask for help. You have to feel that you're not going to be stigmatised and so we try and make that first step as easy as possible.

Michelle K: This is a big area, controversial and sensitive. You're dealing with people's lives and emotions so I've got to ask you right away, are you really qualified to be dealing in this area?

Kerry: You're right, this is controversial and sensitive, but it's also important. I'm lucky enough to have on my team advisors from the top universities and clinics, I've been privileged to gain access to these people through my friends and family and the contacts they have built up over the years. The main thing to say here is that I'm not offering a silver bullet, I don't believe there is one, what I'm offering is a safe place to start.

Michelle K: Before moving on, Kerry, as you know there have been bad experiences in this field some of which have ended up in court, and in some of these cases it seems clear that advantage has been taken of vulnerable people, so how much money are you hoping to make from your blog?

Kerry: Not one cent! I am lucky enough to have private means and any money we make we put back into running the blog and funding research. A lot of my board of advisors operate without a fee and a lot of my team are volunteers although of course we have a core staff that do a great job in keeping everything going. I don't want to make a big deal out of this but my family actually donate funds to help us along and if anyone wants to check us out beyond the financial and ethical codes that we've already been assessed against then they're very welcome.

Michelle K: Thank you, I hope you don't mind me being so frank.

Kerry: Not at all Michelle, it's a very important question and I want, as far as is possible, for people to feel it is both safe and easy to start their own journey by approaching our blog. We are, of course, not the only route through which help can be sought and to anybody who needs it I just say please find whatever is the right first step for you and please take it. It's an old saying but no less true for that, that the longest of journeys starts with the first step.

Michelle K: I want to move on. Can you tell me a little bit about treatment for trauma, it seems quite disparate and complex to me.

Kerry: Yes, it can seem like that. We've learned a lot in the last 20 years or so and I think we understand more about trauma and reactions to trauma than we ever have. That's good news. But we're all individuals and we react differently to situations so I don't think it's a surprise to find that different people in different situations need different forms of help. Personally, I don't think there will ever be a one-size-fits-all solution. Treatment is best, I think, when it's formulated for the client. There's a variety of different options available and that's why our portal is only a starting point.

This whole area of trauma is complex, living with trauma can be a day-in day-out experience even if the traumatising experience was short lived. Putting it another way the fallout from trauma tends to be more of an experience than an event.

We talk to all the organisations we provide links to, it's a big job, but it's a part of our own assurance process, and we look for evidence of outcomes and evidence-based treatments. A common theme that has emerged from our interactions so far is that trauma treatment is an individualised process and that the client needs to retain authority over their own path so we work hard to support that.

The main thing, Michelle, is that we want people to feel that there is help available, that their lives can be improved and that it is worth the risk of taking that first step and asking for help.

Michelle K: That's a powerful message. We're coming to the end of our time now, is there anything else you wanted to say?

Kerry: Only one more thing, Michelle, and that is that as we get better at this, as more people come forward seeking help we need to ensure that the capacity to help is there. Therefore another strand of our work is to support, including financially, the inclusion of trauma in the professional curricula, for more colleges to run more courses and for more people to be attracted to train in this personally exciting and progressive area. My friend Emily over on the West Coast heads up our efforts in this area.

Michelle K: Shout out to Emily.

Kerry: Yea, shout out to my friend, Emily!

Michelle K: Well, thank you Kerry for your time and for discussing this important but often overlooked area. I wish you all the best with your efforts and, if your ever increasing number of hits is anything to go by, you're going to have to grow your team!

Kerry (laughing): I certainly hope so! Thank you for the opportunity to talk, it's been my privilege.

ENDS.

Agaricus

Agaricus is a type of mushroom whose genus contains some of the most commonly cultivated and consumed mushrooms in the Western world. It also includes a stinky variety that can cause stomach cramps, nausea, vomiting, sweating and diarrhoea (although for unknown reasons a minority of people can devour these particular fungi with no ill effects whatsoever) and at least one that is deadly poisonous.

They are distinguished by their chocolate-brown spores and a stem that elevates them above the substrate on which they grow and from which they take their nourishment.

Agaricus Homo: A sub-species generally kept in the dark and frequently fed with lots of well-rotted manure.

ACKNOWLEDGEMENTS

Thanks to all those who have given me support and constructive criticism. Especially to those who have edited various versions of the manuscript over its long gestation and those who have given insightful remarks on plot, pace and character development along the way. All your help has been greatly appreciated!

To Crime & Publishment (C&P), Graham Smith, Michael J. Malone, Matt Hilton, Les Morris and the tens of others who have given me the benefit of their knowledge, their moral support and the encouragement I needed to persevere to the end. Also to C&P my thanks for teaching me the method, structure and process to put a book like this together.

Thanks to Fiverr for the artistic and creative contributions to the cover artwork. It was a collaborative process and I enjoyed it – Thank you.

My respects to Moffat Crime Writers and the 'Twisted Sisters', especially Linda, Ann, Irene, Jackie, Beth, Rose, Fiona, Christine, Andrew and Derek. It is fun talking Crime with you all and learning from each other's experiences on this journey of writing and publishing.

To Janet Williamson for some particularly useful editorial support, and to the mighty M. W. Craven for his time and undiluted feedback (especially on the use and Abuse Of Capitals; and semi-colons!).

Thanks also to Ian Rankin for a brief and chance conversation in Kendal about cruise ships, death and deep freezers.

And finally my thanks to Janet Langley for putting up with the 1000's of hours it took me to write this book, for reading the manuscript and for making constructive suggestions for improvement – most of which I listened to.

Praise for Abuse of Privilege:

"Mark Wilson is like Bond with a conscience"

"Page turner, unexpected twists and turns… a recommended read"

"…a new approach to a traditional genre. Liked it."

"the main characters are flawed and complex, just like us all…"

"Enjoyed it, look forward to the next instalment"

"…a really good read. Recommended…"